Kursk

BASED ON TRUE EVENTS

Clinchandhill

For information contact address: info@clinchandhill.com

Cover design by Frank van Uytrecht. Back cover painting by Dennis Andrews.

ISBN: 978-0-9964-6950-0

First Edition: December 2015

10 9 8 7 6 5 4 3

Dedicated to all the real heroes that gave their lives in the Kursk incident.

CONTENTS

ACKNOWLEDGMENTS

Special thanks to my wife Nathalie who stayed with me despite all my absence from her while writing this book.

--

Thanks to my editor, mentor and critic, Andrea Busfield.

--

For Arthur for who unknowingly handed me the article that got me interested in the subject in the first place.

--

To everyone involved who was willing to speak to me on the subject and handed me (video) material.

--

And especially for my dad who stimulated me to read as a child, and miserably failed (except for comic books).

"Tell me, what happened with the submarine."
"It sank"
Larry King interviewing Vladimir Putin. September 8, 2000

1 The Arrest

April 2000

T HE STREET LOOKED DULL AND GREY. Not a single tree or any spark of green stood out between the low-rise buildings. The year might have been 2000 but everything from the architecture to the parked cars screamed mid-20th century. In fact, with the empty playgrounds and lack of people the scene could easily have been mistaken for an abandoned Eastern European movie set from the '50s. However, one sixteen-story high-rise Stalinist architecture building stood out thanks to a large neon sign above the entrance that read SAYANI HOTEL MOSCOW.

Beyond the large glass doors the only indication that the building was occupied came from a man standing alone behind a counter, reading a newspaper in the otherwise empty lobby. When a column of fast-moving cars stopped with a screech on the road outside, the man looked up – at first surprised and then nervous.

Doors were pulled open and slammed shut. From the first car four men in suits headed towards the hotel followed by a number of men from the other two cars, their casual attire failing to disguise their military training. Finally, from the rear vehicle followed soldiers armed with sub-machine guns. They immediately took up position in front of the large glass doors of the hotel entrance as the other men walked fast-paced into the lobby. The startled desk clerk put down his paper and instinctively took a step backwards, towards the wall, as one of the men approached slowly while lighting a cigarette.

"Can I help you?" the desk clerk asked, unable to control the tremor in his voice.

The Suit calmly exhaled smoke from his cigarette. "I think you can." He paused to stub out his cigarette on the desk. "I'm looking for an American, early fifties, wearing a suit, probably accompanied by an older looking Russian man."

Knowing that asking for papers would make his life only more miserable, the desk clerk glanced at his computer. "Room 701, fourth floor," he said.

The Suit turned to point at two of his men. "You and you, follow me. The rest of you stay here and watch the exits." The three men then headed towards the elevator, which opened as they neared. A woman holding the hand of a small boy exited. She gave the Suit a glance before quickly looking away, pulling the boy with her as she walked into the lobby.

The men entered the elevator. The smell of chemical cleaning solutions was strong, but it did little to conceal the state of decay the hotel was in.

"Four," the Suit ordered and one of the men replied by pushing a button on the panel. The doors closed. When they opened again a large 'four' sign welcomed them; the only distinguishing feature of the floor from any of the others. Before leaving the elevator, the Suit looked down the long corridor to the right, checking the doors on both sides.

"Come," he ordered the other men as he walked into the hallway. As they made their way down the hallway, he quietly counted the numbers of the doors as they passed, "697, 698, 699, 700". Finally arriving at Room 701 he saw the door was open. Inside of the room, a man walked towards him, clearly intending to close it.

To all intents and purposes, Edward Payne looked like any other middle-aged American businessman. His blue suit was modern but worn casually with no tie and his flat, grey, two-thirds parted haircut coupled with a pair of horn-rimmed glasses gave him the look of a banker crossed between a character from a '70s movie. Payne looked the Suit in the eyes and though he didn't say anything his frown clearly expressed a desire to know what he wanted.

"A talk," the Suit replied calmly. He stepped into the room, put a hand to Payne's chest and gave him a gentle push backwards. With no other option, Payne turned and led the way into his suite, noting how the two men accompanying the Suit were holding video cameras.

Through the small hallway they entered the living area. The room was typically old-fashioned in décor with an aged and plastic-looking fire-red couch standing out like a sore thumb amongst all the beige. On the couch were three men, two of them relatively young and seated either side of a grey-haired older man whom they were obviously accompanying and who looked increasingly nervous as the strangers intruded on his meeting with the American.

In his late sixties and dressed in a cheap brown suit, Boris Lukin could have passed as a college Professor or a rocket scientist. However, there was no mistaking the fear on his face when Payne walked back into the room followed by the Suit and his men.

Ignoring everything and everyone, the Suit focused on Payne, staring him straight in the eyes as though daring him to lie. "Are you Payne, Edward Payne?"

The color drained from Payne's face. "Yes, I'm Payne. Who –"

"Who I am is of no importance," the Suit interrupted as he turned to Lukin on the couch. "And you? I know who you are. Boris Lukin, a brilliant scientist and most recently head of the rocket engine faculty at the Bauman Technical University in Moscow. Am I missing anything?"

Lukin remained silent.

"Mr. Lukin, Mr. Payne, I have orders to escort you to FSB headquarters where you will be charged with espionage and treason against the Russian Federation."

2 The Issue

IT WAS A SUNNY SUNDAY at the almost 1,000-acre joint base Anacostia–Bolling military installation. At the Defense Intelligence Agency Headquarters a young naval officer in a clean white uniform rushed through a long hallway reminiscent of a sterile hospital corridor. At the end of the hallway he stopped at a glass door engraved with an American Bold Eagle. Below the eagle, a sign read: CMDR, M. JAMES, NATIONAL SECURITY COUNCIL. The officer pulled open the door and stepped into a small front-office where a young secretary kept guard.

"You can walk right through," she said without looking up from her desk. Appearing to pay her no attention, the officer raced towards the door at the back of the room and knocked urgently.

"I said you can walk right through," the secretary snapped only to be ignored once again by the officer who opened the door and entered the room without a backwards glance. Immediately in front of him, sat behind a mahogany desk flanked with two patriotic flags was Mitchel James.

As the officer entered the room, the half politician half naval officer's eyes narrowed slightly as the chill of a problem looming ran down his spine. Mitchel James was only in his mid-30s and relatively young to have made a mark on Capitol Hill, but though he was ambitious he was not reckless in nature and problems were only okay if they belonged to the mistakes of someone else.

"So what's the rush?" James asked a slight lisp apparent as he spoke. "You look worried."

"They've got Payne commander," the officer responded, still trying to catch his breath from the long run through the hallways.

"They've what?"

"Payne. The FSB took him from his hotel along with a contact he was meeting," the officer almost shouted as he spoke, his arms flailing with exasperation and concern.

James stayed calm and hooked a thumb under the waistband of his trousers, an action that reminded him he wanted to lose a few pounds. "Take a breath, officer. Do we know why the FSB took him?"

"Nothing official, but my contact in Moscow tells me he was meeting with Lukin when it happened."

James's face lost its composure almost immediately. "Did we get it?" he demanded, and the officer coughed nervously.

"I couldn't say, but the last I heard was that Payne was supposed to meet Lukin only the one time. So if this was it, we have to assume – "

"We didn't get it," James interrupted. "Any idea where they took him?"

"No," the officer replied honestly before taking a handkerchief from his pocket to wipe the sweat from his forehead. "There's been no contact, although I would expect to hear from him or from official Russian channels fairly soon."

James frowned for a second before pushing the intercom on his desk.

"Yes, sir?"

"Get Mr. Turner on the phone and if they say he's not available tell them it's urgent and have him call back ASAP."

"No problem, sir."

"Thank you, Mary." James turned to the officer. "Please keep me informed if there's any more news."

The officer nodded and left the room. As he passed the secretary he saw her push the intercom. "I have Security Advisor Turner for you on Line Four."

In his office, James reached for the phone and pushed a lit button at the bottom of it.

"Mr. Turner?"

As he spoke, he pictured the middle-aged Harvard man at the other end of the line. At 55, Turner still looked every inch the corporate lawyer he once was. Coming from a humble background, his parents were shopkeepers, his legal training and no-nonsense upbringing had enabled him to keep his head while others struggled to do so and as a result he had already survived his share of political storms as National Security Advisor.

-"Charles," Turner insisted, even though he liked the reverential tone in the young politician's voice. "How many times have I told you George, call me Charles? Now, what can I do for you?"

"It's Payne," James replied, cutting to the chase immediately. "He's been arrested."

On the other end of the line, there was a pause before James heard Turner rising from his desk to close the door to his study.

"Where?" he asked.

"Moscow. He was meeting with Lukin to obtain the plans. I need to get confirmation but it looks like we'll need to find another way."

Turner said nothing as his brain scanned through all the possible repercussions of Payne's arrest. As James was about to ask whether he was still there, he finally replied. "Is there anything Payne can tell them about us?"

This time James took a moment to think before answering. "Payne believes he's buying declassified information so it's unlikely."

Turner nodded to himself, but the slight hesitation in James's voice hadn't convinced him. "OK. I'll try my contacts to find out what happened and I suggest you do the same."

"Will do."

When the line went dead, James looked at the phone for a while, wondering what his next move should be, and how quickly the Press would find out about Payne

3 Vidyayevo

June 2000

VIDYAYEVO, POPULATION 5478, MURMANSK OBLAST it said on the sign when entering the closed-to-civilians village in the uppermost north-western region of Russia. Immediately before the secure military area there was a small public-housing community where concrete buildings, built like barracks, stood out in the rural wasteland. Only the Eastern European-made cars in front of the barracks revealed there were people living behind the closed curtains and the plain colors and lack of plants or trees revoked memories of the Soviet era. It was as though time had simply stopped here a long time ago.

A young woman carrying heavy grocery bags walked up to a small house built with concrete and wood. Dressed in a thick warm coat against a backdrop of grey, she could have been dressed for winter rather than the beginning of summer. As she entered the house she lowered the hood from her head revealing black hair to her shoulders, fair skin, dark eyes and full lips. Unsurprisingly, Sophia Kastamarov was considered to be a pretty woman in this region.

"I'm home," she yelled into the empty living room.

A female voice yelled back.

"We're in the kitchen!"

"Of course you're in the kitchen, you're always in the kitchen, you live in the kitchen," Sophia mumbled to herself.

"What's that, dear?"

"Nothing, *Mama*."

Sophia took off her coat and crossed the living room to take her groceries into the kitchen, which was clearly the centerpiece of the house, with a large stone countertop on one side and a wood-burning stove on the other. At the top of the room, a television was constantly set to the news channel while in the center of the room, at a small table, a young man in his mid-twenties with a military brush-cut to his blond hair and a playful look in his eyes read a newspaper. With his plain clothes, jeans and stained white T-shirt, Mischa Kastamarov looked more like a construction worker than a naval officer.

As Sophia entered the kitchen he stretched out his arms to her.

"There's my wife, come here and give your husband a kiss."

Sophia looked at her husband and threw the shopping bag into his outspread arms. "Kiss this before you put it away and grow up. You're twenty-seven years old, act like it," she said, but she was unable to stop a smile from softening her harsh words or the kiss she then blew to him. God knows her husband wasn't the easiest of men, but she had never met another like him. He was her world; something she discovered when she left him only to find she couldn't live without him.

At the stove, Mischa's mother, Elena, was preparing food for that night's dinner. Her long, colorful dress, printed with flowers, dragged over the wooden kitchen floor.

"Stop teasing, *Mama*," Sophia cried, trying to nip the older woman's playfulness in the bud. "You like a clean house and your doting son here has faithfully sworn never to go to the pub again without me."

10

"And you believe him?" Elena laughed, again oblivious to the undercurrents of Sophia's replies. "You are of good faith." Mischa, however, was not so deaf to his wife's sensitivities and he intervened by jumping to his feet, straightening his shirt and giving a military salute. "I always make good on my promises," he declared, and both the women had to laugh at that because it blatantly untrue.

As Elena turned back to the stove her attention was caught by the mention of her president and President Clinton in the same sentence on the news. She turned to the television, intrigued.

"Shh, I want to hear this," she said and waved her hand to make the others pipe down. A second later President Clinton's White House Daily press briefer, came on the screen.

"This election shows that the ballot box has indeed become the undisputed way for Russians to select their leaders. I think this is an important milestone in the consolidation of democracy in Russia. The United States would like to see a Russia that is not only consolidating Democracy, but one that is consolidating the free market economy and instituting the rule of law that is helping the Russian people to get back on their feet after these difficult years of transition."

Mischa glanced at his mother. "Well said, don't you think, *Mama*?"

Elena looked less than convinced. She wasn't well-educated, she'd broken her back working on the land for most of her life, but she had experienced enough over the years to know that change doesn't come with simply a new face at the top. "Son, whether it's a Tsar, a General Secretary, Chairman or president, as long as one man is in power nothing much will change, I'm afraid." She turned down the gas on the stove, set the lid on a pan and turned to her son to further explain herself when the doorbell rang.

"Saved by the bell," Mischa joked and Elena stepped forward to playfully box the ears of her only child.

"I'll get it," Sophia said, partly to get away from the mother-son love-in and partly because she was curious; visitors were rare during the day when most people were at work on the base.

At the front door was a large man in an even bigger fur coat poised to ring the doorbell again. The relief at finding someone home was evident on his red-cheeked face when Sophia opened the door.

"Oh, thank God. I was starting to think I would have to come back later in the evening," he said.

Sophia smiled. "So what can I do for you?"

"Ah yes," he replied and quickly unclasped the brown satchel hung over his shoulder to take out a letter. "I work with your husband and our boss wanted me to bring this to him, today." As the man handed the letter to Sophia, she noticed it was actually addressed to Elena.

"Do you want to come inside?" Sophia asked.

"No, thank you," the man replied with a warm smile "I have to get back to base. We're having a special party for the officers this evening to celebrate the last mission of our captain this summer. Will you please say 'hi' to Mischa for me? I'm Lieutenant Vitaliy, and tell him I'll see him this evening at the party."

Though Sophia was surprised and a little rattled by the revelation she didn't show it. "I'll be sure to give him the message. Thank you." She closed the door and glanced at the letter before turning away, deep in thought.

"So, who was it?" Mischa asked when she returned to the kitchen.

"When were you going to tell me about the party?" she sweetly demanded of her husband, and recognizing the danger, Mischa immediately put down the newspaper he was reading to better concentrate on the best way to answer his wife without getting into an argument.

"I wasn't going to go," he lied.

"Then why did your friend say otherwise?" Sophia asked not even trying to hide the disbelief in her voice.

"He doesn't know. Everybody expects me to be there, but I seriously wasn't planning to go."

"I don't understand. Why would you say you were going if you weren't planning to?"

Mischa emitted a deep sigh, as though he was about to make a confession. "Look, I didn't want the men to know why I can't be there. I was going to call in sick at the last minute. Nobody would be any the wiser."

Sophia looked at him. On the one hand she was more proud of him than she could possibly say, on the other hand she didn't know if she could trust a word he had just said. This was where they were at. This was the bittersweet nature of their love. But when all was said and done, she had been the one to come back and she had been the one who promised they would face his demons together. So she took her husband's hand in her own.

"It's OK. We'll get there," she said, and because Elena was looking at them in confusion she left it at that and quickly changed the subject. "Look, I've got a letter from your boss, Captain Yaroslav Kuznetsov."

Mischa raised both eyebrows and gestured for her to pass the letter over.

"Not so fast," Sophia teased. "It's not for you. It's addressed to your mother." She then handed the letter to Elena.

"Why would he write to you?" Mischa asked his mother. "Open it."

Enjoying her son's frustration, Elena took her time as she inspected first the front and the back of the letter. Then she picked up a knife from the countertop and meticulously started to open the envelope as if the contents were highly breakable. It was provoking Mischa and he was doing his best not to react. When his mother took the letter from the envelope he could see it was one sheet of paper with a small amount of handwriting on it. Elena started to read to herself, mumbling.

"Out loud, please, out loud," Mischa begged while Sophia smiled at Elena, encouraging her to continue teasing him.

"Ok, so here it goes."

> *Dear Ms. Kastamarov,*
> *I was very pleased to hear that your son Mischa has extended his stay in the proud Russian Navy.*
> *I am particularly pleased to re-welcome him under my command as Captain Lieutenant in charge of the Turbine Department of the Navy's Royal Submarine Kursk.*
> *I would also like to give you my personal assurance that I will do everything in my power to keep him healthy and bring him back to you safely after each voyage."*
> *Yours truthfully,*
> *Captain Yaroslav P. Kuznetsov*

Sophia threw her hands in the air in exasperation. "What about me?" she demanded. "What about bringing him safely back to me?"

Instead of answering, Elena turned towards Mischa who shrugged his shoulders. "Your captain knows how it's done," she said. "A sailor belongs first to his mother no matter how old he is or whether he's married, especially when you don't have any kids to show for it."

Sophia raised an eyebrow at the remark because she knew it was in jest, but the joke was starting to wear thin and Mischa would have to have a word if his mother didn't let go of it sometime soon. "I still think you should have got out when you could, Mika," she said, her tone turning serious. "I've always thought this is a dangerous job. Not only that, the pay is terrible, the environment is unhealthy and you are surrounded by people all too eager to lure you back into bad habits." She leant forward to brush her lips against her husband's ear so only he would hear her next words. "I tell you, Mika, if you ever want children you better show it to me."

Mischa quickly turned his head to catch Sophia's lips on his own. "I'll prove there's nothing dangerous about my work and that there's nothing to fear," he gently assured his wife. "My love, my work on Kursk is probably the safest in the entire navy. In fact, next week on Wives' Day you can come and see for yourself."

Although Mischa didn't intentionally try to make fun of Sophia's concerns his face was habitually set in the kind of a smirk that made it near impossible to assess his true feelings, and Sophia's scowl grew deeper as she sensed he was toying with her. Sensing a fight brewing, Elena decided to intervene, as she always did because she knew from bitter experience how a fight could escalate between couples. "Not one more word," she told the pair. "You two have a lot going for you and an entire future ahead. So stop bickering and help me get this food to the table."

4 Zapadnaya Litsa

THE DOCKYARDS OF ZAPADNAYA LITSA LOOKED CLOSE TO EMPTY and sad. With little to no vegetation, the sandy, windy plain was home to just a few old buildings, and the entire scene brought to mind the demise of the once mighty Soviet Union. Most of the operational nuclear submarines were based at the dockyard. Built in the 1960s, the Zapadnaya Litsa complex consisted of eight large wooden piers, most of which were empty now and stood like a memory of better times. A lot had changed following the end of the Cold War and the navy had taken the brunt of those changes. Today, only a few submarines remained at the dockyard. A handful of guards walking their rounds were the only sign of life on the ground. In the center of the docks, an old wooden building was notable for its size, if nothing else.

In the distance, a large dust cloud rose from the sandy plains signaling a car was approaching. As the vehicle neared the gated entrance to the docks, a lone sentry left a small wooden shed and took his place near the barrier. The vehicle, a luxury town car, drove up to the barrier and stopped. As the window opened, the guard noticed two

Russian officers in the front. The passenger wore an Admiral's insignias on his uniform. In the back of the car were two Asian-looking men, one of whom was also wearing a military uniform.

"Papers, please," the guard said as he stretched out an arm ready to receive them. The Admiral handed some documents to the chauffeur who passed them through the driver's side window. The guard looked at them briefly before handing them back and opening the barrier.

"You know where you need to be?" he asked, while pointing in the direction of the old wooden building some 200 meters away. The chauffeur nodded his head and drove away.

As the car stopped in front of the only building in their immediate surroundings, the Admiral and the two Asian men exited and walked up to a large steel staircase snaking up the side of the building.

"Mind your step," the Admiral cautioned. "These stairs can be slippery under the dust layer." As the men walked up to the first floor, the door at the top swung open to reveal a captain in his late forties. With his big, round head, beady eyes and a thin layer of dark hair, he wasn't the best-looking officer in the navy, but he was one of the most experienced and his loyalty to the greater glory of the old Soviet Union had no match

"Welcome, gentlemen," Captain Yaroslav Kuznetsov greeted.

Kuznetsov waved his guests inside and the men entered what looked like an old classroom with school benches stacked up against the walls. In the center of the room was a table with ten chairs. On one end of the table sat a laptop, placed in front of an old blackboard covered with what looked like a white sheet used as a projection screen. At one side of the table two men were already in position.

"Please take a seat." Kuznetsov pointed to the chairs opposite the seated men. "I suggest that when we are all comfortable we start with an introduction from everybody."

Once everybody sat down, Kuznetsov was reminded of a warzone negotiation scene from the Second World War, somewhere in the pacific.

"Shall I start?"

One of the men dressed in Russian uniform asked. And without waiting for an answer, he did just that.

"I am Northern Fleet Admiral Nikolai Petrov of the proud Russian Navy."

In his mid-fifties, the Admiral looked every inch the seasoned seafarer with a large, reddish mustache, slightly over-heavy build and starched uniform. He was an officer who managed to look both Navy and family man; a man to whom you might trust your secrets. After his introduction, he looked to his left.

"Michail Federov, Defense Minister of the Russian Federation," the man next to him said. In his sixties, Federov had only a little grey hair left on both sides of his head. His large, round glasses gave him the air of a scholar if not the brain of one.

"And I am Captain Yaroslav Kuznetsov of the Russian submarine the Kursk that you might have seen in the dock when you arrived." Kuznetsov pointed at a small window, not that anyone could see the submarine from where they were sat. He turned to the Asian military officer, inviting him to introduce himself.

"Colonel Xu Junping, Ministry of Defense of the People's Republic of China, intelligence department."

Junping was in his forties and in full dress uniform. Though he spoke pleasantly it was clear from his eyes that darted between Petrov and Kuznetsov that he had reservations about being there.

Finally, the last man at the table introduced himself. "Qiungian Wang, civilian contractor for the Ministry of Defense."

Admiral Petrov nodded briskly and rose from his seat to walk up to the computer.

"Welcome gentlemen to Zapadnaya Litsa and thank you all for being here at such short notice," he began. "Forgive me for the poor conditions in which this meeting takes place. I'm convinced the low profile of this arrangement will suit our privacy the best." The Admiral paused to survey the faces around the table. "I will try to keep this briefing short and to the point as much as possible," he assured them. "As you all know, the Russian Navy's been much criticized in the past years since the demise of the Soviet Union and though it's true that due to budget cuts there have been some dramatic changes, we now have the means to take back some of the worldwide naval leadership advantage that we once had."

As Petrov worked to get his first slide on the screen, Junping and Wang followed his every move without saying a word. On the screen the first slide showed what appeared to be a regular, green torpedo with a strange chrome nose. Instead of a propeller at the rear it had eight small rocket exhausts. Junping straightened in his chair as he looked at the screen.

"Is that what I think it is?"

For the first time in the meeting, Petrov allowed a small smile to escape. "The VA-111 Shkval," he said before pausing to enjoy the silence in the room. "With its roots of development some 30 years ago during the time of the Soviet Union, the Shkval will tip the balance in marine warfare in our favor again. Ask yourselves, what's the weakest attack point in submarine warfare?" Petrov walked away from the screen, confident that it would take several seconds before any of the men ventured a reply, but Junping answered the question quickly, as if taking part in a quiz.

"Surprise."

"Indeed, surprise," Petrov confirmed. "The fastest torpedo currently travels at a maximum speed of 50 knots. This gives the enemy plenty of time to react to it with all kinds of counter measures." Petrov rushed back to the computer to put on the next slide. On this sheet were more specifics and numbers, created to impress the Chinese visitors. Petrov gave them a second to absorb the statistics before resuming his performance. "Not with the Shkval. The Shkval reintroduces the element of surprise to submarine torpedo warfare," Petrov stated proudly. "The Shkval is launched from a submarine at 50 knots and accelerates to a speed of up to more than 250 knots. The enemy will never see it coming."

Up unto that moment, Michail Federov had remained silent, now he weighed in to help sell the torpedo to the Chinese. "What's more, these weapons are cheap, very cheap," he said. "At about 10 percent of the cost of a conventional torpedo, we can deliver you the fastest and meanest torpedo ever designed."

"And how is this any different from the concept you tried to sell us some five years ago?" Wang replied.

Realizing Wang must have been to the table before, most probably during the period under Mikhail Gorbachev, Petrov kept his face unreadable and answered him by putting up a slide showing the torpedo traveling underwater. "Here you see our perfected concept of the supercavitation of the Shkval. You notice the silver nose on the torpedo? This nose creates a long bubble of gas under water, large enough to encompass the entire torpedo traveling through the water. Therefore, there is no more friction from the water to slow down the torpedo, allowing it to reach far greater speeds. At the back you see eight small rocket thruster pipes. These thrusters control the direction and speed." Petrov smiled proudly again.

"I've heard about this theory," Wang replied, not even attempting to disguise the skepticism in his voice. "I also heard that the Americans experimented with the same technology, but abandoned it because of safety issues."

Federov smiled easily. "We have been developing and perfecting this principle since the late '60s. I can assure you that we wouldn't be using them ourselves if we didn't consider them to be totally safe."

Wang stretched out his arm to Kuznetsov. "You are a submarine captain and responsible for your crew. What do you think of this torpedo?"

Kuznetsov thought for a moment before responding. "I think - no, I know - that risk comes with the use of all weapons." Again, Kuznetsov paused as he searched for the politically correct answer so as not to embarrass his comrades. "I don't think that the Shkval brings any extra risk to the ones we take every day. If I didn't think the risk was acceptable I wouldn't subject my sailors to it."

Federov and Petrov both looked at Kuznetsov, relieved that he'd made a good job of the answer.

Seemingly convinced by Kuznetsov's response, Junping cleared his throat, indicating he was ready to move the discussion on.

"And what about the warhead?"

"Glad you asked." Petrov put up his next slide; a table of figures listing the variations of payload the torpedo could carry and the damage it could do. "As you can see, the Shkval can carry any kind of warhead up to 269 pounds, from conventional to nuclear. You can also use it without any payload at all but with a dummy head. Due to the speed of the Shkval you will shoot straight through any ship, sinking it or at least rendering it defenseless in the water."

From Junping's expression it was clear he was falling for the sales pitch yet he remained concerned about the dangers of deploying such a weapon. "This all looks very interesting but I would like to get back to the topic of safety," he said. "Originally, there were safety issues on the propulsion system."

For a second, Petrov glanced at Federov asking for permission to take back the conversation. Federov nodded in consent.

"The torpedo runs on a mixture of 95% hydrogen peroxide and kerosene. Together they form HTP, high-test peroxide. Once in contact with the catalyst, in this case kerosene, the hydrogen peroxide decomposes into a high-temperature mixture of steam and oxygen and forms a bi-propellant. We also use it to fuel our Soyuz rocket. As long as we keep it away from air and corrosion there's nothing to fear. Regarding its effectiveness, well, the numbers speak for themselves."

Federov stood up from the table and walked up to the front. "Gentlemen, you can find all the details in the folders in front of you and read them later. I'm sure they will satisfy all your curiosities about the performance of the Shkval. There will be plenty more time for questions later. After all, you didn't come here just to talk and watch a presentation." Federov paused for dramatic effect. "You came here to see the Shkval with your own eyes."

Petrov nodded and took the lead from Federov. "In two days you will join us at our summer naval exercise. Mr. Wang, you will travel with Captain Kuznetsov on the submarine Kursk to see the weapon being fired. Colonel Junping, you will witness the demonstration from our command ship and exercise target, the Peter the Great. I'm sure our demonstration will answer any questions you might still have. I thank you for your attention and I'll be glad to welcome you again in a few days."

5 Wives' Day

Thursday, August 10, 2000

B Y CAR IT WASN'T FAR from Vidyayevo to the Zapadnaya Litsa dockyards. Mischa and Sophia had declined their friends' invitation to share transport because Sophia had thought it best to have some time alone with her husband; without friends, parents or comrades to sway Mischa when she was trying to keep him on the straight and narrow.

"So, what do you say?" Sophia raised her hands to show she was serious.

Mischa took one hand from the wheel and pointed to the barren landscape on either side of the road.

"You see that? The land? That's me, Sophia. I'm as much part of it as a grain of sand in it. I grew up here, as did my father who was a submarine officer before me. This is what I am. This is what I know."

"I'm not talking about what you are or what you know," Sophia interrupted. "I'm talking about what it does to you and what you could become. How much like your father do you want to be, Mika?"

Mischa flinched at the attack. It was an unnecessary blow, but he understood it. However, one mistake by the son does not make a man his father.

Perhaps sensing she had overstepped the mark, Sophia continued more softly. "Don't you see what it does to you, Mischa? Your work is dangerous and it keeps you in touch with friends who are a bad influence on you. Don't you see that? It's dangerous; it's stinking; and it leads you into bad habits." Sophia's gestures became increasingly wilder as she struggled to make her point.

"That's not true," her husband finally answered, his patience wearing thin. "You shouldn't talk about things you know nothing about. My work on the submarine is safe, as I will show you, and as for my friends, I haven't had a drink with them in over two weeks. Trust me, I don't have a problem."

Sophia shook her head, but kept silent. Her disbelief was apparent enough and as she folded her arms she sighed.

As they approached the docks, the road became more crowded. Though the traffic still flowed the fact that there was more than a handful of cars about meant it was the closest the region got to a traffic jam. At the entrance to the docks, the barrier stayed open and the guards barely checked the passing cars as they chatted and smoked together. Once inside the grounds cars appeared to be parked everywhere and a large crowd of men and women were clearly having fun while enjoying the sun. It was a rare sight because the dockyards were usually only staffed by men, some of whom were wearing their best uniforms while others dressed more casually to show their loved ones around. Most of the women were dressed up for the occasion.

Near the piers, two large Oscar II class submarines rose up from the water. More than 150 meters in length, these were the largest nuclear submarines in the Russian fleet. Originally built during the Cold War, the submarines were redesigned in the early '90s to create space for

26

more technology as well as for new solid fuel propelled missiles. Mischa and Sophia stopped their car roughly a thirty meters from the submarines.

Sophia hadn't spoken to Mischa since he denied having a drinking problem and her husband realized it would take more than a wink and a smile to warm his wife back up again so after parking the car he jumped out and ran to the passenger door, which he opened with a flourish.

"My lady," he said and gave a small bow.

"That's one small credit for you." Sophia smiled before throwing her hands back into the air in exasperation. "Are you going to film everything?"

Mischa grinned and gave a wink over the small video camera he had taken from his pocket to film Sophia getting out of the car.

'I'm only capturing your beauty," he joked. Mischa walked backwards away from Sophia all the while filming her. With his free hand he gestured she should follow him. "Come, you'll see, you'll take it back."

"Huh? Take what back?" Sophia asked.

"'Dangerous, stinking, bad habits'; all your prejudices against me and my job."

"Ah, you think that I might change my mind just because the weather is fine and your navy buddies can actually behave themselves in front of their wives for a day? I don't think so."

Mischa lowered the camera and adopted a childlike expression as he tilted his head a little. "My Sofochka, you will change your mind because of this…."

As Mischa stopped talking, he lowered his camera and turned his wife gently to face the pier. Sophia looked up. They were standing in front of the two huge submarines. On top of one was a man who sat in a small deckchair with his eyes closed and his face aimed at the sun hoping to get a tan. On the identical ship on the left, people were coming and going along a fragile-looking wooden gangway.

"This is why." Mischa repeated more enthusiastically. "This boat is what it's all about. This submarine depends on me like I depend on her. She keeps me safe but she also keeps you and every other Russian safe. Really, when I am on my boat you should actually sleep better at night."

"Well, I don't," Sophia said sniffily, "and I still don't see what could be worth risking your life for every day for a measly 100 dollars a month."

"Don't you believe anything that man says!"

From somewhere in the crowd a woman's voice cried out. Seconds later a young, pretty, blonde woman in her early twenties walked up to Sophia and Mischa. She was accompanied hand-in-hand by a 25-year-old handsome young man in full uniform.

"Grisha, Galina, I'm so glad to see you," Mischa greeted them cheerfully and walked up to Grisha with his arms wide open. The two men gave each other a firm hug and patted each other on the back while Sophia and Galina greeted each other with two kisses on the cheeks.

"So finally we get to see the happy couple again. You've been missing since your wedding. Have you been on permanent honeymoon?" Grisha joked.

"Almost four months," Galina joined in. "That must be a new record?"

"Laugh while you can, my friend," Mischa warned Grisha. "Because tomorrow is your maiden voyage and who knows what may happen on a first trip."

"I'm not afraid. I was born for this. I can feel it in my bones," Grisha replied. Though he'd heard rumors about initiation rites the stories never tended to be the same so he concluded they couldn't be true meaning there was no reason to fear.

Sophia stepped in, smiling. "Come Mischa. Let's leave these two low-ranking Russians to themselves and check out this submarine you're so in love with."

As they walked up the gangway onto the submarine, leaving Grisha and Galina playfully bowing and curtseying behind them, Sophia noticed that although the sub was enormous in length there had to be even more of it underwater. Mischa was forever talking about all the space on board as well as the luxuries.

On deck, the couple first walked up to the large sail that housed the conning tower with all the antennas and periscopes. The tower also had a small deck that could be used when sailing surfaced. A large, red emblem was painted on the side of the tower, a two meters high insignia with two silver eagles on it. Mischa pick up his camera again as he waved Sophia to go stand in front of it.

"What is this?" Sophia asked even as she affected a model pose. "That's great." Mischa encouraged. "And that, my dear, is the coat of arms of the Russian Federation. It is said that the first version of it was created by Peter the Great himself." As a colleague passed by, Mischa called out to him. "Excuse me comrade, could you please take our picture?"

"Sure, no problem," the man replied, taking hold of Mischa's camera before taking a few steps back to capture the couple posing in front of the emblem. Mischa placed an arm around Sophia's waist and she placed her head on his shoulder, feeling the warm sun on her face. Dressed in a long, black winter coat she felt a little envious of Mischa who was more dressed for summer wearing brown pants and open khaki jacket.

"Perfect," the sailor said as he took the couple's photograph and handed back the camera.

"Thank you, really, very much." Mischa smiled and turned to Sophia. "And so now we have proof."

"Proof of what?"

"Proof of you and me sharing my work. It might well be the first and last time, but this picture will last forever." Mischa smiled and then dropped his voice to speak to his wife more tenderly. "But seriously, dear, welcome to my home. My second home, away from you, the great K-141, Kursk; the biggest and most feared of all the submarines in the world. More than 150 meters long and almost 20 meters in diameter, the Kursk weighs more than 16,000 tons and boasts most of the luxuries of a cruise liner."

Sophia looked at her husband, frowning as if he were a car salesman trying to sell her a car. It was not that she didn't want to believe him, but rather that she didn't want to hear what he had to say because she knew that if she let herself believe he was safe, it would be harder on her if something were to happen to him. Therefore it was better to stay firm and strict.

"Sure – you and all your luxuries – you better show me everything if you want me to let you go."

"It's one more time," Mischa told her, "just one more time."

"That's what you said the last time. Why would this time be different? Why should I believe you now?"

Mischa walked towards her as he nodded his head. "You're right. I've said it before but you have to believe me. This isn't easy. All my life I've been convinced that this would be my work, my future, our future. My father always told me that if I wanted to be an independent man who could provide and care for his family, the navy was the best place to achieve just that."

Sophia put both her hands to his cheeks and softly asked, "Your father of all people said that?"

"I know," Mischa replied, "but though he might have failed as a man, a husband and a father he was right about what the navy can provide for the man who actually wants to look after his family. Come, I'll show you what I'm talking about." He then ran, almost dragging her, to the front of the ship.

Above a large open hole, the flag of the Russian Federation waved in the light breeze. "It's not the most elegant way to enter a submarine but this is how we do it. Do you want to join me?" Mischa asked.

Sophia bowed her head above the hatch and looked down. Deep below, inside the hole, she saw light and shadows and heard voices. A dark metal staircase descended about four meters towards the light.

"Don't worry. It isn't too far. It will only take you to the first floor. There are three floors, you know."

Looking doubtful, Sophia grabbed the steel railing above the hatch with one hand. With the other hand she reached out to Mischa and waved to hurry him to grab it. Mischa took her hand.

"Ladies first," she said, as she took the first two steps down. Not daring to take any chances, Mischa held onto her, so firmly in fact he almost lifted her up again.

"You can let go of my hand now. If you hold on I will never get down," Sophia shouted up at him.

"Sorry," he apologized and slowly, Sophia disappeared from the surface and into the submarine.

Mischa waited until she was completely down because. He wasn't taking any risks today and he most certainly wasn't going to risk dropping anything on his wife's head, not when his future might possibly depend on it. Then he went down as fast as he could. "Welcome to the belly of the beast. If you will please follow me to the left and down, we'll start our tour today."

The room they descended into was filled with meters, equipment panels and gauges on all the walls yet there were no desks or chairs, nothing to reveal that there might actually be people working in there.

"People work here?" Sophia asked.

"Well, yes and no. This space is largely unoccupied. But sometimes when we have to take special readings we can do it here."

They walked on, almost to the end of the room where a normal-looking staircase disappeared downwards. As they neared the staircase, the noise of people in the room below became louder; it sounded busy. As Mischa walked down the stairs he looked back to see if Sophia was following. As the room became visible, he smiled at the amazed look on his wife's face. The room was about 13 meters deep, 10 meters wide and 5 meters high. Every free inch of the walls was filled with screens, levers, buttons and gauges. Despite the fact that about 20 of Mischa's comrades were giving tours in the room it didn't look cramped. In the center of the room Sophia recognized the periscopes.

"I know these; from the movies. The captain of a submarine always looks through them before firing at the enemy."

Mischa laughed. "Amongst other things. This is the central command center. The heart of operations. This is where it all happens. Normally more than 40 people work in this room."

"This is where you work?" Sophia asked while touching all the levers and buttons on the walls.

"Can you please not fire any nuclear missiles?" Mischa joked. "No. My workstation is right at the back. We'll have to cross the distance of one and a half soccer fields to get there. We'll see that later. Do you see those staircases on both sides going up?" Mischa pointed at four staircases that seemed to end at nothing against the ceiling. "Although this ship is the safest to be in if anything were to happen, these staircases would be our escape route."

"Where do they go? Outside?" Sophia asked.

Mischa laughed at her remark. "Of course not. What would you plan on doing when you're at the bottom of the sea? Swim up?"

Sophia looked at him, annoyed that he was not taking her seriously.

"No, silly," Mischa continued. "These staircases take us into the seal on top, the part where we took the picture earlier. In that seal is a large escape vehicle. If we were in trouble all the men would fit into the vehicle, then it would detach from the submarine and take us up safely. It's as simple as that."

"Still convincing me, I see," Sophia said, smiling at him. Then she walked up to the periscope. "Can I look?"

"Sure." Mischa turned the periscope towards her. Sophia put her hands on the handles that protruded from the sides and put her eyes to the viewfinder.

"As I said I saw this in the movies and -" Sophia suddenly stopped speaking and pushed her eyes more firmly against the viewfinder. "Wow. This is great. Everything is so clear and close by."

Mischa stood behind her and put his hands on her hands. Slowly he started rotating the periscope.

"Wow," Sophia exclaimed softly. "This is absolutely amazing."

"Well, I guess it is when you think that, theoretically at least, we can be underwater for 120 days. Come on, I'll take you on the next part of the tour."

As they walked towards the front of the sub, Mischa walked backwards in front of her again, filming Sophia's every move. Sophia inspected every detail of the ship.

"Do you approve, madam?" Mischa asked, a little afraid of the answer.

"Hmm, I don't know yet. It looks cleaner than I expected. But the problem is not how it looks. The problem is that it's dangerous. I imagine there are so many things that could go wrong in a submarine."

Realizing his wife was not ready to give up, Mischa worked to reassure her. "Sure, things could go wrong. But that is why the crew takes such good care of her. The beauty of a submarine is harnessing all of her power and controlling it until you need it. And I tell you, this crew and Captain Kuznetsov are the best in the business." Mischa paused and lowered the camera. "We are at the next stop on the tour; the torpedo compartment. Please enter, my dear."

Mischa stepped from the corridor into a remarkably small opening in the steel wall. Sophia followed him inside.

The torpedo compartment was about 10 meters deep and surprisingly narrow at about 7 meters. The cranes, pipes and levers filling the room from top to bottom made the place feel cramped and claustrophobic. On both sides of the walls, at the front, stood large, empty racks where torpedoes could be stored. Across the front wall were four rows of large, round, steel torpedo hatches, two in each row. In the middle of the hatches a large opening let in the daylight. Sophia looked out to see the clouds in the sky.

"This is where we load the torpedoes into this room," explained Mischa.

"Sunlight," Sophia said with a sigh. "I've just realized how you must crave the sunlight when you're under water for so long."

"You get used to it. I don't even think about it anymore when I'm on board." He walked up to her and put his arm around her for a second as she continued to stare at the sky.

"OK, so much for the sky, let's continue. As you can see, the room is still very empty, but after tonight all of these empty spaces will be loaded with torpedoes for the exercise. You may not believe it, but at any given time up to ten men will work in this room -"

"I want to see where you work," Sophia interrupted, getting a little board with the whole tour thing.

"Patience, dear, we still need to go all the way to the back for that, but maybe you're right. Let's go." Mischa turned and walked back through the command station. They left the room through a much larger steel door than the one they had entered and walked into a large area that looked to be sleeping quarters. On both sides of the room, steel beds, stacked three high with thick green mattresses, protruded from the wall giving the person sleeping about a 30 centimeters of headspace. Down the center of the room were another two rows of beds.

"This is where we sleep," Mischa said, sounding almost proud.

34

"What, you too? I thought you were an important officer?"

"You know I am, but everyone other than the captain sleeps here. It's only for sleeping after all. At any given time, half the crew works while the other half sleeps or enjoys free time. You see, we have the luxury of having two crews aboard."

Mischa walked up to the front of the living quarters and indicated another door.

"Here, take a peek behind this door. You'll like it."

As Mischa opened the door, Sophia looked inside and giggled.

"This is our recreation room," he said with a smile.

Inside the small room, on top of a grass-like carpet, were four rocking chairs. The walls were plastered with wallpaper imitating bricks while a large photo on one of the walls gave the impression of a city landscape as seen through a window.

"Wow. It's almost like home, although the chairs are better," Said Sophia before adding a little more sarcastically, "Do you come here often?"

"For relaxing, whenever there's time," replied Mischa who had either missed the dig or decided to ignore it. "But I don't come too often I can assure you of that. There's always work to be done. Or I sleep, which is also very important. You need to be well rested to do this job."

"Now that I believe." Sophia pointed a finger at him as if to imply he had spoken the first truth of the day to her.

Mischa looked at her, searching for a response, but he couldn't find one. "Let's go through that door," was the best he could think of.

The wooden door was closed and Sophia had trouble opening it.

"Here, let me help you." Mischa put his hand over her hand on the door handle and pulled. As the door gave way they almost toppled backwards. Balancing himself before checking if Sophia was OK, Mischa made a quick recovery. "You see how sturdy everything is?"

Sophia raised an eyebrow and glanced through the door, which hid a small swimming pool. As she stepped into the room, she smiled and opened her coat as though she was about to undress.

"I dare you!" Mischa challenged, his eyes twinkling. "You know, come to think of it. I don't think a woman has ever swum in a submarine swimming pool. You would be the first."

"Do you swim here?" she asked.

"Never. I'm afraid of water, as you know. But maybe I could be tempted to go skinny dipping with you."

"Keep dreaming sailor, keep dreaming." Sophia slowly pushed her husband through the door back into the recreation room. "I think we'd better move on before we do something we might regret," she added.

"I think you're right." And Mischa smiled because he loved the way his wife liked to tease him.

Walking on, towards the back, they reached a compartment with what looked like two separate smaller chambers in the middle of the room. The doors into both chambers looked like large industrial refrigerator doors with large metal handles and locks. Next to the doors was a small window made with extremely thick glass. Outside of the two smaller rooms the walls were filled with the same riggings Sophia had seen elsewhere on the ship: panels, levers, buttons and gears. One thing was different though. On every wall in the room a yellow warning sign screamed the words:

DANGER, RADIATION RISK

Mischa held Sophia back with his arm in front of her before she could walk up to the small chambers.

"This is a very dangerous place on the ship," he said. Though he tried to sound serious Sophia wasn't going to fall for it. She shook her head in disbelief.

36

"No, seriously," Mischa insisted. "Behind these doors are the nuclear reactors that power the entire ship. Come, have a look through one of the windows."

Although Sophia wasn't sure she believed him she wasn't going to take any chances. Slowly, she walked up to one of the windows and without getting too close she took a peek through it. Behind the window, the center of the room, steel pipes rose from the floor, coming to a halt in mid-air.

"This is the entire reactor?" Sophia asked in disbelief. "It looks a lot smaller than I expected. And it doesn't seem so dangerous to me."

When Mischa spoke again, Sophia was left in no doubt that he meant what he said. "There are two of the reactors, there's one in each room. Maybe to you they don't seem so dangerous, but I assure you I'd rather spend all my time underwater in the torpedo compartment than just one day with these things. Just because you cannot see the real danger it doesn't mean it isn't there. It gives me the creeps."

Sophia took a small step backwards and then took another look through the window.

"You're fine," her husband reassured her. "As long as you stay on this side of the wall I'm told nothing can happen."

"And you believe them?" Sophia asked.

"Sure. Look at me. I still have all my hair, don't I?" They both laughed at that and Mischa pointed Sophia back towards the door. Without the need to say anything more, they walked on and arrived at the propulsion control compartment. This was Mischa's domain. Again, the walls were filled with grey levers and valves. The chairs looked like they had been taken from a regular office, but of course this was no regular office and about halfway into the room lay two large pipes, each about one meter in diameter, that disappeared through the back wall, and presumably out of the ship.

"My empire, my kingdom," Mischa exclaimed proudly, spreading his arms widely. Sophia looked around the room absorbing everything in it as if she was doing a thorough safety inspection.

"What is it that you do all day?" She sounded baffled. "Look at these walls, press buttons and rotate wheels?"

"It's a very important job, I'd have you know. Without me, the sub wouldn't be able to come home again."

"Or go away in the first place," she replied. "I'm sorry, but I haven't changed my mind, yet. I still think your job is dangerous and a submarine is no place for a -"

"For a what?" Mischa's tone was agitated. "It's really no more dangerous than being on a surface ship. The Kursk is the safest boat in the navy. By many it's considered to be unsinkable."

Sophia smiled sadly. "Where have I heard that before?"

Mischa immediately realized that he should have chosen his words more carefully. "Look, I know you're worried, but there is one big difference between us and the Titanic. We are built to be under water. Really, the Kursk has a double hull that's almost 2 meters wide. Even a direct torpedo hit wouldn't get through the walls but get stuck in between. Besides, it's not like we're at war. Who would be shooting at us? You should really stop worrying."

With one look at Sophia's face Mischa knew he had made his point. Maybe she wasn't totally convinced, but he was getting through to her, making his case. In truth he only had one real goal; to convince her to let him go on one more mission. If she later decided when he returned home safely that navy life wasn't so bad after all he might even be able to convince her to allow him to continue with the career he loved. If not he would change it because he loved her too, more even.

Perhaps sensing his mood, Sophia came dancing towards him and Mischa picked up his camera to film her.

"*Tanets, rebenok, Tanets*", "Dance, baby dance," he cheered, but she stopped a few centimeters from him.

38

"Take me with you to the sea."

"If only I could," Mischa smiled. "But I can't. Anyway, it's bad luck having women on board a submarine."

Sophia pouted her lips and tilted her head as she put her face a few inches in front of Mischa's. "But please." She sounded almost pitiful. "I promise to be nice to everyone and always smile?"

"That's it. Now you're definitely not coming with me if you're going to be nice to everyone." Mischa smiled as he softly pushed her away from him. As Sophia walked away, she danced the last few steps before stopping to look straight into his eyes.

"I'll only be nice to your superiors so you can get promoted to admiral. Please? Please?"

Mischa took a deep breath and exhaled with a smile on his face. "Sorry, no," he whispered.

6 The American Way

IT WAS A BRIGHT, SUNNY DAY in Washington DC. From his office on the top floor of the Defense Intelligence Agency building, Charles Turner had a clear view over the Potomac River. Turner had recently joined the DIA as Special Assistant to the president for National Security Affairs. Experienced as he was, however, he didn't feel especially comfortable with having to conduct yet another meeting about what might easily become the next international incident between the USA and Russia. As his secretary walked in, he was looking out of the window, deep in thought.

"Sir... Sir."

It took Turner a moment to hear her before he turned around.

"Commander James is here to see you."

"Please, send him in," Turner replied before turning back to the window.

James had been to Turner's office before but never as the bearer of bad news. "Morning, Sir."

"Morning, George," Turner less formally greeted him. "Did you know that only 46 percent of people living in the DC area are born here? The rest of the population is made up of people like us; politicians, lobbyists and lawyers, drawn to the nation's capital to get their share of good political fortune."

"Are you ready?" James replied, not even bothering to answer the question. "And has there been any news?"

"About Payne? Not much. The latest we heard was that he's being held at Lefortovo Prison. There's no direct contact. Intelligence sources from inside the prison tell us he's doing well but that's about it."

Turner finally turned away from the window and looked James in the eye. "And what about the plans?"

"We're now sure the documents didn't change hands at the meeting where he was arrested. So I guess that's good news."

"Only in America, only in America that's good news," Turner corrected him. "In Russia they don't care if the evidence changed hands or not. A suspected CIA agent and a top Russian scientist are caught in the same room with secret documents. That's enough for them to put Payne away for life, not to speak of what a newly elected Russian President will do with the incident. There are so many ways that this can go wrong without us having anything to show for it."

"What do you mean?"

"Well, we are still none the wiser as to any information about the weapon."

"That is correct, sir, but isn't that why we're all here," James said, as if he had the solution to everything.

"If you say so," Turner replied with little faith apparent in his voice. "I suggest we get going then. We don't want to keep them all waiting."

42

James and Turner left the office and walked through the long hallway without talking. When they reached two large milk-glass doors, two soldiers in navy uniform opened both doors for them.

The room they entered was exceedingly bright, filled as it was with sunlight streaming through the floor-to-ceiling windows. A large, mixed group of civilians and military men were sat waiting for them at a long table in the center of the room. Some were involved in hushed conversations, but most of them were quiet. James couldn't help but notice that the only woman in the room was a secretary behind a laptop. Most of the Joint Chiefs of Staff were present, along with the Secretary of Defense. Although James was relatively young he had already met his share of political and military dignitaries yet never so many in one room at the same time. For the first time in his career he felt something close to intimidation. One wrong step and these men could make or break him on Capitol Hill.

On the table in front of each person was a dossier. The beige folder had a sealed red band around it that read CLASSIFIED and James noticed that nobody had yet touched their dossiers or even broken the seal.

A lectern was placed at the head of the table and with one remaining empty place next to it, Turner nodded at the seat. "You sit there," he told James. "I'll just make a short introduction and then the floor will be yours."

James walked to the end of table, giving the dignitaries a small nod as he passed and mumbling a quiet, "Good morning" before taking his seat.

No one paid Turner much attention as he took his place behind the lectern and for a moment he stood in silence, taking the opportunity to look over the table and make eye contact with each delegate, one by one. It was a tactic he had learned early at college and he had used ever since. He was convinced it gave the delegates a feeling that he was aware of each and every one of them, and he was not a man to be messed with. He next took a slow, deep breath.

"Gentlemen, please can I have your undivided attention?" The room fell silent. All eyes were now focused on Turner.

"Thank you all for being here at such short notice. As most of you are aware, since the end of the Cold War Russia has been attempting to regain her military supremacy on land, at sea and in the air. Naturally, we've been keeping up with her development, most notably her pursuit of another Cold War relic – the supercavitating torpedo."

Some of the younger delegates frowned and Turner felt obliged to explain further. "From the '70s until the '90s, most nations, including the United States, experimented with similar technology. Most nations, as far as we know, also abandoned the research because of the risks that were involved. The idea was to develop a torpedo that could be fired from a submarine or even surface ships that could travel at up to four times the speed of regular torpedoes. That's up to 250 knots and maybe more."

"It's never been done," General Corey Aimes, the Chairman of the Joint Chiefs of Staff, interrupted Turner.

"Are you sure?" Turner challenged. "Because we have serious intel that tells us otherwise."

Aimes sat back in his chair.

"A few months ago," continued Turner, "we became aware of claims that the Russians had picked up their research from where they left off in the '70s and had made serious progress on developing the VA-111, or Shkval, a supercavitating torpedo that far exceeds the speed of any standard torpedo currently used by NATO. The speed is a result of supercavitation; the torpedo is, in effect, flying in a gas bubble created by the outward deflection of water. It creates this with a specially shaped nose cone that emits expanded gases from the engine. That way, the water doesn't come into contact with the surface of the torpedo so there's zero drag, allowing speeds of 200 knots and more,

44

compared to the current torpedoes that don't travel any faster than about 50 knots. I'm sure I don't need to tell you how serious this is, gentleman. At current speeds, we have the balance between firing time, detection and subsequent destruction of enemy torpedoes. However, a super-speed torpedo creates a clear advantage over the enemy because it retains the element of surprise. In short, once you see it, it's too late. Some have dubbed the Shkval the Aircraft Carrier Killer because a torpedo reaching such speeds will simply not allow us enough time from the moment of detection to launch counter-measures. In other words, if this rumor is true, we will have nothing to stop the Russians."

Turner stopped talking and looked around the table. Many of the faces revealed disbelief and he wondered whether his speech had lacked impact. He decided to make a few last remarks before giving the room to James.

"In a more detailed response to your question, General Aimes, "we believe - or rather, we know - that the Russians are now ready for live weapons testing and that they will do so soon. Very soon."

At this, the room started to buzz with shocked responses. Turner let the weight of his words hang in the air before glancing at James who gestured it was time to move on. Turner moved away from his lectern. As he did so, the room hushed and he purposely walked behind each and every member at the table as he began to speak again.

"So, what else do we know?" His tone regained everyone's attention and he continued his slow pace around the table. The delegates turned in their chairs as he passed, trying to keep eye contact. "Well, we know that the deterioration of the ex-Soviet Navy has forced Russia to speed up sales of the Shkval to China. With the new Russian President in place, we suspect that he'll use these funds to restore his navy back to the glory days of the Soviet Union. We also believe China may want to buy these torpedoes with an eye on a possible Taiwan invasion, Pearl Harbor style. Now, I don't have to explain our disadvantage if both

Russia and China have these torpedoes and we, say, were called on to help Taiwan fight off a Chinese aggressor."

Turner glanced at James, warning him to get ready for the next part of the presentation and for the first time, James started feeling a little nervous. Turner had set the tone of the meeting and soon it would be in his hands to continue that tone if they were to get everyone's approval for their plans.

"Commander James," Turner waved a hand in his direction, "As an experienced naval officer Commander James is Assistant to the president on matters of Russian, Ukrainian and Eurasian Affairs and for the National Security Council. In this matter he will liaise with us and the White House and fill us in on the orders from the top."

James stood, picked up his papers and walked to the lectern. After carefully placing his documents down, he took a moment to steady his breath so as not to sound nervous. As Turner took his seat at the table, James glanced his way and he mouthed a silent, 'Good luck'.

"Thank you. Mr. Turner. All right, if you'll all please open the folder in front of you I will fill you in on all the details."

It took only one sentence for James to find himself back in his comfort zone and there wasn't a single sign of nerves visible in his demeanor as he watched the men before him release their folders from their CLASSIFIED bands. Inside the folder they found reports and documents filled with rumors about the new torpedo as well as an artist's impression based on speculation. In the back of the folder was a photo of a regular-looking guy in his forties or fifties. James gave the room a minute to browse the folder before he continued.

"Last April, an ex-Navy, now American civilian, Edward Payne, was in Moscow trying to obtain the plans for the Shkval from one of its inventors, Boris Lukin. We'd used Payne before but always kept him in the dark as to what he was really obtaining, so he didn't know what he was about to receive. We felt that as a respected businessman who travelled regularly between the US and Russia, Payne's low profile would give us the advantage of not getting noticed. However, before the plans for the Shkval could change hands, both Payne and Lukin were arrested in their hotel during the exchange."

James paused to let the information sink in. "Now, Payne is still in Russian hands and we don't know too much about his condition but we are working on that. The fact remains, however, that we need to know more about this torpedo and we think we have a new chance of doing just that."

James took a small break to look around the room to see if anyone was planning to ask questions. From experience he knew that once he started a speech he tended to ramble on. This time everybody seemed to be waiting to hear more of what he had to say.

"On August 12th, the Russian Northern fleet will start their summer exercise in the Barents Sea. Now we don't know much about the exercise but from what we've learned the president is planning to make a big showcase of it. His intentions seem to be focused on both showing the world that Russia is a navy to be reckoned with and also impressing Asian allies with new technology."

"And what does this exercise have to do with the plans for the Shkval?" interrupted a civilian in his fifties, waving the folder impatiently in one hand. James didn't recognize him.

"And you are, sir?"

"Bill Brown, Director of Information Operations in Advanced Technologies for the NSA."

"Well, Mr. Black, the dossiers in front of you may appear to contain specific information on the torpedo but actually they're pure speculation. In reality, we know next to nothing about it. What we do have is reliable intel that the exercise will be used to test and demonstrate the torpedo."

"Demonstrate it to who?" interrupted Black again.

"If you'll let me continue for a few minutes more I think your questions will all be answered. If not, you can ask me at the end of the presentation," replied James, clearly agitated by Black's interruptions.

"To answer your question, it's the Chinese. As Mr. Turner previously stated, the Chinese are very interested in this development."

"And you want us to catch one of these torpedoes for you?" joked one of the men.

A ripple of laughter broke around the table and James had an uncomfortable feeling they weren't taking him seriously. Before his irritation got the better of him, he noticed Lieutenant General James Hill, DIA Director and Turner's boss. James swallowed his pride, took a deep breath and came back with the shortest and most astute reaction that he could think of.

"No, I don't want you to catch one, I want you to listen to one of them." The men fell silent and James found all eyes on him once again.

"We'll have to wait for another opportunity to get the plans, but the DIA and more specifically the Measurement and Signature Intelligence, MASINT, would like to create a profile of the torpedo's signature. As you know, submarines are always listening to what happens below the sea to identify any threats. For exactly that purpose the United States Navy has the largest dictionary of sound signatures of almost any foreign and domestic naval weaponry. If this weapon was to be used in action at this moment we are completely defenseless against it. We probably won't even recognize it if it was fired at one of our ships. So if we know what it sounds like we might be able to identify it in time.

"In time for what?" Rear Admiral James Braiden, Chief of Naval Research, asked looking particularly interested now.

"We're not sure at this point. That still depends on the specifics of the torpedo. But whether it's sooner or later, having enough time to react is always going to start with recognizing it in the first place."

A discussion between the members at the table broke out. Turner stood and put his arms in the air in an attempt to silence the room.

"Please, gentlemen, please. If we could just have another minute of your time because time is of utmost importance here. If we are in any way to succeed in this mission we need to act quickly. So, if you please."

Turner lowered his arms and the room silenced. James resented the fact that Turner had come to his rescue, but he continued as though nothing had happened.

"Our plan is simple," he said. "We have two subs in the region: the SSN-806, USS Baltimore; and the SSN-709, USS Detroit. Both are Los Angeles-class submarines and both are perfectly equipped for an operation like this. Their crews have already received shipping orders to sail to the region in the Barents Sea where we think the exercise is being held."

"On whose orders?" asked General Hill, leaning forward across the table, his broad frame lending authority to his rank. The anger in his eyes also told James that he was less than pleased not to have been informed of this decision

"My orders, General," Turner stated firmly, coming again to James's rescue. "The submarines' captains are not informed on the content of the mission so we can scrap it at any time," he continued, "but I would urge you to give your consent. In the folder are the detailed orders we intend to give to the Baltimore and the Detroit. As Commander James stated, time is of the essence. In less than two days, the Shkval will be launched. We need to be listening."

Turner decided it was time to end the meeting. The delegates had enough information to make an informed decision and they were starting to become noisy.

"Thank you, Commander James," He said and the younger man returned to his seat, secretly glad that the meeting was over. "If there aren't any further questions at this time I would like to close the meeting," finished Turner. "You have about six hours to reach a decision, but I hope to hear from you well before this deadline so that we can get this show on the road."

"I have one more question," said a man in a suit from the far end of the table.

Turner sighed. He didn't know who the man was and at this point he honestly didn't care. "Yes?" he responded, impatiently.

"How dangerous is this mission?"

Turner smiled in acknowledgement, now recognizing the man as Bill Jones, director of the National Threat Assessment Center, NTAC.

"That information is also included in the folder you received. But to answer your question, we expect a minimal threat level on this mission. The Russians know we always monitor their exercises so this will be nothing new to them. Now, if there are no further questions I suggest we all use the little time we have to review the matter."

As the delegates began to pick up their papers and rise from their chairs, James joined Turner at the lectern and shook the man's hand.

"I want you to be there James." Turner held on to James's hand as he spoke his order carefully hidden in a request.

"I'll be there." James replied without hesitation as Turner let go of his hand. As the men prepared to leave, another voice called to them from the back of the room.

"Do we know which vessel they're using to launch the Shkval?"

Turner looked at James, who nodded and pulled a piece of paper from his folder. He tilted his head, looking around the room for the man who had asked the question. He decided it didn't matter.

"We do. We learned it's an Oscar 2 Class submarine. The K-141, Kursk."

Kursk

7 Old School

Friday, August 11, 2000

CAPTAIN KUZNETSOV stood in front of the pier at the Zapadnaya Litsa dockyard alongside Anatoly Markoff, captain of the Kursk's sister ship, Voronezh. The sun was starting to appear behind the trees that shielded the harbor, lighting the low mist skimming the water and making silhouettes of their two submarines. Behind them, working in deep red overalls a number of men could be heard better than they could be seen in the weak morning light as they shouted to each other over the noise of welding torches and heavy machinery from the hulls of both submarines. The work looked intense and chaotic with no apparent sense of cohesion, but this was the way of the Russian Navy; working to outlines rather than specifics, making it fast, practical, last-minute and dynamic. The Russians had won wars this way; defeating Napoleon two hundred years earlier and driving back the Germans in the Second World War.

Unlike Markoff, Kuznetsov wasn't dressed in full military uniform. It was to be his last voyage and he thought he had earned the right to dress that little more casually and so he wore a black fur coat trimmed with a brown collar that almost covered his ears. Topping off the ensemble was a large black hat baring the silver insignia of the Russian Northern Fleet that was stationed in and around Murmansk in the northern Kola Peninsula, directly on the border of Finland and Norway in the west.

Unlike their captains, the submarines looming behind Kuznetsov and Markoff looked identical in every way, apart that is from the impressive red emblem on the Kursk's conning tower picturing two eagles. In contrast, the Voronezh had no distinctive markings on the black matte, almost rubberlike finish that she had in common with the Kursk. Another thing she had in common was an experienced captain in charge of an experience crew. Despite the apparent chaos of the scene, each and every man knew exactly what was expected of him and because both captains trusted their men they paid little attention to the work as it was carried out.

Kuznetsov was born and raised in the Volgograd region. He wasn't from a military background. He simply joined the navy in 1972 to provide for his family. After graduating from the Submarine Navigation Higher Naval School in Leningrad in 1977 he served as a weapons officer aboard several submarines. In 1984 he served as Captain Third Rank on the K-77 that was tasked with spying on American submarines during the Cold War. After making the Advanced Special Officers' class in 1986, he served a few years on the Voronezh as First Officer. A little over a decade later, he was given command of the Kursk, where he had been ever since. Now, it was hard to believe, but he was at the start of his final journey with the old girl.

Looking out over the dockyard, a feeling of melancholy overtook him and he instinctively patted Markoff on the shoulder.

"Marko, Marko, Marko. Will they leave her with any of her dignity?"

For a few years, Markoff had served Kuznetsov as XO, Second in Command on the Kursk before getting his own submarine. Though

Markoff was some years younger than Kuznetsov at 35, the two men were familiar enough with each other to consider themselves as friends.

"You know how it is these days," Markoff replied, an air of resignation weighing heavy on the words as he spoke them. "I guess we'll all have to sacrifice something to get back on our feet."

Kuznetsov nodded his head in agreement. "You and me, we are old school. Well, at least I am. You? Maybe a little." Kuznetsov shrugged his shoulders and gave a little smile. "And you still have time to maybe get your chance to be new school again."

"Meaning?"

"Meaning if our president gets his way in the coming years perhaps our fleet will regain some of its former glory. The good old days, you know?"

"Like the Tsardom, the Russian Empire?" Markoff asked, the doubt clear in his voice.

"I mean the Soviet Union," Kuznetsov clarified, "and maybe a little of the early Russian federation. You know, before the adoption of the current Russian Constitution. You may think me an old fool, and perhaps I am, but even though the Cold War wasn't the best of times, it at least gave the world a form of balance, some equilibrium. Today everyone must look to America or possibly the emerging power of the Asians. You know, it's as if Mother Russia doesn't even matter anymore in the realm of international politics and that pains me deeply."

"And you believe our Comrade President can give us back what we've lost?" Markoff raised both eyebrows. "To be honest, I have serious doubts about the benefits of the past. All I remember from those days is my parents having to survive on food stamps because they earned next to nothing leaving them with nothing to spend but free time. At least now we roughly take home one hundred and fifty dollars. It might not be much, but I'm not sure I'd be willing to kiss it goodbye in the hope that we might one day become a great nation again."

Kuznetsov frowned at his friend's response and gathered his thoughts before answering. It was hard for him to grasp the lack of ambition in the younger generation. To his ears Markoff's words almost smacked of disloyalty, but the fact was times had changed and those who remembered the glory days of the past were getting older and taking their memories to the grave.

"Well, maybe you're right," Kuznetsov said. "Maybe I am the only one here that's still old school and maybe it's time to make room for new thoughts and ideas. I guess that's the price you pay for getting old."

Kuznetsov gave Markoff a tight-lipped smile and sighed.

A large steel crane that looked like it had been welded together from old railroad iron rose some five meters above the back of the pier. Manufactured in the '60s the crane had suffered from a lack of proper maintenance after the Cold War and as a result many of its systems no longer functioned like they ought to and it had to be directed manually. This made some jobs more intense than others and right now the crane was being used to transport a large, green, cigar-like torpedo which was swinging precariously from a steel chain. The torpedo didn't have any distinctive markings only a chrome-looking nozzle at the front and the back. At the nose and tail of the torpedo were four ropes, all of which were attached to a man on the ground, all of whom were struggling to steady the 10 meters long Shkval. With only one chain to lift the weapon the men were finding it hard to control what was essentially a 6,000lb cigar-shaped problem with a mind of its own as the crane slowly swung above the Kursk, its nose wide open in the center like a giant peeled banana awaiting its cargo. As the men shouted orders at each other, Markoff and Kuznetsov continued to stand on the dock with their backs turned to the activity.

Markoff was unhappy. "Right now they are stripping my boat, your former boat, just to get you on the way tomorrow. I really hope it's worth it."

Kuznetsov looked at his friend and for a moment considered sharing what he knew, but only for a moment.

"I can't tell you anything, Marko. I would if I could, but I can't. But you have to trust me on this because this exercise might ultimately be my legacy to you. If all goes as planned it will define your future, allowing you to continue serving in the water whilst I spend my retirement safely at the side of it fishing."

Markoff looked across at his friend and smiled before slowly shaking his head. He wanted to believe him but how?

"With our budgets and the condition they're leaving my boat in I'll be lucky to set sail again in two years, but..." Markoff fell silent. Unfortunately, when all was said and done nothing mattered. Even as captain of one of the Fleet's greatest submarines he was but a small cog in a far bigger machine.

"We had some good times," Kuznetsov told Markoff after the pause began to hang heavy between them. "It was always an honor serving with you. For me, my time is almost done; one last exercise, one last chance to--"

Before Kuznetsov could finish his sentence a loud bang finally attracted both captains' attention. They turned around in time to see the tail of the torpedo hanging from the crane and bouncing off the nose of the Kursk. The four men hanging onto the ropes were furiously shouting and cursing at each other even as they battled to rebalance the torpedo, now swinging in the wind like some kind of enormous and dangerous kite.

Kuznetsov and Markoff revealed little surprise and cocked their heads at each other.

"Need I say more?" Markoff asked and Kuznetsov responded in the only way he knew how; as the 'glass half full' optimist he had always been.

"With our annual budget already spent in the first six months of the year we should be happy we're still at work."

"And receiving even this small salary," Markoff added, to which both men laughed before turning to approach their crews who were clearly in need of more superior instruction on how to handle the crane.

8 Toma

August 12, 2000

AT SUNRISE the Bolshaya submarine dockyard now looked more like a market place in the early morning then a military base. Everywhere you looked men, and some women, were walking around, carrying materials onto the Kursk.

In the chaotic picture on the dock both civilians as men in military uniforms dominated the scene though the civilians seemed to do all the work and the officers seemed to be busier with each other. In these last minutes before departure all the fresh supplies were brought on board to sustain the crew on this five-day exercise. Although five days were just a short period for a mission the Russians always loaded their subs as if they were months underway. The reason was simply because they always needed to be ready to switch from exercise to a real threat situation. On the other hand this had to do with superstition. Better to be safe than sorry. That same principle applied to the weapons on board. In the past days an almost full complementary off arms was loaded onto the Kursk. Twenty-four, P700 Granit cruise missiles with various payloads, from ballistic to nuclear and twelve, type 65 torpedoes in part with dummy and part with ballistic payloads and then there were the two new Shkval torpedoes. The Shkval's only had a dummy payload and were only to be tested for their speed and navigation. Still it was believed that at the high speed the Shkval was supposed to travel it was expected to drive itself straight through the hull of any conventional ship.

The last thing to do before they could sail was the loading of the perishables. Men were driving carts up and down the pier and unloading their crates with fruits, vegetables, boxes and bottles onto the Kursk. A row about 5 trucks long was still waiting to be unloaded. A foreman at the end of the pier was shouting and waving at the trucks to get to the front for unloading. Then his attention shifted to the men with the carts walking up and down between the trucks and the Submarine.

"Come on men, hurry, hurry, hurry." he shouted. "We've got less than an hour to finish. This way the fruit will have perished long before it's on board." A man pushing a cart full of bottles shouted back.

"We need more men. You can shout all you want but we need more men to finish in time."

A black town car stopped in front of the pier. Kuznetsov, this time back in full uniform, accompanied by Qiungian Wang in a thick winter coat, got out of the car. As they started to walk up to the pier Kuznetsov noticed the foreman shouting at the workmen and walked up to him.

"You need help?"

"If you can spare a few men captain? My men are doing the best they can but because the loading of the equipment last night was delayed we had to wait and now we are far behind." Kuznetsov waved a small group of sailors that were talking to each other on the pier."

"You!" At first the men didn't notice him "He, you there." He rose his voice. Straight after every member of the group looked his way.

"Yes you, if you want any fresh fruit or vodka during the trip you better start helping them finishing up the loading." The men now all saluted back to Kuznetsov and walked up to the trucks to help unloading. Even if they didn't like helping, they knew better then not to obey even an informal request from their captain.

"Thank you Captain. I'll be out of your way in forty-five minutes."

Kuznetsov nodded to confirm and looked around to see were Wang had gone. Some 10 meters onto the pier Wang was talking to a Russian soldier smoking his probably last cigarette before leaving port knowing that once submerged he wouldn't be able to smoke for a while. Kuznetsov walked up to Wang greeting every soldier he passed on his way.

"Morning, how are you? Ready to sail? One last time left." He had unique greeting for each and every one taken into consideration everyone's merits. Wang looked at him approaching and expected him to stop at his place. Instead Kuznetsov past him straight by while summoning. "Are you coming?" Wang immediately took a few firm steps towards him and match his pace towards the running-board onto the Kursk.

In the back of the dockyard Mischa and Sophia walked hand in hand up to the pier Mischa wore his military uniform with his cap on his head. Over his shoulder he wore a greenish duffel bag, the same duffel bag that every officer seemed to ware on the docks. Sophia wore her long fur overcoat and a beige shawl over here mouth covering almost half her ears as if it was mid-winter. With her hand in his hand Mischa swung forward and backward as if they were walking up to a carnival. Then Sophia held back on his pace and his enthusiasm.

"What's wrong?" He asked.

"I'll miss you. Will you miss me? She solicited.

"Sure I'll miss you and you, you won't have time to miss me. In five days I'll be back to finish our honeymoon." He now had a boyish grin from ear to ear.

"Finish our honeymoon? We got married 4 months ago. I consider it finished. Come to think of it I considered it finished straight after the honeymoon" She teased him. Mischa grinned back.

That's what you think. He replied quickly. Wait until I get back well see who's right. If I come back!

"You make fun of it but I'm really worried, all the time. There's nothing you can do about it but returning to me in five days unharmed."

"*MEWOW*"

A beige, black sported cat suddenly screeched as he rubbed against Sophia's leg.

"Oh my" Sophia reacted startled and put up her hand to her mouth while Mischa laughed exuberantly and picked up the cat and started stroking him as was it his own cat.

"Don't be scared. It's only Toma. Toma is our Mascot. I'm glad he is here. Now he can come with us." Sophia reacted amazed as she slowly put her hand back down again. She frowned her eyebrows.

"You take a cat with you?"

"Sure. For good luck." Mischa replied without noticing he was walking into some kind of trap.

"And I can't come?" She said. Mischa felt he should have seen that one coming. While he was still looking for a way out Grisha and Galina Sokolov walked up to them as Grisha yelled at Mischa.

"Always playing with the cat!"

"Jealous? How long have we known each other? I thought that by this time you would know better than to be jealous." Mischa countered. Mischa opened his arms as Grisha walked straight into them. The men gave each other their standard warm and firm Russian hug. Sophia and Galina kissed each other on the cheek. Mischa put the cat on the ground and stretched his arms as he firmly grabbed Grisha at the shoulders as he pushed him a little away from him.

"Ready for your first trip?" He asked Grisha. Grisha was carefully considering his answer. In the back of his head he knew this was his first trip so he knew that anything he said from here on could be used against him. While he was thinking Galina answered the question.

"He hasn't been talking about anything else in the past days." Sophia replied to Galina as if she was predicting her future.

"Well. Prepare yourself because it's going to be like that from now on."

"Nonsense." Mischa cut into the conversation. "You'll see. It'll be great. Are you nervous?"

"Anxious would be a better word. Anxious to get on the way." Now Grisha's answer came quickly. His confidence seemed to build up rapidly. Grisha looked around to all the workmen still running around with materials. "They're still doing such a lot of work. Any idea when we'll leave?"

"I heard they were planning to sail within the hour. We better get ready to get on board." Mischa sounded enthusiastically. "We better say our good-byes."

"Will you take good care of him?" Galina sounded almost commanding. Mischa's response was pertinent and short.

"Always."

"You better." Sophia added. She couldn't hide her own frightened feelings on leaving the two of them with their favorite deathtrap. And you, Grisha, you keep my Mika on the straight pad on this trip away from all temptations. On this trip I need you to be me.

"Will do Sophia." Grisha said smiling.

"You know I'm serious about this"

"I do, I know you do. Trust me. I'll be you."

Mischa looked Sophia in the eyes as he took her hands and they moved a few meters away from Grisha and Galina.

"Come home safe Mika." Sophia whispered in his ear.

"As always." Mischa whispered back "As always." Without saying anything else the held each other tight for a minute. A tear rolled down on Sophia's cheek.

"You know you can count on me my Sofochka. Give me five days and I'll prove it to you."

A little further on the pier Galina and Grisha did the same thing.

"Don't let them get to you." Instead of whispering like Sophia Galina used a really loud noise as if to make an impression.

"What do you mean?" Grisha smiled a little. He loved his Tasha especially when she became a little worried. This way he always knew how much she cared.

"I mean. I hear stories about rites during first missions. I just want you to have a great time so whatever they are planning to do with you, don't let it get to you."

"Don't worry. I'll survive, and have some fun in the meantime. I love you dear. I'll be back before you know it. Grisha pulled her tight towards him one more time.

"I love you too."

While still hugging Sophia Mischa looked over her shoulder to Grisha and Galina as he shouted. "Are you ready, let's go then?" Sophia immediately pushed him away from here, grabbed her ears and with a big smile she yelled at Mischa. "All right, so now I'll need the five days to get my hearing back." The two couples rejoined and Grisha hugged Sophia while Mischa kissed Galina on both cheeks.

"You all take care now and hurry back." Sophia said.

"I love you my Sofochka."

"I love you my Mika."

Sophia and Mischa kissed one last time. Then the men walked onto the pier towards the gangway onto the Kursk. The woman stayed waving constantly while they both yelled and gave hand kisses. "I love you. Come back soon. Don't do anything stupid. I'll think of you. Think of me!" The women were yelling waving and shouting. Around them there were dozens of other woman doing the same for their friends, husbands and sons as all the sailors were now walking up on the pier onto the Kursk. Just before walking up to the gangway when he stopped to look back one more time he felt something rubbing his lake. Looking down there was Toma again. Mischa picked up the cat with one hand and looked back to Sophia who waved him a hand kiss. With his free hand Mischa caught the hand in the air and put it to his heart as he mimicked with his mouth. "I love you too."

Mischa and Grisha looked at each other one more time before walking up the gangway. Silently they gave each other a firm nod with their heads and started walking up the gangway. This was it. There was no turning back now. On deck of the Kursk both men looked once again into the crowd if they could find their woman. But they couldn't find them so they walked up to the 'hole' in the submarine where they lowered themselves and disappeared from sight.

In her apartment Mischa's mother Elena sat down at her kitchen table. In the back there was a television set with a round the clock news casting. She wasn't worried about her son going on another mission. She was used to it as Mischa's father also was a submarine man and she had seen them both going on missions more times then she could count. They always came back with lots of stories to tell. She unfolded the newspaper with on the front a big picture of their new president. While looking at his picture she whispered in herself. "Same old, same old." The newscaster on television sounded in the back.

"Today, just after 4 months in office the president gives himself an already well-deserved vacation. Here we see him leaving the Kremlin in his limousine on his way to his holiday mansion in Sochi along the Black See. It's not known –"

When the apartment door opened Sophia and Galina entered the small hallway. While they hung their coats on the rack Sophia called out.

"Mom? Are you there?"

"I'm in the kitchen."

"You're always in the kitchen." Sophia said smiling while looking at Galina. Sophia and Galina walked through the living room entering the kitchen.

"You brought Galina." Elena noticed.

"Hi Ms. Kastamarov. How are you doing?" Galina replied.

"I'm good dear. How are you and how's your mother?"

"We're both a little sad." Galina said in a gloomy voice.

"So am I dear. I am always a little sad when they leave on a mission. But I know it'll be al OK soon. "A drink?"

"Before Galina could answer she noticed Sophia's eyes wandering off to a small brown cupboard in the kitchen." Sophia seemed startled.

"What's wrong? You look like you've seen a ghost." Then Galina noticed Sophia looking at a small necklace hanging from one of the wooden knobs on top of the cupboard. At closer look she sees that on the necklace there's a small crucifix. Sophia walked over to the cupboard and picks up the crucifix and looked at it in her hand.

"What is it?" Galina asked concerned.

"It's Mika's crucifix." Sophia replied. "He always wares it with his dog tags. It is for good luck he says."

Oh child. Stop worrying. Elena intervened. You young people and your superstitions. I'm sure he'll be fine. Now put that away and let's have some tea."

Sophia took one last look at the crucifix and then hung it back on the knob.

9 The Marjata

THE BARENTS SEA was named after the Dutch navigator Willem Barentsz. Prior to this it was known as the Murman Sea, a name that still lingers in the region of Murmansk. Located off the northern coast of Norway and the western borders of Russia much of the sea lies within Russian territorial waters, which once made it strategically valuable during the games of the Cold War. More recently it had become the strategic playground of NATO thanks to Norway's proximity to Murmansk, which also happened to be home to Russia's biggest naval force, the Northern Fleet.

That morning, the sea was dark blue in color and reasonably calm. The sun lit the water, decorating it with twinkling stars on top of each and every wave, and as far as the eye could see the vast expanse of the Barents Sea was empty save for the lone figure of the FS Marjata.

The Marjata was a small, 75 meters electronic intelligence-collection vessel belonging to the Norwegian military. Large soccer-ball-like antennas sat on top of the grey ship's bridge that rose far above the sea line. On the green deck at the rear a helicopter pad displaying the name 'MARJATA' occupied nearly half of the ship. At 9:00am a sailor exited from a door on top of the bridge. From the balcony he panned over the empty waters, looking through binoculars before focusing on the area west. A few seconds later a Norwegian Bell 412SP helicopter in full camouflage colors could be seen heading towards the Marjata. The sailor lowered his binoculars and made his way down the steel staircase towards the deck. By the time he reached it the helicopter was only about a 100 meters from the ship. On deck he was joined at the helicopter pad by a man in a bright yellow oil-coated jacket whose job it was to guide the helicopter in.

With the chopper blades still rotating, the sailor approached the helicopter just as the side door opened. Commander Mitchel James exited the helicopter. Dressed in his United States Service Dress Blue uniform and his short, blond hair and model good looks, he saluted the sailor that ushered him away from the noise.

"Commander James," the sailor shouted. "on behalf of the Norwegian Intelligence Service, welcome. If you would please follow me, I'll take you to the bridge."

James duly followed the sailor to a side entrance.

"You had a nice helicopter ride?" the sailor politely enquired as they made their way up the stairs to the bridge. "Did you see any whales? With a little luck this season we might spot some Bowheads. They can grow up to 35 meters and weigh seventy-five tons. Quite a spectacular sight."

"No whales," James curtly replied.

"That's a pity," the sailor said, and decided to leave the conversation there.

The two men climbed up the long metal stairs to the bridge and stopped at a closed metal door with a small sign reading 'STYRHUS'. The sailor stopped and opened the door for the officer. James looked inside and found himself confronted by a bank of computers, radar screens, knobs and keyboards. Directly ahead of him was a commanding view of the deck of the Marjata and the Barents Sea.

Despite there being some thirty men working at their stations the room was quiet, 'library quiet' James thought as he entered the bridge. After shutting the door behind them, the sailor pointed James in the direction of Rear Admiral Fredrik Anders.

Inspecting the vast expanse of water before them, Anders cut an imposing figure; large with fair skin, blond hair and tiny eyes, the 45-year-old managed to look not only serious but also like a man with an appetite for life. As James neared he turned around.

"Fredrik Anders," he said by way of introduction.

"Lieutenant Commander James."

"How was your flight?"

"Fine."

The two men shook hands before Anders turned back to the window, raising the binoculars that hung from his neck to look over the seemingly empty waters.

"Any whales?" James asked.

Anders turned and smiled.

"No whales. The Bowhead migrate at this time of year. Three days ago I saw two of them in the distance. I've been looking for them ever since without any luck."

"Shame," James responded, "I saw no whales on the flight either, but helicopters aren't really my thing so I wasn't paying that much attention. Oh, and thank you for speaking English by the way. Back in the US they didn't pay much attention to foreign languages at military training."

"No problem. So, you're frightened of flying then?"

"Frightened of crashing," James responded with a smile and Anders replied with one of his own.

"So tell me, is this your first time in the neighborhood, Lieutenant Commander?"

"I've attended NATO's Joint Warfare Center in Stavanger before but I've never been at sea in this area," James replied truthfully. Though his back was straight he felt a pang of inadequacy hit his chest like it always did when he came up against combat soldiers, sailors and pilots. Intelligence was an increasingly vital role in the protection of the state, but it still felt like a copout on occasion.

"Ah, the sea," Anders said wistfully. "Tell me Lieutenant Commander, what do you see when you look outside?"

James glanced through the large glass window, but his mind was as empty as the view. He was more a city man.

"I see water, blue sky, lots of water more sky and more water," He replied, only half-joking.

"You know what I see?" Anders asked, though he didn't wait for an answer. "I see an endless sea holding infinite diversity. You know why? Because I choose to. The world offers you anything you want to see; you simply have to choose for yourself."

James gave Anders a sideways glance; he knew he needed his full cooperation so he didn't want to contradict him from the outset, but he kind of thought life was a little more complicated than that.

"I guess that if the world really works as you say one could also choose to see something completely different."

Anders reacted with a smile; Americans were so, well, one-dimensional. "OK, so why don't you tell me why you're here Lieutenant Commander."

"You don't know, Admiral?

"I suppose I do but I'd like to first compare my notes to yours."

James felt the hairs on the back of his neck bristle, but he couldn't help but respect the man's straightforwardness; when a mission starts the goals are not always in sync. "Can we go somewhere a little more private?" he asked.

"Sure." Anders pointed towards a small door at the back of the bridge. The sign on the door read: "KONTROLLROM"

70

Please, join me," invited Anders and he led James into what looked like a conference room with a long, grey table at the center and ten chairs around it. "Please take a seat."

"Thank you." James sat down. "Admiral, my orders are to set up communications between the White House, the D.I.A., and two US Submarines, The Detroit and The Baltimore, which are both in the neighborhood." James paused, but Anders gave nothing away. "And you, the Norwegian Navy are here on behalf of NATO to make that possible."

"And that's it?"

"That's it."

"OK. So let's go with the obvious; why do we need these communications?"

James scraped his tongue along his teeth and decided to come clean; he needed the Norwegian's full cooperation and he saw that honesty might be the best way to get it.

"As you know, the Russians have started their summer exercise in the region. We believe that one of the Russian subs is carrying a new type of rocket torpedo called the Shkval and that they will test fire it during this exercise. If this torpedo is as advertised it's a one-off and potentially devastating. So, the big picture is about discovering the truth and if the Shkval does exist, what we can do about it."

"And what's so special about this...Shkval?"

"Apparently it can travel up to speeds exceeding 250 knots and carry any payload. As you can imagine, this will give anyone who has it a considerable advantage in sea warfare."

"And do I sense there's more than one party involved?"

"Yes, we believe the Russians are trying to partially fund their new naval plans by selling sell the Shkval to the Chinese. If the rumors are true and should China get this weapon it might be used to facilitate an invasion of Taiwan; something the US and NATO cannot allow to happen. I'm sure I don't need to explain to you the casualties that might be incurred if we're required to come to Taiwan's defense."

"If true, this torpedo would, as you say, put us at a serious disadvantage at sea," Anders admitted. "So what do you need us to do?"

"The mission is fairly simple. We have intel that the K-141 Russian nuclear and ballistic missile submarine the Kursk will fire the torpedo during the coming exercise maneuvers. When that happens we plan to be in the area. The USS Detroit will guard the waters at the borders around the exercise while the USS Baltimore will near the Kursk to take readings."

"What kind of readings?"

"For now we simply want to record any sounds and radar images we can get from the Shkval in order to ascertain whether we can devise a method of detecting these torpedoes in the future."

"And do we have any idea when the launch will take place?"

"No." James shook his head and had to admit they were not operating under ideal conditions. "We know that the exercise will take about five days and that the Kursk hasn't even left dock yet. When it does our subs have orders to take their positions near the boundary of Russia's territorial waters and get as close as they can to the Kursk for the duration of the exercise. The Marjata will be in position as the command ship during the length of this operation. If it's OK with you I'd also like to set up a command center in this room, but I will need communication and radar devices to do so."

Anders rubbed his chin, took a deep breath and set a smile on his face. "OK. I guess your 'notes' are in sync with mine," he said. "I'll have someone help you set up shop."

"Thank you, Admiral."

10 Underway

Saturday, August 11, 2000

ON THE ZAPADNAYA LITSA PIER the workmen were leaving as the last sailors walked onto the Kursk. The dockyard was almost empty, the families all gone. As the departure of any ship was considered to be a classified movement in the navy no civilians were permitted to watch.

On the bayside of the Kursk two tugboats maneuvered into position and moored themselves to the front and the back of the submarine. Though they were small, the tugboats stood out from the Kursk thanks to their red bellies and yellow bridges. It took only a few minutes to tie up the tugboats after which a wave of hands signaled the all-clear to the Kursk. On top of the sub's conning tower, Captain Kuznetsov and his first officer Kolya Bodrov acknowledged the signal and ordered the Kursk to be released from the dock.

In contrast to Kuznetsov who hailed from Volgograd and was therefore considered to be a 'true Russian', Kolya Vladimirovitsj Bodrov was a career officer from Belarus, commonly thought of as a 'lower' Russian region. After the Cold War Belarus had attempted to bolster relations with the West, something the new president had wasted no time in expressing his dissatisfaction at when he took office. As a result, the Belarusians in the military found themselves with second-rate reputations even if they were first-rate officers, such as Kolya Bodrov, not that he was overly concerned about any of this. Now 31, he had joined the navy as a fifteen-year-old boy and though he wasn't as outspoken as some his loyalties lay undisputedly with Russia.

"Release all lines and release the boat," Bodrov ordered an officer waiting below them on the deck of the submarine.

With a firm salute, the sailor turned to signal the men onshore who quickly began to reel in the lines attaching the Kursk to the pier. Then, with a smoothness that comes from years of practice, the Kursk began to inch away from the mainland. As she did so, the tugboats started their engines to propel the submarine, and slowly the Kursk slipped away from the pier, covering a few meters every ten seconds. Once the tugboats had maneuvered the Kursk to the center of the bay the submarine would have the freedom to take charge of her own movements.

Within minutes the Kursk was drifting in the center of the bay and the tugboats released their lines and sailed away. Kuznetsov was the last man standing above the conning tower. He looked at the mainland one more time because it was not only his habit but also his privilege to be the last one to go down into the sub. Taking a final breath of fresh air deep into his lungs, he descended the stairs and disappeared from the outside world. At the bottom of the staircase he pushed a big red button that closed the hatch above his head.

"Captain on the bridge," a voice stated over the intercom system as Kuznetsov entered the central command center, which was basically a room roughly 10 meters long, 5 meters wide on the second floor of the submarine. The walls were busy with buttons and gauges and they filled the blue-grey panels from the floor to their ceiling. Working at the panels on yellow upholstered seats were sailors dressed in blue overalls. All the men worked their stations in silence, talking only when it was absolutely necessary. The mood was one of calm professionalism; it was a job they knew blindfolded and more than that most of the men loved it.

In the front of the command center was a large access hatch to the forward torpedo compartment. To the back another hatch led to the stern which housed the crew facilities and nuclear reactors. In the center of the compartment two work benches sat next to each other. One was setup for communications and the other was covered with maps and navigational aids. In front of the work benches, two large steel periscope cylinders descended from the ceiling.

Kuznetsov walked up to the center of the room.

"All stations prepare to get under way," he ordered.
The room hushed as the men concentrated on their instruments and most of them ignored Qiungian Wang as he appeared from the stern hatch.

"I trust everything is to your liking?" Kuznetsov asked him.

"It is Captain, and thank you for ceding your quarters to me for the mission, though it wasn't necessary."

"Anything for our clients," Kuznetsov said.

"Are we already on the way?"

"Not yet," Kuznetsov smiled. "The Kursk is a silent boat but not that silent. You'll know when we're underway and about to go. Is this your first submarine trip?"

"It is."

"Are you nervous?"

"Excited would be a better word. I always wanted to go on a submarine but now I'm on it, I guess you could say that I'm a little nervous."

"If you wish you can take a seat at navigation." Kuznetsov pointed to the desk next to him.

"Thanks, Captain. I won't be in your way."

At the stern of the submarine, in the propulsion control compartment, all chairs were manned and all eyes were focused on a wall of instruments. By now Mischa had changed into his own blue overalls and was stood in front of the 1MC Intercom Radio waiting for their captain to speak

"All stations report," Kuznetsov ordered.
Mischa looked around the room and his men nodded to show they were ready. With a loud firm voice he stated, "Propulsion ready, Captain."

Back in the command center, Kuznetsov stood waiting for the same response from all of the Kursk's stations.

"Navigation ready, Sir."

"Reactor and auxiliary systems are go, Captain."

Kuznetsov looked over at Bodrov who was inspecting a screen over the shoulder of a young sailor.

"Mr. Bodrov, propulsion, one third power," he commanded.

"Aye, propulsion one third power, Captain." Bodrov picked up another 1MC from the panel and repeated the order to the propulsion room.

"Propulsion, one third power," Mischa informed his men.

"One third power coming up, Sir."

"XO, all compartments secure?" Kuznetsov asked Bodrov who immediately checked a panel on the wall where a series of nine lights, representing each compartment of the submarine, were lit green bar one. A second later that also changed color. "All compartments secure, Captain."

"Thank you, XO. Check speed zero six knots and take us underway."

"Checking speed zero six knots and taking us underway sir."

Outside, the water slowly started to swell around the stern of the Kursk as she surged forward towards the Kola Fjord. The five-mile wide inlet was lined by a precipitous coast to the east and a relatively flat shoreline that ran the 35 miles from Murmansk in the south all the way to the Barents Sea in the upper north-west part of Russia. Home to the military ports of Murmansk, Severomorsk and Polyarny, the Fjord had always been the main waterway for Russia's Northern Fleet to enter the northern territories. And as the Kursk sailed on the surface she looked a fraction of her true size as she navigated the many sharp-rocked islands that blocked her way to the open sea. From the command center, Kuznetsov watched their progress with a mild sense of nostalgia. Slowly, but surely, their journey had begun.

11 One Control

I N THE MARJATA'S CONFERENCE ROOM James flicked some switches on the radios and screens that Anders had freshly-installed. Within hours the conference room had been transformed into a high-tech communications center with state-of-the-art materials. As he turned on the radar screen to reveal a large part of the eastern Norwegian coastline in green graphics, Anders walked in.

"Are you comfortable?"

"Everything looks great. Your men have just finished setting up and we now have radio and radar. I was about to try and make contact with the Detroit and Baltimore."

"Good for you, though I wouldn't expect too much from this radar as it's chiefly designed to locate objects above water and given that we're looking for subs...." Anders smiled. "I'll have them set up more applied and sensitive equipment for you later on today, but don't mind me, please continue."

James nodded to Anders as he picked up the 1MC. "Listener One this is One Control, do you read, over." He let go of the microphone for a moment and waited for a reaction. When no reply came he changed frequencies and tried again. "Listener One, this is One Control, do you read, over."

Deep in the waters of the Barents Sea, in the hushed confines of the USS Baltimore, the submarine's captain flashed a smile at his crew.

"One Control this is Captain Stephen Cook of the SSN-806, Baltimore. Reading you loud and clear, over."

Sailing north of the Kola Fjord, submerged at periscope depth, the USS Baltimore sat quietly in the deep like only a Los Angeles Class fast-attack nuclear submarine can. At 361 feet in length she was only two-thirds the length of the Kursk and half as wide making her a good deal faster than the hulking Russian sub. However, there was one thing the two had in common and that was a full complement of arms including torpedoes and cruise missiles.

Inside the Baltimore space was at a premium yet everything looked more organized than on the Kursk. Whereas the Russians used loose fabric to cover free-standing chairs, the Americans used tight blue leather to upholster steel seats that were bolted to the submarine. In fact, everything was where it was supposed to be, including the crew who were jammed into the command center.

Captain Stephen Cook II stood at the radio in the center of the room. He was thirty-five, a few pounds heavier than he would like to be, and wearing glasses. Well over six feet tall, when he spoke his voice boomed with a rich southern accent and when he moved he had to bend in order to avoid hitting his head on the overhead pipes. After graduating with honors from the Naval War College, Cook had proved himself as an officer and was widely respected in the service.

"Captain Cook, good to hear from you. This is Lieutenant Commander Mitchel James on the Marjata commanded by Admiral Anders of the Norwegian Navy. How are things going?"

"Good morning, Commander, good morning Admiral. We're in position about twenty miles north of the Kola Fjord with zero movement awaiting your orders."

80

"Thank you, Captain. We've set up our Command Center on the Marjata and are awaiting contact with Listener Two. When we have contact we will get back to you. In the meantime, I'd ask you to wait and hold the line."

"No problem, Commander, we're not going anywhere. Cook, out."

Sailing on the waterline of the Barents Sea, three officers of the USS Detroit stood at the top of the conning tower looking out over the vast expanse of water. One of them was Captain Jack Coleman. In his late thirties, wearing sunglasses and a cap, the man was known to have a ready smile and a fair few talents. On one occasion he managed the first ever on-time and below-budget shipyard depot modernization in the history of the US Navy and he was proud of it. It was also that kind of efficiency he expected from all of his men on board.

Enjoying the wind in his hair and a much-needed cigar, his attention was stolen by the radio crackling to life.

"Listener Two, are you receiving me? Over."

Coleman paused before picking up the 1MC, unwilling to wave goodbye to the fresh air, summer breeze and sunlight just yet. After a second or two he reluctantly picked up the microphone.

"One Command, this is Captain Jack Coleman on Listener Two," he replied, without bothering to take the cigar from his mouth.

"I've been listening in on our secure comlink. We're about fifteen miles east of Listener One sailing the fair weather over the Barents Sea. Over."

"Welcome to the party, Captain. Captain Cook are you still there?"

"Still here, Commander."

"Hi there Stephen, how are you doing?"

Cook smiled as he heard the familiar voice from the Baltimore's sister submarine the Detroit. Judging by the rush of wind coming over the intercom he guessed Coleman was enjoying the weather topside and possibly a last cigar.

"Doing great, Jack, thanks. How's the weather up there?"

"All good," Coleman answered "Fine down under too."

"Gentlemen," James interrupted. "As you are no doubt aware by now, satellite has confirmed the Kursk has set sail. Additional intel informs us that the battle cruiser Peter the Great will command the coming exercise and will be the likely practice target for the Kursk. We expect you to pick up the Kursk within two hours of her leaving the Kola Fjord. We don't know whether she will sail topside or submerged so I suggest you keep your eyes and ears aimed at both. Get back to us when you've established contact. We'll be sailing the coastline at approximately 50 miles awaiting your call."

"Will do. Cook, out."

"Talk to you soon. Coleman, out."

James hung up the 1MC and turned to Anders who had not stopped looking out of the window throughout the brief conversation with the US submarine commanders.

"Worried?" he asked.

"Not worried," Anders replied easily. "Just thinking. I've had word that Admiral Petrov of the Northern Fleet will be in charge of the exercise and positioned on the Peter the Great."

"Do you know him?"

"I met him once at an embassy dinner. He struck me as a proud man with an unshakable belief in a new and invigorated Russian Navy. I must admit, I kind of liked him."

"Why?"

"I liked his conviction. Petrov loves his country and wants the best for Mother Russia and her citizens. Is that so different from what we want?

"No, which is kind of ironic."

"Ironic?"

"Well, in a way our job is to prevent that dream from becoming a reality by stopping the Russian Navy from finding the means and the finances to become great again..."

12 Sea Baptism

THE KURSK CUT THROUGH THE KOLA FJORD as smoothly as a hot knife through butter. In the torpedo compartment, leaning casually against the weapons, were a number of sailors surrounding a chair upon which Grisha was sat. On one side of the room some of the men were hanging an old, rusty hammer on a chain from the pipes attached to the ceiling. From the back door Mischa entered the room singing the national anthem:

> *Russia – our sacred homeland,*
> *Russia – our beloved country.*
> *A mighty will, a great glory –*
> *These are your heritage for all time!*

As he reached the chorus, the rest of the men joined in and Mischa walked about the room waving his arms in the air as though conducting a choir.

> *Be glorious, our free Fatherland,*

Age-old union of fraternal peoples,
Ancestor-given wisdom of the people!
Be glorious, our country! We are proud of you!

All the men cheered and clapped their hands as Mischa walked up to Grisha. His friend looked up at him warily, but Mischa put a hand on his shoulder and winked. With the other hand he pulled a microphone down from the ceiling.

"Comrades…comrades, if you would please keep your mouths shut for a moment I can start our business here today."

Slowly, the room quietened.

"Thank you, comrades. My name is Mischa Kastamarov and I will be your host today." Mischa paused and waited for the laughter to subside before continuing. "As you know, we are gathered here for the sea baptism of Grisha Sokolov who is undertaking his first mission with us; his maiden voyage, if you will." Cheers and clapping erupted once again, reaching deafening levels in the cramped confines of the torpedo room. "Please comrades, please. Let me continue," Mischa theatrically begged his fellow sailors. "Grisha, it's a very important day for you; today you become part of a heroic submarine crew."

Grinning from ear to ear, Grisha threw his arms wide and repeated with a joyful shout: "Heroes!"

Around him, the rest of the crew echoed his cry. "Heroes! Heroes! Heroes! Heroes! Heroes!" they chanted.

"All right, all right. Enough already!" Mischa waved his arms to calm the crew, who were getting boisterous. "Grisha, I promise you, you will remember this day for the rest of your life. Right, let's get this over with!"

One of the sailors handed Mischa a white cup, which he proceeded to hold with great reverence as though he was in possession of the Holy Grail rather than cheap enamel.

"Grisha, this cup, filled with salt water from 75 meters deep, represents all life in the sea. Therefore, to begin your baptism you will drink this water, all at once, so that the sea and also your crew mates can witness your devotion to her and to them and, in doing so, unconditionally accept you as part of them."

Mischa handed the cup to Grisha who inspected the contents by smelling it. It smelled salty, fishy and pretty much how you would expect the sea to smell. He looked up to face his fellow crew members.

"Today, I drink water taken from the depths of the Barents Sea," he said loudly. "I do this so all will be well on this mission and on the many missions to come." Grisha put the cup to his mouth, with both hands, and after a slight hesitation he drank deeply as the men cheered.

"Drink, drink, drink, drink!"

Grisha gulped to keep down the seawater, which was fighting to come back up again after hitting his stomach. When the cup was empty he turned it upside down and placed it triumphantly on the ground. Beside him, Mischa gestured for silence.

"Of course today you don't just express allegiance to the sea and any old crew. No, today you become a member of the proudest crew to man the biggest and toughest submarine in the Northern Fleet, if not the entire Russian Navy, if not _" the sailors in the room took a breath to help Mischa finish his sentence, "-the whole wide world."

"Therefore, in order to prove your worth, to show that you too are tough enough for this boat, the K-141, and to show us that, yes, you love her, here we have..." Mischa took a step to the side to reveal the rusty hammer hanging from the ceiling. "... the hammer! Do not be fooled, this is no ordinary hammer. This is the hammer that built this boat and your first official assignment is to kiss this hammer to show respect for a job well done. Kiss it .... while it's swinging. And kiss it as if it was Galina herself!"

Grisha nodded seriously and walked up to the hammer as one of the sailors swung it from the pipe.

"Kiss, kiss, kiss, kiss..." the men chanted as the hammer swung wildly from side to side. When Grisha tried to kiss it the first time it almost smacked him in the face. The second time he lunged for it he succeeded and the men appreciated the effort with a loud cheer and furious clapping before stepping forward to shake hands with the newest member of their team.

"Congratulations," Mischa said, and his broad smile told Grisha he had conducted himself well. "You are now a member of our crew, manning the toughest submarine in the fleet and we are proud to have you with us. Now, as for the rest of you – get your lazy butts back to your stations and let's start this mission."

As the Kursk neared the exit of the Kola Fjord, the hills to the left and the right of the boat gradually faded into the distance as the inlet met the Barents Sea. In the command center, Kuznetsov readied his crew to dive, always the most thrilling and tense part of a new mission.

"Diving Officer, have all compartments rig for dive. Prepare to take us down 15 meters," Kuznetsov instructed.

The officer relayed the command as the rest of the crew took to their stations whilst keeping an extra eye out for leaks because their submarines were known to take in water from time to time. "Torpedo control, rig for dive. Navigation, rig for dive. Propulsion rig for dive. Reactor room, rig for dive."

As the orders boomed over the intercom, the diving alarm sounded, a deep almost eerie wail that blared twice through the speakers throughout the boat. A second later, the command center turned crimson.

Next to Kuznetsov, the XO relayed the next command.
"Dive, dive," Bodrov instructed the crew, and the Kursk gracefully disappeared from view, diving beneath the waves as it passed the last island of the Kola Fjord.

13 Let the Games...

AS THE BALTIMORE SAILED SUBMERGED in the clear waters of the Barents Sea the crew anxiously worked at their screens searching for anything 'abnormal' in the vicinity.

"We've got something sir!" a voice sounded from the sonar station and Cook immediately went to investigate.

"Are you sure, son?"

"Well Sir, I've got something on sonar, but the computer is having trouble determining what it is," replied the technician as he pointed at a blurred smudge on the screen.

"Could it be a natural phenomenon?" Cook asked.

"It could be, Sir, but due to the regular speed and straight movement of the object my guess would be manmade."

"Thank you, lieutenant." Cook walked to the radio station trying not to smile and picked up the microphone.

"One Control, this is Listener One. Over." As he spoke a hush descended on the room and all eyes turned to him as the Marjata answered the call.

"Listener One, this is One Control. Commander James here. Over."

As James spoke into the microphone he used his free hand to switch off the video game he had been playing. Most men needed a way to pass time on a mission such as this, and this was how he passed his. He glanced around the room, loving the professionalism and sense of anticipation within the boat's newly established communications center. Over the speaker, the captain of the Baltimore sounded.

"Listener One, we've picked up something large that we're still trying to get a definitive confirmation on via sonar," revealed Cook. "However, there are positive signs that we may have hit our target which is travelling in direction two-seven-zero at a speed of twenty-five knots."

James raised an eyebrow and flipped a switch on the panel in front of him to discuss the development with the captain of the Detroit.

"Listener Two, can you confirm?" he asked. "I repeat: Listener Two, can you confirm the target's direction and position? Over."

For a second there was the sound of static through the loudspeakers as the captain of the Detroit quickly checked his own radar and sonar screens.

"Still nothing?" Coleman asked his sonar technician.

"Nothing Sir, only Listener One, and some as of yet unidentified background noise."

Coleman frowned; he never liked to be last to the party. In fact it was this competitive edge among US personnel that made their counterparts in the Russian Navy dub them submarine cowboys. "OK thanks, keep looking and listening." Coleman turned to his XO, Mitch Garret. Mitch had joined his crew a few months back and though it was

90

his first term as Senior Officer Coleman thought he already showed great promise as a potential commander.

"XO, help them look for that Russian. I don't like it one bit when there's something down there I cannot see." Coleman picked up the 1MC and the tone of his voice clearly conveyed his irritation to not only his crew, but the others listening in. "One Control, this is Listener Two. We cannot confirm, I repeat, we cannot confirm anything at this time. This could simply be that we are too far away from our target"

"Roger that Listener Two. No problem," answered James from the Marjata, keen to ease the tension he heard in the other officer's voice. "At this stage, none of us have much on the Kursk's signature. However, I think we can safely assume that the Russian sub's outer hull is layered with some sort of sonar-absorbing rubber, which would make any signal hard to identify. Furthermore, according to our readings, there's nothing else in the water in that neighborhood, so let's accept Listener One's readings as a working theory until we are given a reason not to. Listener One, stay on the suspected target and record all activity and every sound she makes. Listener Two, keep your position, keep searching and keep monitoring overall fleet movements. Captains, you are both specifically instructed to use active sonar to let the Russians know we are here. Be loud. We don't want any misunderstandings, or any accidental collisions."

As Cook hung back the 1MC he turned to his XO.
"Mr. Garret. Please lock on to the probable target bearing two-seven-zero, mirroring depth and direction." He then turned to the rest of his crew in the command center. "Let's get in close gentlemen, and every thirty seconds inform them of our presence."

At the captain's command, the Baltimore swiftly changed course. As she picked up speed the propeller softly hummed at the stern, a noise that was barely audible at the depth they travelled. A second later a sharp 'ping' sounded, slicing through the density of the water. It was repeated half a minute later.

As the Kursk entered the open sea, Kuznetsov prepared to address his men. It was customary for all captains to say a few words at the start of a mission and though he had done it a hundred times before, this time it would be different. It was his last voyage, the last time he would speak to his men in such a way, and it felt strangely emotional. While he was looking forward to spending more time with his family, he knew he would miss being there for his men. A good commander never simply gives orders; he leads by example and he takes care of the crews that take care of him. In many ways, he would miss the respect he had earned from his men over the years, but also the camaraderie and, yes, affection. Of course, when he saw Qiungian Wang approach him, he also realized there was one thing he wouldn't miss about the job and that was the political and commercial reality of today's Russian Navy.

"Can I help you, Mr. Wang?" Kuznetsov asked the frustration he felt clear in his voice at the Chinaman's presence during this part of the exercise. Though he was all for a reinvigorated Russian Navy he couldn't shake his dislike of the politics or, indeed, the Chinese. He had never trusted them.

"Am I in your way?" Wang asked, having obviously picked up on the restraint in the captain's voice. He took a small step backwards and bowed slightly. It was a movement that perfectly symbolized Kuznetsov's distrust of the Chinese because it struck him as insincere; no race of people could be so universally subservient and respectful without having something to hide.

"No, you're not in my way," Kuznetsov told his guest, being careful to keep any signs of emotion out of his voice and off his face. "However, I'd kindly ask you to keep your distance from the instruments, just in case."

"Of course, I will. You won't even know I'm here."

But you are here, Mr. Wang. You are here. Nodding curtly, Kuznetsov picked up the 1MC.

"Comrades," his voiced boomed through every compartment and corridor of the boat, immediately silencing every man on board who knew the drill and now waited for the captain's speech to commence. "Today we sail once more for the glory of the Russian Federation. This exercise will be the beginning of a new era for the Russian Navy. Under a new leadership we have the opportunity and the desire to reign supreme once more, above and beneath the water." Kuznetsov paused for a moment to appreciate the cheers and applause echoing throughout the Kursk. "Today men, we are not simply conducting an exercise, we are telling the world that we are still here and we remain a power to be reckoned with, perhaps more than ever before. My fellow comrades, many of you are the first of a new generation. You are the ones who will deliver a new era of greatness, not only as sailors, but as Russians. From this moment forward it is your duty to continue the job I began. This is my last voyage and I am honored to stand before you not as your captain but as a fellow sailor and proud Russian. I thank you for your trust in me over the years and for allowing me to guide you towards the first step of a new Russian prosperity. So comrades, let us find our target and show what we are capable of."

As Kuznetsov finished, the Kursk exploded with loud cheers and Mr. Wang nodded his head in admiration. "They follow you like we followed Chairman Mao," he said.

Kuznetsov shook his head. "It's different," he said, or at least the way he viewed it was. "The Chinese followed Chairman Mao in order to eat, to get food. We Russians; we follow because we are proud to follow – whether it be the tsars or the communists and whether we are fed or not."

"And that makes you, what?" Wang asked. There was an edge to his voice and Kuznetsov smiled.

"I don't know," he replied. "--Russians?" Kuznetsov turned to his XO. "Take us closer to our target Mr. Bodrov."

As the Kursk continued its slow journey, the Baltimore edged closer until it came close enough to the Russian sub that the crews could have waved at each other if there were windows to see out of.

Every man concentrated on his screen. Every thirty seconds a ping sounded from the active sonar, slowly travelling through the deep blue and fading away. Although it was now apparent they were close by and Cook could have safely killed the signal, he knew it kept the crew on their toes. While the atmosphere was calm, the men were completely focused.

Breaking the quiet, the sonar technician called to the Baltimore's XO, Eric Sanders. "Sir, Sir!"

Sanders looked up and wandered over to the young man.

"Calm down, son. What's up?"

"We're right on the target, Sir. Speed 15 knots, distance 150 yards and closing at 50 yards a minute.

"No problem, we've plenty of time." Sanders remained characteristically calm. Turning to face the command center, he ordered the speed to be pulled back to three knots. "What's our depth?

"Fifty feet, Sir. Our friend is at approximately equal depth."

Sanders nodded. "Navigation, keep us 500 yards apart and maintain mirrored heading and distance."

"Aye Sir, making our distance 500 yards keeping heading and distance."

"Sir!" called out the sonar technician urgently. "It looks like they're taking her to the surface."

At that, Sanders and Cook both walked up to the technician's station.

"Show me." Cook ordered.

"Here, Sir." The young man pointed to the screen.

"They're probably preparing for an exercise attack round," Sanders said.

"Agreed," replied Cook and he called out to the command center. "Take us back, but make sure our distance is at least 500 yards, then take us up to periscope depth and keep on sending those pings. She must know we are here."

As the Kursk moved upwards to a shallower depth the periscope came out to peek above the waterline. The sea was fairly calm with a five-knot wind blowing from the east, which made small whitecaps dance around the bottom of the periscope. Inside the submarine things were not quite as calm. It was the first part of the exercise and the men were pumped and ready for action. Only Kuznetsov looked visibly relaxed as he eased into the central role in the command center and took hold of the periscope handles.

"Let's see what's out there," he said. Maneuvering left he quickly found what he was looking for. "There's our American friend," he half-smiled. The Baltimore had surfaced completely and waited some 500 meters astern of the Kursk. Kuznetsov looked up from the periscope. "Bodrov, it seems they have no shame at all. They are right behind us."

"I guess they want to show us that they know everything and they're watching every move we make," Bodrov replied, somewhat stating the obvious but Kuznetsov let it pass. He appreciated the XO for his diligence and dependability rather than his searing wit.

"Well, I'm sure we won't disappoint them," he said.

"Sir?"

"I mean that after today's demonstration they'll have something to talk about for quite some time to come."

"We better make it worth their while then," Bodrov replied with a shy smile.

"Yes, let's give them a show they'll never forget," Kuznetsov said before returning his eyes to the periscope and searching the sea to the right by a fraction. "There she is!" he said with some satisfaction."

Some 1,000 meters ahead of him he saw the pride of the Northern Fleet; their flagship Peter the Great, looming starboard.

Built in the 1980s, the huge Kirov-Class nuclear-powered battle cruiser was originally christened '*Yuriy Andropov*' after the General Secretary of the Communist Party, but after the demise of the Soviet Union she was renamed '*Pyotr Veliky*', Peter the Great. Weighing in at almost 25.000 tons, and standing more than 275 meters long, the Peter the Great was equipped with an arsenal of weapons to combat, air, sea, and land targets. As far as that day's exercise was concerned, the ship, with its crew compliment of more than 700 sailors, served as the central command of the exercise, as well as a target for several of the practice attacks so the navy could test their latest weapons and detection systems. Though the USA currently dominated the seas when it came to nuclear battle cruisers, it was Russia who took the prize for the largest and most heavily-armed surface combatants. The bridge of the mighty ship alone rose 45 meters above sea level and on the flat surface it could be seen for miles around. Inside the huge bridge, up to a 100 men could be working at any time. Their stations were lined up in rows of desks that reminded Fleet Admiral Petrov of the mission control center used for the Apollo missions to the moon. As Petrov walked the bridge with Colonel Xu Junping beside him the traditional sailor in him made him salute every sailor he passed before gazing down from the bridge to survey his small empire.

"You know, I'm a big fan of Sun Tzu's 'Art of War,'" he told Junping, more out of cordiality than earnestness, though he had enjoyed the ancient study of military strategy.

"Really? I'm more a fan of Wáng Jìngzé's 'Thirty-Six Stratagems'," Junping replied, "Where the 'Art of War' describes a fairly practical view of battle, the actual wisdom of war, if such a thing even exists, can be found in the 'Thirty-Six Stratagems'. It's also been said Sun Tzu based his views on the works of Wáng Jìngzé."

"That's interesting," Petrov said, and he actually meant it. He'd never heard of Jìngzé and he relished any chance to broaden his knowledge. Some of his colleagues were against the contamination of foreign thinking within the great Russian Navy, but he believed it was such close-mindedness that had been the navy's biggest downfall over the years. One should always be willing to accept the new, even if the intention was only to recreate the glories of the past. "Maybe you could be so kind as to get me a copy of this man's work when we return," Petrov said to Junping, but before the Chinaman could reply a young lieutenant approached the two of them. "What is it, sailor?"

"We have *Vintic* on the coms, Sir.'

"Ah, our own *Conqueror*, the Kursk," Petrov said with a nod to Junping. "Thank you, Lieutenant. Put her through."

Smiling proudly, Petrov approached the desk to speak to the captain of the Kursk, or as the Fleet had fondly dubbed the mighty sub *Vintic*.

"Big Peter, Big Peter," came a familiar voice over the intercom. "This is K141, Vintic giving final notice as we begin the summer exercise. Please, confirm."

"Vintic, this is Big Peter. Fleet Admiral Nikolai Petrov here and honored to welcome you to these waters on such a fine day. Please state your position?"

"Admiral Petrov, this is Captain Yaroslav Kuznetsov grateful, as ever, for the warmth of your welcome. However, forgive me for refusing to state my position at this time as I think we both know this may defeat the purpose of our exercise."

Petrov almost laughed under the huge red moustache he wore and the crew closest to him saw the twinkle in his eye. "Still as sharp on your last mission as your first, Captain, but in all seriousness, let me say it's an honor to work with you one last time, Yaroslav."

"The honor is mine, Admiral," Kuznetsov replied honestly before briskly continuing as his voice threatened to crack at the unexpected kindness. "The Kursk is ready to begin the exercise on your command, Sir."

"All right, Captain Kuznetsov. Give us your best; we are ready for you and on our guard."

"Copy that, Sir. My crew knows nothing other than their best. You'll be hearing from us soon. K141, out."

Bodrov nodded and picked up the bridge microphone "Comrades!" he began, "this is your Admiral-Captain speaking. We've made contact with our comrades on the Kursk and I have a feeling we'll be attacked within the hour. Secure the bridge; rise the alert status to high; and keep on the lookout for anything suspicious. Be aware that the Kursk will be testing missiles as well as torpedoes during this exercise and we don't know in what order they will come."

"Then how will we know what to look for?" Junping asked at his side.

"We'll know it when we see it, Colonel, either on the sonar, radar or simply through the window. It's our job to try and prove the ineffectiveness of this new weapon; a job I would think you don't want us to succeed in." Petrov smiled at that, but there wasn't a man on the crew who believed the Admiral was joking. The competition between the various arms of the navy was fierce during peace time. Every crew wanted to prove its worth and this exercise was no exception. Petrov turned to his sonar operator.

"Sailor, I want you to alert me when so much as a goldfish on your sonar moves. The Kursk is almost impossible to detect and I need you to be the one to save us today."

"Will do, Sir." The sonar operator replied. "So far there's nothing new and we're still being watched by the westerners who insist on pinging away like they're in a video game."

Petrov laughed at the joke. "OK, stay sharp and keep K141 informed about the activity of our American friends."

The Kursk slowly came to a full stop and the crew waited. Seconds later the lights dimmed to a faint yellow throughout the sub and three slow 'whoops' sounded over the intercom – the exercise was active.

"Comrades, this is it," Kuznetsov's voice told them. "As of now we are the most feared enemy in these waters and I can finally reveal the specifics of our mission. During this exercise we'll perform two missile and torpedo tests. All of these weapons will be fired at our comrades aboard the Peter the Great. First we'll fire the P-700 Shipwreck missile, targeted half a mile in front and astern of the battle cruiser. If all goes well we'll change our position and fire our first test torpedo, the VA-111 Shkval. From now on I expect you all to be alert and performing at your best. We'll begin our first missile run in a few minutes. I wish you luck and may your god be with you."

Kuznetsov smiled at the expression knowing it would be enough to cover most of the faiths on board including the Orthodox Christians, Muslims, Buddhists, and Judaists. "XO, do we have the distance and coordinates for launching the first shipwreck?"

"Sir, we have the target on bearing one-two-zero, range five-zero-double-zero," Bodrov replied.

"Secure the hatches. Zero bubble. Take us down to 20 meters."

"Taking us down 20 meters. Secured."

Kuznetsov glanced at his men before taking a breath to keep his voice even and calm. "Open Missile Hatch 6, Tube 13 and ready Shipwreck One," he ordered. As he spoke the lights changed from yellow to red and the crew braced themselves for action.

Positioned 20 meters underwater, the Kursk was motionless save for the opening of a missile hatch on the starboard side. There were twelve hatches in total and behind every one of them were two missiles packed with different payloads. The P-700 Shipwreck missile was an anti-ship cruise missile that could carry a nuclear warhead or traditional payload to its destination at speeds exceeding Mach 2 and over a distance of 300 miles. Of course, the warheads on the missiles fired today were dummies, balanced for weight to support the guidance system. And although the crew was hugely experienced and had recently been lauded for its excellent performance under command of Kuznetsov, only a handful of test missiles and torpedoes had been fired from the Kursk since its launch in 1994. Therefore the tension that Kuznetsov saw in the faces of his crew was very real and very understandable.

"Shipwreck One ready. Awaiting your order, Captain," Bodrov stated.

"Thank you, XO. On launching, take us down to 30 meters immediately and set course zero-zero-six for 17 miles at 15 knots."

"Yes, Sir."

Kuznetsov took one more look around the room to make sure everyone was focused and ready before giving his next command.

"Fire when ready," he told Bodrov.

Bodrov nodded. "Firing Officer, get ready to launch Shipwreck One on my command."

To his left, a young officer reached for a row of lights numbered from one to twenty-four. Below every light a silver cap covered a firing switch. The firing officer opened cap thirteen and put his thumb against it.

"Ready to launch on your command, Sir."

As the submarine awaited the command, the air turned thick with expectation and every member of crew seemed to fix his eyes on the ceiling. In those compartments of the Kursk not involved in the firing of the missile the only indication they had that something was about to happen was the dim red light that picked up the sweat on their upper lips, and the feeling of anticipation that thickened the air.

"Fire Shipwreck One," Bodrov ordered, and the switch was flicked.

"Shipwreck away, Sir," came the confirmation as the submarine slowly began to shake and emit a low growl as Hatch 13 opened and the missile fired from its tube, slicing though the water leaving a fizz of bubbles in its wake as it shot to the surface. Though the rumble of the launch quickly subsided, the crew continued to sit with bated breath.

"Missile successfully launched and clear of the waterline," the firing officer called out and the men began to breathe again.

Kuznetsov smiled and picked up the 1MC.

"Wait for it," he told his crew.

On the bridge of Peter the Great there wasn't a man not staring at his screen or looking out of the window so when the shout came the relief was almost tangible.

"Sir, we have a missile inbound, south-south-east, and it's nearing fast."

Petrov picked up his binoculars and looked out to sea. "Damn," he whispered.

"What should we do, Sir? The sonar operator asked.

"Nothing," he replied. "Let this one go." Petrov raised his voice so he might be heard over the entire bridge. "Would someone care to tell me why we seem unable to find a 150 meters long submarine, our own submarine, I'd like to add?"

Though it was clearly a rhetorical question, not a man on board would have liked to answer it. Petrov tightened the grip on his binoculars as his eyes followed the white stripe in the sky heading for his ship.

"Counting down to simulated impact," a voice sounded over the intercom. "Eight, seven, six, five, four, three, two, one, impact."

Petrov winced as he watched, effectively powerless as the missile hit the water some 200 meters in front of him. There was no explosion simply a splash a few meters high, but the missile might as well have torn a chunk from the hull as far as Petrov was concerned; he was close to furious.

"We have impact," Kuznetsov informed his men and the submarine erupted in cheers and the smack of high fives. Feeling just as pleased, he allowed himself a small smile and let the men have their moment of fun; it was wise to cut them some slack after the tension of firing a first missile, even if it was for practice purposes rather than combat. He also knew the successful 'hit' would bolster their confidence for the rest of the exercise, and he would need a confident crew for the first-time weapon test and demonstration of the new torpedo later that day.

Kuznetsov picked up the 1MC. "Comrades, congratulations," he said, as the submarine quickly hushed to hear what he had to say. "Our first exercise was a great success and we are now on our way. We will arrive at our next location in half an hour. You did good men, better than good, but for the next part of the exercise I need you to be great."

The sonar operator on the Peter the Great looked perplexed. "I couldn't say for sure, Sir. It sounded like we had something on sonar for a second but now it's gone again."

"Thank you. Please keep looking," Petrov said before tuning to Junping.

"Do we have any idea as to when the demonstration will start?" the colonel from China asked and Petrov could barely retain his sigh. He wasn't used to babysitting guests and being a loyal member of the proud if decayed Soviet Union it pained him that they now had to rely on others for help, even if they were allies. Like Kuznetsov, he also felt uneasy about being part of this new commercial arm of the navy, yet he also understood the necessity of it.

"Of course we don't have any idea when the demonstration will start," Petrov said somewhat harshly before remembering his manners and managing to smile in a jovial manner. "If we knew that we would be at a welcome advantage during the exercise. But as you can see, we are all a bit tense right now, myself included."

Junping nodded. "I understand, Admiral. You're not only responsible for the success of this mission but also at least in part for our successful cooperation in the future not to mention the rebuilding of the Russian navy."

"No pressure then?" Petrov responded with another smile.

"I'm sorry. I didn't mean to…"

"No need to apologize, Colonel. I'm afraid Captain Kuznetsov of the Kursk is free to create his own timetable in this matter. However, I think I know the man well enough by now to know it won't be long before we hear from him again. So just a little more patience."

"Do you have any other means detecting a launch early?" Junping asked.

"Well, if we don't find the Kursk, we'll see the torpedo coming. Of course, it will be too late to do much about it, which is why it would be particularly beneficial if we could locate her."

"And what will happen when you find her?"

"We will signal the destroyer that's closest by and depth charge the Kursk, simulating her destruction before she can fire."

Junping frowned and Petrov read his mind.

"Don't worry, Colonel. You'll still get your demonstration whether we find her or not. It's just a question of who wins the game."

"Do you believe the rumors about the Shkval to be true?" Anders asked James as they gazed out to sea from the window inside the Marjata's conference room.

Without turning from the view, James replied that he did. "To some degree," he clarified. "We know with certainty that the Russians have been experimenting with the technology since the '60s. So I guess they've had enough time to make something work. But whether they have a working prototype, well…"

"This is Listener One calling One Control, do you read, over." The sound of Commander Cook's voice over the intercom shook both men from their trance-like watch of the sea. In one fluid movement, they turned to the control desk where James picked up the 1MC.

"This is One Control, we copy. It's good to hear from you, Captain. We were starting to get a little bored here."

"Wouldn't want that to happen, Sir," Cook replied. "Besides, we just picked up a tactical missile launch from the Kursk. The missile appeared to be part of a practice attack on the battle cruiser the Peter the Great and it went down with a splash a quarter of a mile in front of the ship."

"That's good news, Captain. It means the Russians have started their war games, which raises my own hopes of completing our mission possibly today. Is there any sign that they are aware of your presence?"

"I would say yes, Captain. But all's quiet. They left the scene straight after the launch and are still moving. Unfortunately, because of their stealth capabilities we keep losing them every now and then. However, as we haven't stopped pinging, they can always see us and steer out of harm's way."

"Agreed," James replied. "Stay focused on the target. I hope it won't be long now. One Control, out."

"Will do. Listener One, out."

James turned to Anders. "To come back to your question about whether I believe the rumors are true about the Shkval, it seems we may both soon find out."

14 Collision Course

"WHAT ARE YOU DOING?" Grisha yelled as he walked into the aft propulsion control compartment after shoving open the large steel door that separated the last two compartments. Mischa looked up, his face smeared in grease and black dirt. Dressed in dark blue overalls, he blended in with the room that was covered in, what looked like, some kind of tar.

"You look like Baba Yage, The Boogeyman." Grisha teased.

"Laugh all you want, but if I didn't look like this there's a good chance you'd be drowning right now," Mischa replied.

"What do you mean?"

Mischa took a deep breath. Grisha was his friend, his best friend, but even so he really wasn't used to babysitting the new guy. "OK, you see those shafts down there, the ones that are disappearing into the back of the boat?" He pointed at two, one-meter round steel tubes running the length the room. "Inside those shafts an axis rotates that runs the propellers outside the boat. When we're running at speed the rotation of the axis distributes grease inside the tubes that keeps the water out."

"And when they're not running....?"

"When we lay still, water slowly seeps into the boat through the shafts. It's nothing we can't handle as long as we keep pumping out the bilge in the fourth compartment and greasing the shafts right. As you can see, it's not a very glamorous job, but it's a necessary one."

"So why not get one of your men to do it? Isn't that why you became an officer?"

"Do you want to do it?" Mischa asked smiling. Before his friend could answer there was a small 'screech' and Toma ran into the room to jump into Mischa's arms. "Great," Mischa sighed. "You left the door open."

"And?" Grisha asked clearly unaware why this might be a problem.

"And, we keep the door closed because every time Toma comes up here he leaves filthy and then merrily contaminates the last five compartments of the boat." Mischa held the cat tightly in his arms and scratched his head. Toma purred in response.

"Does that work with your wife too?" Grisha joked as he knelt down beside them.

Mischa laughed and shook his head. "If only marriage was so simple. So, what do you want here?"

"OK, so I was wondering if you'd heard anything about the next test?"

"What do you mean?"

"I mean that there are all sorts of rumors going around about this Shkval. They say it's a very special torpedo and the test launch is top secret and very dangerous."

"My dear friend," Mischa answered calmly to counter the excitement he saw in Grisha's face, "welcome to the Russian Navy. There's always something top secret going on and everything we do is 'very dangerous'." Mischa's voice dripped with sarcasm. "However, if you're so curious about our next exercise why don't you get your butt

106

out of my compartment and go to the front where you'll find Senior Lieutenant Vitaliy Polyakov who's in charge of firing all the test torpedoes and ask him what's going on?"

Grisha got up from his knees, smiled and saluted before heading for the door. "Aye, Captain."

"Not so fast," Mischa ordered. As Grisha turned to him he found Toma thrust in his direction. "Close the door behind you both when you leave."

Grisha saluted again, tapped his heels together and gave Mischa a wink.

"Go," Mischa ordered wearily.

As Grisha worked his way up to the front he passed the XO who was preparing to address the sailors over the intercom.

"What are you doing with that cat, sailor?" Bodrov demanded.

Startled to be addressed by the senior officer, Grisha stammered an answer: "I'm bringing him to the front, Sir. He snuck into the ninth and was getting all dirty so I took him with me."

"Well, you're in the front now so you can let go of him and get back to your station. We're about to begin the next phase of our exercise."

Grisha immediately released the cat to walk quickly back to his own station in the third. After watching Toma disappear under a desk to lick his paws, Bodrov turned to the communications desk and picked up the 1MC.

"Comrades," he addressed the crew. "We will soon perform the most important part of our mission. When we shortly arrive at our location we will fire two prototype torpedoes. As you will understand, it is imperative that we reach our designated area undetected, therefore we are running silent and I need every man to be as quiet as can be. Secure everything, but don't make a sound. Watch where you walk and be careful not to drop anything. If we can fire at our target undetected I will personally serve you free vodka when we are back on dry land. So from now on, not a peep." Bodrov hung up 1MC and joined Kuznetsov who was standing at the Navigation desk with Qiungian Wang.

"It looks like Big Peter isn't planning on giving us too much trouble. She has remained stationary at her initial location," Kuznetsov noted.

"Why would she do that?" Wang asked.

"The weapons test is of far greater importance than practicing our tactical skills. Her main motive is to detect us before we fire. Should she succeed I will lose the last battle of my career."

"And we wouldn't want that, Sir." Bodrov smiled before adding, "I'll keep the sub running as smooth as a feather on the water. Trust me, they'll never know what hit them."

Kuznetsov nodded his thanks before directing the attention of his second in command to a position on the map. "Take us there and put us at optimal firing depth," he ordered.

"Aye, Sir." Bodrov picked up the 1MC. "Navigation Control, take us to 69 degrees point 38 north and 37 degrees point 19 east, put us at 10 meters below periscope depth and keep us there." As navigation control set course, Bodrov continued to giving orders over the 1MC. "Propulsion, rig for silent running. Keep us below whisper speed."

"I'll keep her quiet, Sir, even if I have to push her," Mischa responded, only half-joking.

The men then fell silent, eager to give their captain one last victory, especially those who had sailed with him many times before and considered him to be a father-away-from-home.

James leant back in his chair concentrating on the small screen of the Gameboy he held.

"Ah, shoot," he muttered and raised the console in his right hand as though he was about to throw it at the wall.

"Problems, Commander?" Anders asked as he walked into the Marjata's conference room in time to witness James's fit of pique.

"No problems," he replied. He then looked at the Norwegian as if to weigh up what to say next. "Remember that slight diplomatic problem I told you about?"

"Edward Payne?"

James nodded. "Well, I've just spoken to my boss and it seems that Payne has been arraigned and sentenced to twenty years in prison. There's nothing official yet, but apparently he has been charged and found guilty, on the orders of the highest political authority no doubt, of smuggling classified military equipment out of Russia as scrap metal. Our sources believe he has already been sent to Lefortovo Prison."

Anders shook his head, his cool Nordic eyes softening with sympathy. "If I'm right that would make him the second American in about forty years to stand trial for espionage in Moscow."

"Gary Powers," James said by way of confirmation.

"Indeed, Mr. Powers. 1960, wasn't it or thereabouts?"

"1960 exactly and he got ten years for espionage – until he was 'spy-swapped' a few years later at the Berlin wall."

"The Cold War years," Anders replied sounding close to nostalgic. "Things seem more civilized now but to tell you the truth, I doubt if they really are."

"I couldn't say," James said with a shrug of his shoulders. "But I have the feeling there aren't as many spy-swaps' as there used to be so I guess we'll have to wait and see what happens to Payne."

Anders nodded before looking out to sea. "And any news from our friends out there?"

"Thirty minutes ago we knew the Kursk was sailing a course towards a probable new location, I assume to perform the next test. Unfortunately, our people are having a hard time keeping up with them, or rather keeping them in their sights."

Kolya Bodrov paced up and down the command center, and when he wasn't pacing he was looking over the shoulder of one of the officers checking on their performances. Although he felt the pressure of giving the captain a successful send-off, he also knew the exercise was his chance to prove himself as Kuznetsov's replacement on the Kursk.

"69 degrees point 38 north and 37 degrees point 19 east," came the confirmation from the navigation station. 'A good start', Bodrov thought and he took two steps to the navigation desk to stand next to the Kuznetsov.

"We have reached our destination, Captain."

"And our range and distance to the target is?"

"Eight miles east of target, Sir, and there's no indication she's seen us."

"Any sign of our American friends?" Kuznetsov asked with a tight smile.

"Sonar reports one element steady nearby that cannot be identified as ours. Earlier on we also confirmed a second bogey, but that one got lost among our other ships taking part in the exercise."

"OK. As long as they give us space we'll let them be."

Kuznetsov nodded at Bodrov confirming it was time. He then picked up the 1MC. "Torpedo Compartment, how are you coming along?"

At the front of the boat the excitement and pressure was written clearly on the faces of the seven-member team. Taking up the wall space were 6,000lb torpedoes, all of them 10 meters long and 1 meter wide. The standard torpedo on the Kursk was the type 65 and even in peacetime the submarine carried a full armament of live weaponry. Today, the Kursk carried 24 of these torpedoes all armed with a standard high-explosive payload capable of destroying aircraft carrier battle groups, merchant targets and enemy submarines. These torpedoes did their job well and the Chinese had already proved to be satisfied customers, but the Shkval was a different fish altogether. Painted a brighter green color

110

and smaller in size than their type 65 counterparts, the two Shkvals stood out in the torpedo room. However, in order to fire the Shkval, special modifications had to be made to the Kursk's firing tubes and as of yet these modifications had never been tested.

As two men 'chained up' one of the Shkvals to the winch the man responsible for their safe launch picked up the 1MC to speak to their captain.

"Senior Lieutenant Vitaliy Polyakov here, Sir. I'll be your torpedo specialist for this trip. We have one '*Tolstushka*' in chains and awaiting your orders."

"Please load the Shkval into starboard tube number four and keep me informed."

"One Shkval loading in starboard tube number four," Polyakov echoed before hanging up the 1MC. "Alright men, let's pick her up and put her in number four."

As the chains tightened the torpedo slowly lifted and four men worked to keep her straight and try to stop her from bumping against the walls. As the torpedo moved it scratched the trestle she had sat in and the men winced of the sound of metal on metal.

"Comrades, if you want to give away our position or get us blown up, please continue what you're doing," Polyakov harshly whispered. "Now, take it slowly – step by step, piece by piece – our target isn't going anywhere."

The torpedo was guided towards the designated tube. When it neared, one of the sailors opened the torpedo hatch. As the torpedo was put in position the silence in the room was almost unbearable as the crew waited for the 'ready' signal.

"What's a '*Tolstushka*?'," Qiungian Wang asked Kuznetsov in the control room.

"*Tolstushka*' or 'Fat girl' is a nickname then men have given this new torpedo. I've no idea how they came up with it."

"Sir, sonar reports the American is getting near and at high speed over on starboard," Bodrov stated as he came to join the two men. The concern was etched on his face. "At this speed she will be right on top of us when we are ready to fire."

Kuznetsov expelled a harsh sigh. He would have loudly cursed the Americans for getting in the way, but the success of the exercise necessitated silence. He reached for the 1MC.

"Lieutenant Polyakov, how long do you need?"

"She's entering the tube as we speak, Sir. We'll be ready to fire in two minutes."

"Thank you, Lieutenant. Hurry, but continue with care."

As Kuznetsov hung up the microphone he felt the eyes of the men on him. He knew he had to act decisively. It was something every crew expected of their captain. They either had to fire in the next few minutes or abort the launch until the Americans got out of the way.

"Comrades," he said, addressing the room. "We came here to do a job and nothing in that order has changed. Most of you have been in these situations before and we all know what to do. XO, please make all preparations for an evasive maneuver and be ready to send one active ping in case it becomes clear she hasn't seen us."

"Will do, Sir," Bodrov replied.

"Captain, I take it this will not interfere with the demonstration?" Wang asked Kuznetsov, whose face immediately made it clear that he hadn't chosen the most opportune time to ask such a question.

"My dear Comrade Wang, the demonstration, as you call it, is foremost a test to me; the difference being that there are a great many things that can go wrong with a test, very wrong. So if you don't mind, I will put the safety of my crew before all things. If I'm convinced that it's not the right time to proceed I will postpone the test to a later time in this exercise."

All men in the room were now following the conversation as Kuznetsov's voice seemed to rise an octave with every word. "You'll get your demonstration," he continued. "and we'll get our test. All in good time." Kuznetsov turned abruptly away from Wang to speak to Bodrov.

"Continue loading procedures," he ordered more quietly. "Keep a close eye on the Americans."

"Aye, Captain."

It was a confirmation that was whispered by the sailors close by eager to prove their loyalty to, and belief in, their captain.

15 Hit

Saturday, August 12, 2000: 11:15 am

UNDER WATER the Baltimore and Kursk looked about the same size as they came within half a mile of each other. On the bridge of the Baltimore the tension was tangible as the crew poured over their screens, looking for any sign of the Kursk. Commander Cook pointed at several dots on the sonar screen.

"Where is she?" he asked, nerves tightening the sound of his voice.

"I don't know, Sir," the sonar operator answered honestly. "I'm picking up multiple signals in the neighborhood, but I cannot get a lock on her. She must be close by. For all I know we…"

A loud bang shook the Baltimore to the core. It was immediately followed by a deafening screech and for a second the submarine came to a shuddering halt before continuing on its course. Cook knew instinctively from the impact of the collision that the Baltimore's nose had struck something – and something big.

In the darkness that consumed the lower depths of the Barents Sea, a buoy became detached from the Baltimore's hull and floated to the surface unnoticed. Also passing unseen was the shadowy form of the Kursk. Its antenna was all but obliterated by the weight of the Baltimore's belly as it passed over the Russian sub and a 10ft long strip of its nose was also ripped open by the power of the Baltimore's rotating propeller; efficient as a can opener.

Cook and the rest of his crew, hastily returned to their feet after the force of the collision had thrown the men forward and then back again before the sub steadied itself. Shaking his head to regain his wits, Cook rubbed at his wrist which had smashed against a metal chair bolted to the floor that he had used to keep his balance after the initial impact. Around him he saw the confusion and fear in every man's eyes before a siren sounded and the lights dimmed. Grabbing the chair next to him in case anything else should occur, he shouted one order: "Report!"

"Did you feel that?" A young sailor asked Mischa, his eyes wide and startlingly white beneath the grease on his young face. As he finished speaking, the Kursk shook again as though caught in the aftershock of the earlier quake. The worried crew looked left and right before they settled on Mischa.

"Sure I felt it," he answered, keeping his voice calm in order to soothe the younger man's nerves.

"But, but, what happened are we under attack?" Another sailor stammered and Mischa couldn't help but notice the sweat pouring from his face. He could lie, but what would be the point?

"I don't know, but I'm sure it's nothing. I once ran aground while training on a 670 Skat. We took a bang far worse than this one without any problem. We didn't even have to return to the dock for maintenance. I'm sure this was something like that."

116

"But didn't you feel the sudden dive before we flattened out again?"

Mischa laid down his tools and put his arm around the sailor and looked him straight into his eyes. "Listen, trust me. There's really no reason to worry." He relaxed his voice to lighten the atmosphere because he knew the rest of his men were not only watching, but listening and right now he didn't want them panicking. "How many times have we sailed together? Six? Seven?" He didn't wait for the answer. "And have I ever lied to you or given you bad advice when you came to me for guidance?"

He looked Mischa square in the eyes, took a deep breath and exhaled. "No, I guess not."

"Then trust me now. When I know what happened, you'll know what happened, but right now I need you to get back to your work."

Mischa walked him to his station. As he did so he could hear the whispers of his crew and he knew he had to act decisively. "Everyone," he ordered sternly, "get back to work. We're OK, there's nothing going on, so stop muttering and do the job you came here to do."

The men all fell quiet, but the bewilderment remained etched on each and every face. It was a similar scene in the command center where the crew quickly gathered all the loose items rattling around the floor before returning to their work stations and looking at their captain. Kuznetsov kept his face composed even as his mind raced through the possibilities. Beside him, Wang looked about to speak and Kuznetsov silenced him by raising his forefinger.

"Bodrov, tell me what happened. Did we hit the bottom? Was it an attack?"

"I'm trying to find out, Sir," the XO responded. "It felt like we definitely hit something or something hit us, but we're still trying to find out for sure."

"Why was there no warning?"

"I don't know, Sir. Please give us a moment."

Bodrov ran from one station to the next while Kuznetsov picked up the 1MC. "All compartments: status report in two minutes. Vitaliy, how are you doing in the torpedo room?" For about ten seconds there was only silence in the command center. "Commander Vitaliy Pavlov, are you there, over?"

It took a few moments more before the senior lieutenant answered and when he did he was clearly breathless. "Senior Lieutenant Polyakov here, Sir. Sorry for the delay we're a little busy."

"Report, sailor," Kuznetsov demanded.

"A little water, Sir, leaking from the pressure pipes, but nothing we can't handle. Whatever we hit didn't go through the double bulkheads. We're almost back in control. We just need another minute."

"And the Shkval?"

"Fine, Sir. A few bangs, but she's still in her chains and half-loaded in Tube 4. We'll need two minutes to bail the water and then we'll be ready to continue our work as planned on your command."

"Listen very carefully Lieutenant Polyakov. First, I want you to fully load the Shkval and secure her. Then I want you to load Tube One with a fully-armed USET-80 and let me know when you're ready."

For a moment there was silence.

"Can you repeat that, please Sir."

The uncertainty in Polyakov's voice was audible; the USETS on board were equipped with live conventional payloads powerful enough to bring down an aircraft carrier.

"You heard me, son. Load the USET in Tube One and flood the chamber when ready. When you are done, get back to me."

"Sonar, what happened? Sanders?" Cook cried out to anyone who could hear him.

Sanders struggled to get to his feet as the Baltimore recovered from the impact before shouting out an answer. "It felt like we scraped a brick wall, Sir, but nothing showed up on sonar or otherwise." As he finished he glanced up in time to see a large spot appear in the middle of the sonar screen. The sighting was followed by a loud ping. "Ah, there she is, Sir," Sanders confirmed. "At least she was for a second, but I'd say we've just passed her nose."

"Helm!" Cook commanded urgently. "Emergency dive, one hundred feet. Navigation: keep our course straight to clear, one quarter speed."

Kuznetsov turned to Bodrov awaiting an explanation.

"Another sub on sonar, Sir, turning away heading zero-five-eight at slow speed. It's the Americans. They must have grazed us."

"Why didn't we see here before?" he asked impatiently.

"I don't now sir, not yet anyway." Bodrov's voice sounded guilty.

"Our heading?" Kuznetsov asked.

"Three-one-zero."

"Alright," Kuznetsov replied, beginning to relax for the first time since the collision. At least now we can be certain it was a collision, something that can't always be taken for granted when rival countries have subs in the same waters. Even so, precautions still had to be made. "Let's be careful out there. Take us around slowly, heading zero-five-eight and maintaining a distance of 500 meters. I want to get ahead of this thing and I need you to keep track of her every movement – the US sub's commander is obviously drunk."

Around him the men laughed quietly and Kuznetsov felt the air lift.

Bodrov also smiled. "I'd say it's clear from the sub's direction that she lost sight of us for a moment and failed to anticipate our course."

Kuznetsov nodded and picked up the 1MC. "All compartments: damage report."

Within seconds, the crew of the Kursk stood up to be counted.

"Torpedo compartment here: still having a few minor problems, ready for response in two minutes."

"Living and kitchen: no visible damage, a bit shook up, some men fell from their bunks, some cuts and bruises, all in control."

"Nuclear control reporting: nothing worth mentioning, Sir. We've been through worse."

"Mischa Kastamarov, turbines and propulsion: we're all good, a little unnerved, but waiting to hear what happened."

"We're working on letting you know, comrade. Don't worry, is all I can tell you for now," Kuznetsov responded. As he hung up the microphone he looked at Bodrov, tilted his head and sucked on his lips before grumbling: "Looks like we got away with this one, but keep an eye on the torpedo compartment. I want them to be one hundred percent ready for what's coming next."

Bodrov nodded and left the command center through the small corridor heading for the torpedo compartment. When he got there he noticed steam hissing from a couple of pipes and a number of small leaks, but otherwise the place looked in fairly good order. Ignoring the water collecting slowly at their feet, the crew were busy loading the Shkval into Tube Four. The torpedo slotted into place with a screech, like nails down a blackboard.

"More lift, men! Hold her tight, a few more meters Release the forward chains and let's put her to bed," Polyakov directed the men.

"Report," Bodrov commanded.

"The starboard crane broke and the men have loaded manually. Almost ready for closing up." Though Polyakov sounded calm he brought a hand to his forehead to wipe away the sweat.

"Captain wants the USET loaded ASAP. Does the port winch function?"

"I believe so, Sir. We'll close this one up and get right on it." Polyakov turned to three of his men. "You, you and you, chain up number eight for Tube One."

"Thank you, Lieutenant. Continue with your work," Bodrov told Polyakov and he was about to return to the command center when it became clear that a problem had developed with the Shkval. With its 'tailpipes' visible outside of the tube the torpedo appeared to have jammed.

"She won't go any further, Lieutenant," said one of the crewmen trying to push the Shkval in by hand.

"Leave it," Bodrov ordered from the other side of the compartment. "Close her up as far as you can and then help over here with the loading."

Polyakov glanced at Bodrov his gaze clouded by confusion before echoing the senior officer's orders.

"You heard, men. Close her up now."

Three men grabbed the steel hatch and tried their best to close it before looking for further instruction.

Polyakov saw the hesitation in their faces. "Just turn the security bolts as far as they will go," he told them. "She won't be going anywhere for now."

"Closed, but no lock, Sir," one of the men said.

"Good, now get to the port-side and help load Number One."

As the men did as they were told, the hatch remained open by an inch and with the steam emitting from the pipes and the water still seeping into the room no one noticed the clear, thing liquid dripping from Tube Four.

"One Control this is an emergency, do you read?"

In the Marjata's conference room Cook's anxious voice sounded through the loudspeakers and James ran into the room from the bathroom still zipping up his pants. Almost tripping in his hurry to reach the table he snatched at the microphone.

"James here, what's your emergency?"

"We've hit something or someone," Cook admitted in a controlled voice that did little to hide his upset.

Anders walked into the conference room. "What's going on?"

James raised his hand to silence him. "Captain Cook, what's your status?"

"We're a little shook up, but structural damage seems minimal. Power, maneuverability, the radios and audio are still being assessed, but it looks like most of our sonar and radar capabilities have been lost."

"Any idea what caused the collision and the damage to the other party?" James asked.

"We cannot get any confirmation, but my guess would be a brush contact with our target."

At the captain's words, James felt the hairs on the back of his neck bristle. Contact with a Russian sub was not going to be an easy mistake to trivialize to the grown-ups back home. Nor would it be easy to second guess how the Russians would take it. "OK. Listener One, hold on while I check for confirmation from Listener Two."

As James let go of the microphone button he turned to Anders. "I have a bad feeling about this," he muttered.

"Let's try and figure what happened before jumping to any conclusions," Anders suggested.

"It's not a conclusion, just a feeling," James replied before pushing the button on the microphone.

"Listener Two, this is One Control, please come in."

"This is Listener Two, we're here and have been monitoring the coms following your conversation."

"Can you confirm?"

122

"I'm standing next to my sonar officer looking at two clear spots on the screen, one of them being Listener One. Cook are you listening in? We have you on radar. It looks like you have a bogey on your six."

"We figured as much," Cook responded. "Our sonar may be gone, but we have received audio on the bogey."

James glanced at Anders again. Were the Russians now tailing their men and if so for what purpose? "Cook, can you put through the audio you're receiving?" he asked.

"Yes."

Over the Marjata's radio speakers a strange metallic sound filled the room like someone twisting a bottle cap under water. James again looked at Anders to see if he recognized the sound, but his face was unreadable.

"Did you get that?" Cook's voice asked over the system.

James flipped some switches on a screen to his right.

"Got it and running it through our pattern recognition software."

"Cook, do you read? This is Jack Coleman on Listener Two. Sonar has just confirmed the bogey has turned in your direction and looks to be heading your way, perhaps to redress some of the damage you may have inflicted on her. We'll keep you informed."

Although Coleman sounded like he was trying to make light of the situation, James was having a hard time finding any of it funny. He looked at the screen and then turned to Anders his face drained of color.

"Do you see this?" he asked quietly.

Anders looked at the screen. "Is that what I think it is?"

"What do you see?" Cook asked over the intercom.

"One second, please," James responded. "I'm just confirming."

James flipped a number of switches on the screen in front of him. He then looked again at Anders who confirmed his fears with a slight nod of his head.

"Listener One, Listener Two, it looks like your bogey is loading a torpedo. I repeat, the Russians are loading a torpedo."

Bodrov continued to monitor the progress in the Kursk's torpedo compartment. As the tail of the USET-80 cleared the rim of Tube One the propeller began to rotate before the men had chance to close the hatch creating a high-pitched whine and panic.

"What the hell is going on?" Bodrov hissed wincing at the thought of how far the racket would have sounded under water. "Shut it down and keep it quiet."

"We're trying, Sir. She just started rotating," Lieutenant Polyakov explained.

"XO, what's happening down there?" Bodrov raised his eyebrows and exhaled sharply through his nose at the sound of the captain's voice over the intercom. "The entire boat is listening to the commotion coming from your compartment."

"Sorry, Sir," Bodrov replied, his voice only marginally less-composed than usual. "The propeller of the USET began to rotate in the last phase of loading. The men seem to think they have a Domovoi, a gremlin in the compartment."

"XO," Kuznetsov replied irritably, "Tell your men to shut up and keep their superstitions to themselves!"

"Aye, Sir." Bodrov turned to the men, gesturing fiercely with his arms.

"That's strange," James mentioned, more to himself than anyone else. "Anders, come take a look at this. We've a clear second blip on the screen all of a sudden, about a mile from the Baltimore. That can't be the Detroit; she'll be out of range, so what the hell is going on down there?"

"It's got to be the Kursk, surely," Anders replied.

"Could be, but then why has she chosen to appear on our screen?"

"My guess; it's either provocation or they're preparing to fire."

Both men stayed silent for a moment as they tried to collect their thoughts. When the mission started they had been prepared for many things, but this wasn't one of them.

"I have no idea what they are doing," James muttered, feeling the need to say something, anything. "But it seems to me that this could get dangerous very swiftly. Are we in contact with Washington?"

"We can get contact, but by the time we have everybody lined up I'm guessing it'll all be over. I'll set up communications, but I think it's up to us now."

James and Anders looked at each other, disbelief and fear evident in their eyes as the enormity of the decision they might have to make sunk in.

"You know that this is how wars start, don't you? We could be the 'Stanislav Petrov's of the 21 century and prevent or cause World War 3" Anders remarked.

"What do you mean?"

"Maybe this is not the best moment to brush up on your history. You can look it up later. We need to do something and we need to do it now." Anders replied a little annoyed with what he felt was another American that didn't know his history.

"So, what do we do? What can we do?"

Anders rubbed at his temple, took a deep breath and set his shoulders back realizing the time had come to act decisively. "What's their relative position and heading?"

James looked at the screen before tapping the coordinates into his computer. "They're both heading north-north-west, 340 degrees to be exact. Our bogey seems to be keeping an exact distance of one mile from the Baltimore."

Anders nodded and picked up the 1MC. "Commander Cook, this is the Marjata. Do you have eyes on your tail?"

"Negative," was Cook's almost immediate response.

"Then we'll watch for you, Captain. We have eyes on her here. She's about a mile behind you and following your every move. We'll get back to you. Anders out."

The Norwegian tapped his fingers on the table, drumming his uncertainty like a crazy man as he rubbed at his face with his other hand.

"Do we have any means of communicating with the Kursk or any of the other ships taking part in the exercise?" James asked.

"Not to my knowledge. If anyone should know I'd have thought it would be you."

A painful silence filled the room until it got too much for James. "If we do nothing the Kursk might fire a torpedo at the Baltimore. With their sonar down they have no way of defending themselves. But if we take the initiative it could be misinterpreted as an act of aggression." What did your Stanislav Petrov do?"

"He 'didn't do', and thus saved us from World War 3. But to be frank, with the current state our countries are in and their new president in need of creating his place in history I don't know if the comparison is justly."

"You mean, fire a warning shot across the Kursk's bow?" Anders asked.

"Listener Two could do it."

"To be honest, the thought had crossed my mind, but can we be sure beyond doubt that the Kursk will interpret it as a warning shot?"

"Do we have any other choice?"

Both men looked at each other and let their eyes do the talking before James reached for the 1MC.

"Let's check it out," he said.

"I'll see if there's any response from Washington." Anders replied and walked away, praying for a miracle intervention to take the weight from his shoulders.

"Listener Two, this is Commander James on One Control, come in please"

126

"Coleman here."

"We have a torpedo warning coming from the bogey tailing the Baltimore. Can you confirm?"

"We can," Coleman stated, his voice coming across calm and business-like.

"Do you have a firing solution on a warning shot across the bow of the bogey?" James asked. "It's imperative that the warning is recognized and not understood as a threat."

"Understood."

As James waited for Coleman to come up with a solution, Anders reentered the room. "I've informed Washington, they're gathering the chiefs of staff, but that might take more time than we've got," he said.

"You want to know what I think?" James asked, rolling his pen up and down his fingers. "I think this situation is totally fucked up. Russian arrogance brought us here and we are absolutely not up to the task."

"Well, I think we're all that our boys down there have and that you need to stay calm if we want to give them any chance at all," Anders advised James. He plucked the pen from the American's fingers and set it on the desk. For a moment, James felt an old fire burn in his belly, but he also knew the Norwegian was right.

"I'm sorry," he apologized. "It's just that I didn't come here prepared for something like this."

"No one did, son. We'll just have to make the best of it."

"One Control this is Listener Two." Coleman's voice filled the room again. "We've found a firing solution; high impact, low yield, believed to be safe up to 60 feet right in front of her nose. We are ready to respond on your command."

Both James and Anders hesitated; neither man wanting to be the one to give the order. Eventually it was the American who picked up the microphone.

"Listener Two, please stand-by. Listener One, did you get the message? We are quite certain a torpedo will come your way any second. Do you consent to a warning shot from Listener Two? This thing could get nasty real fast now."

The room fell silent, the intercom went dead and it was clear to every man in the control room that the captain of the Baltimore was discussing their options with his men. Nervous glances were exchanged, sweat dripped from the foreheads, chins and noses of men who recognized how high the stakes were. After a pause that felt like an eternity, Cook came back on air. "That's an affirmative from the Baltimore. Fire a warning because we have no time to evade an attack if it comes. We put our trust in you and may God have mercy on our souls."

"Listener Two. Fire the warning shot when ready," James commanded. "Take it clearly in front of the bow so there can be no misunderstanding."

As James placed the microphone back on the table Anders noticed the tremor in the American's fingers. "Indeed," he said quietly, "may God have mercy on us all."

As Coleman hung back the microphone he saw that all eyes in the hushed confines of the room were focused on him.

"All right men, you heard our orders." Coleman paused for a moment, struggling to find the right words to help the crew understand and deal with everything that was about to happen. "Look, I know that many of you will feel that this is not what we came here to do, and that's true. This is, however, what we have trained to do. With that in mind, I therefore expect nothing less from you than your absolute focus and skill and to listen carefully to my orders and follow them. If there is anyone here who feels unable to fulfill all of my expectations, then I urge you to say so now."

At Coleman's instruction the men turned to read the answer in each other's eyes, and it was unanimous.

"Good," Coleman said, feeling more relieved than his voice revealed. "Let's be the professionals we are."

Coleman turned to his XO and pulled a switch next to the radio. The light on the bridge immediately turned dark blue.

"Garret, get the crew ready for battle stations and inform them of the firing solution we have planned."

"Aye, Captain." Garret turned to face the room and speaking in a clear distinct voice he ordered the crew: "All men get ready for torpedo battle stations. This is not a drill. I repeat this is not a drill. Tracking party; man your stations. Sonar; prepare for active guiding and tracking. Navigation; put us in a 90-degree angle in respect of the target. Helm; take us down to optimal firing depth. Firing officer; report when ready and when we have a clear line of sight on the bow of the bogey."

In the dark blue light, the Firing Officer worked at two screens, glowing green in the gloom. "Checking and collecting right now, Sir."

Garret nodded and picked up the 1MC. "Forward room; order of tubes is one, two, three, four, make ready the forward tubes. Report and stand by."

The reply on the intercom came instantaneously. "Forward; tubes one and two are flooded and outer doors are opened. Ready on your command, Sir."

"Alright Firing Officer, this is it; you heard the man. Give me our firing solution 100 feet in front of the bogey's bow."

The firing officer pushed the buttons on his headset, feeling the heat of a roomful of eyes on his back as he waited to receive the 'all clear' from the sub's other stations. After a minute, no more, he took off his headset and turned to Garret.

"Forward room ready. Torpedo course laid-in and clear, Sir."

"Thank you," Garret replied before turning to Coleman. "Forward room ready. Torpedo course clear and laid-in, Sir. Firing solution ready on your command."

Coleman stood a little taller and spoke without hesitation. "Prepare to fire One on my command."

The Firing Officer opened the capped switch and put his thumb against it. Above the switch a red light burned brightly in the room.

"Fire One!" Coleman ordered in a low, determined voice.

The Firing Officer pressed the switched and the light above it turned from red to green. Immediately the Detroit vibrated to a low rumble followed by silence.

16 Counter Measures

Saturday, August 12, 2000: 11:45 am

A S THE COMMAND CENTER regained control of the Kursk the alarms that had been a constant presence from the moment of impact gradually subsided. As Bodrov walked among his men, patting them on the back and offering reassurances, condensation water from the overhead pipes dripped onto his face and he hardly even noticed. No amount of training could ever prepare a crew for the panic of a collision. There were so many questions to answer following an accident such as the one they had just managed to live through, and so many thoughts and pictures that invade a man's head. For Bodrov it was the image of his wife and daughter as they waved him goodbye at Zapadnaya Litsa. The thought that consumed him was actually a fear; a fear of never seeing them again. A hand landed on his shoulder and he started with alarm.

"What is it?" he snapped.

The sonar officer pointed to the screen in front of him. It took Bodrov a second to realize what he was looking at. When he was sure he knew what it was he looked for the captain.

Kuznetsov stood at the communications desk, a microphone in his hand and his thumb firmly pushed against the send button.

"Command this is *Vintic*, please come in. Anyone in the fleet this is *Vintic* on all frequencies, Is anyone there?" Kuznetsov released the button and waited. As he was about to try again Bodrov called him to the other side of the room and he frowned at the interruption because he needed to reestablish contact. At this stage he couldn't be sure whether the Fleet could hear him and he was simply hearing nothing back or whether no one was hearing anything at all. It was a concern that only grew all the graver when he took a look at the screen Bodrov pointed him to.

"A clear signal on an incoming projectile bearing zero-zero-six, heading straight for us," Bodrov clarified. "Distance seven kilometers. Estimated time of arrival; three minutes, twenty seconds. Shall we surface?"

"Surface?" Kuznetsov asked, surprised to hear such a proposal from one his senior officers. "That might be what they teach you to do in peacetime, but with no idea of what's going on I need to maintain our maneuverability. Subs handle like bricks in mortar once surfaced." The captain picked up the 1MC from the sonar's desk and addressed the crew." All compartments; battle stations. We have an incoming torpedo with an ETA of less than three minutes. Secure all. Seal all doors and hatches."

As Kuznetsov hung up the microphone Wang walked up to him clearly intending to say something, but Kuznetsov raised his hand before he could start.

"Not now," he said curtly. He then returned his attention to his crew. "Helm; take us down fast to 65 meters, course one-one-eight." As he spoke, Kuznetsov heard the strength in his voice and it surprised even him. No matter how he felt or what concerns he harbored, right now his men needed him to be decisive and he would not let them down. But it wasn't easy. Every decision he had made in the past had been made with the confidence of knowing exactly what he was doing because lives were never really at stake, at least not immediately. This time it was not only different, but it felt different – and every one of his 33 years in the navy felt insufficient for the task ahead. The decision he made now in the Barents Sea could have worldwide implications should things escalate. This was his last trip and he had hoped his final role would be to herald in a new era for the Russian Navy; to help bring a new balance of power to global politics and a new sense of hope and pride to his people. Instead, one wrong decision and the dream would turn to ashes.

The Kursk dived to try and outrun the advancing torpedo. As the deepest depths of the Barents Sea at this location reached no more than 100 meters, there was still enough light penetrating the surfacing water to cast shadows on the sandy bottom of the seabed. Kuznetsov knew they had to be careful despite the emergency; pulling out of a dive even a second too late could ground them. During the Cold War a dozen or more subs had suffered the same fate and less than half came back to tell the tale.

With the Kursk's nose angled downwards by 45 degrees her crew attempted to do their jobs while hanging on to anything they could find. In the nuclear reactor station, Senior Lieutenant Bogdan Polakov, was busy shutting down levers and securing all loose items. A St Petersburg man by birth, Polakov was young and vastly inexperienced compared to many of the men, but he had been called aboard at the last minute as first engineer of the main propulsion division in charge of the nuclear reactors because he took his job seriously and there wasn't a machine he was in charge of that he didn't know inside and out.

"I'm here for you, *Babushka*, you hang in there. I'm not going to let anything happen to you on my first watch." The young officer spoke softly, even affectionately, as he placed a hand on the small window separating the crew from the reactor. "I'll get you home in one piece, you hear? Just hang in there for now."

As the Kursk continued to dive, the torpedo room began to fill with ice cold water. When it reached ten inches deep some of the men started to panic as they battled to close the torpedo hatch housing the Shkval.

"Give it all your muscle," Lieutenant Polyakov cried. "Close that hatch now because if it isn't closed by the time that torpedo arrives we are going to be in serious trouble."

As Polyakov finished, the Kursk leveled to a 35-degree angle and the men breathed that little bit easier as gravity now worked with them rather than against them. With a last almighty heave, they finally closed the hatch and locked the last security clamp. Soaking wet, but happy beyond words, Polyakov and his men congratulated each other with hugs and pats as a chorus of relieved cries filled the air.

In the propulsion compartment the men continued to hang on to whatever they could find. For the most part the room was silent; to a man they were scared; and most of the men could barely drag their eyes from the loudspeakers connected to the wall, willing them to emit the next order.

Captain-Lieutenant Andrey Ivchenko was a 22-year-old man from a small village in the Ukraine who joined the navy to provide for his family had done exceptionally on Kursk considering he never felt comfortable on submarines. His mild attacks of claustrophobia had never been a serious issue in the past when he knew operations were going well, but now he could feel his nerves running away from him and he was one small cry away from panic. "What do you think is going on up front?" he asked Mischa, his breathing audibly fast and shallow.

"I really have no idea," Mischa replied calmly. "But I trust our captain to get us through this in one piece".

"Do you think they are trying to sink us?"

134

"No, no I don't. Things happen at sea all the time and they are almost always based on stupid misunderstandings that quickly resolve themselves when people recognize the blunder. Trust me, this will blow over. You'll see."

As the young officer appeared to accept his words, the uneasy calm of the room was broken by the voice of Mischa's best friend calling his name as he came to find him. "Grisha."

"Mischa, where the hell are you?"

"I'm here," Mischa called from the back of the room. "How are you holding up, man?"

He walked over and tried to make light of the situation even though his nerves were as shredded as the rest of them. "What's going on? Are we sinking?"

"We don't know, but we could be," Ivchenko answered dryly.

"Of course we're not sinking," Mischa said quickly and loudly enough for the benefit of all the crew in the room. "The captain is taking us down and out of harm's way. It's going to be OK. Stay calm. It'll soon be over."

"Some kind of a first trip this is," Grisha sighed as Mischa smiled.

"You've got to admit that your maiden trip couldn't be more exciting," He joked and the two friends somehow managed to laugh while Ivchenko watched them with a straight face.

"I cannot believe you find this is funny," he said.

Mischa shrugged. The boy needed to lighten up, but it would be near impossible when it was clear he was petrified. "Look, there's nothing we can do but wait and make the best of it."

"That's easy for you to say," Ivchenko replied icily.

"Yes, it is," Mischa replied honestly, and picking up his tone every ear turned to him. "It should also be just as easy for you too. You know why? Because you're an experienced sailor just as I am and all the rookies on board depend on us to guide them through situations such as these. So man up and let's do just that."

Mischa looked around throwing a challenge out to the room. Not a word was said and within seconds everyone's attention had turned back to the speakers connected to the wall.

In the command center everyone was back at their posts and focused on their tasks. Though the tension in the room continued to thicken the air, everyone felt better for having a job to do. While Bodrov monitored things from navigation, Kuznetsov shadowed the sonar officer, his eyes glued to the green dot that was the US torpedo and his ears tuned to the sounding beep that grew in speed and velocity the nearer the missile came to his boat.

"Bodrov; status?" Kuznetsov asked, not taking his eyes off the screen.

"We leveled safely at 70 meters below. Still heading one, one, eight, speed fifteen knots." Bodrov's voice remained calm and Kuznetsov found himself impressed.

"Time to impact?" he asked.

"Two minutes, 15 seconds, Captain."

"Trajectory?"

"Still coming straight for us, Sir."

"OK," Kuznetsov turned to face the room. "Listen up, everyone. Release rear countermeasures on the XO's command followed by full speed, course zero, nine, zero."

Bodrov saluted the captain and turned to the crew. "Countermeasures: ESM, Rim Hat, intercept. Ready. Release rear countermeasures, change course to zero, nine, zero and full speed ahead, on my mark."

As the last order left his lips Bodrov turned to Kuznetsov and for a full minute both men held the other's gaze because they knew that they had done whatever they could for the Kursk and her men and all they could do now was wait. In little more than a few seconds they would have their answer. Kuznetsov gave Bodrov a small nod.

"Now!" Bodrov shouted, and the command center burst with renewed energy as the men carried out their orders.

"ESM ready?"

"Ready."

"Fire."

"Measures away, Sir!"

From the rear of the Kursk a torpedo sized-object left the submarine only to reach a distance of 150 meters before a cable tightened and it followed the Russian sub's path.

"Two third speed, Sir, and still increasing. Tow is in place. Forty-five seconds left."

Kuznetsov picked up the 1MC.

"Men," he said sternly. "Brace yourself for impact in 40 seconds."

All over boat the crew scrambled to find something to hold on to, some of them even made the mark of the cross on their chest as they waited for the hit, their nerves stretched to breaking point by the continuous rapid beep of the torpedo coming their way. "Sonar report," Kuznetsov demanded.

From his seat, the young officer swung his head in the direction of the captain, his eyes relaying the news before his lips. "The torpedo has changed course to follow our decoy, Sir."

"Thank God," Bodrov muttered.

"Time to impact?" Kuznetsov asked.

"20 seconds"

The torpedo followed a straight course towards the Kursk's decoy in what would have been a textbook example of evasion in the face of enemy fire – or at least a textbook example right up to the point when the missile suddenly veered away from the decoy and headed straight back towards the Kursk's nose. The Russian sub was left with only seconds to react, an impossible task, and the torpedo smashed into the front, starboard, penetrating the outer hull where it exploded. The Kursk shuddered like a harpooned whale in the deep and the command center reacted as though hit by a tidal wave. Pipes and screens ripped free of their moorings, crashing into the sailors to leave them bloodied and bruised upon the floor. For some, the force of the impact was instant and deadly and the crew suddenly found themselves clambering over the bodies of men they classed as friends. From the center of the room, Kuznetsov hauled himself to his feet, the distress clawing at the lines on his face.

"Tchert poberi!" he screamed "The devil take you!"

17 The First Aftermath

Saturday, August 12, 2000: 12:05 pm

"**W**HAT THE HELL HAPPENED?"
Jack Coleman shouted amid the chaos of the command center where every man present was pushing buttons and flicking switches to discover just that.

"We hit her, Sir!" the XO reported, the horror of the words churning his stomach as he spoke them. "We don't know why, but we hit her. We did everything by the book to get a clean and simple warning shot out there, but it went into the Kursk's starboard bow. We are continuing to assess the situation."

"Thank you, mister Garret," Coleman responded even as he felt the blood turn to ice in his veins. "Any report on the damage yet?"

"No Sir, but with the high impact, low yield load of the torpedo I guess we'll be waiting to see whether the rumors about Russian subs are true and whether they are unsinkable. If I had to hazard a guess as to what happened I'd say our torpedo mistook the decoy for the Kursk because our readings suggest the torpedo then tried to correct the mistake but had no time to make a course correction before impact. What do we do now, Sir?"

"Get me One Control on the radio," was all Coleman could manage.

"Status report, Bodrov. Where are you?"

Kuznetsov cast his eyes over the wreckage of the command center's starboard side. Every last piece of equipment had been ripped from the wall to bury his crew in bolts, gears and knobs. "Bodrov, where the hell are you?"

Kuznetsov's voice sounded distant even to himself. He simply couldn't get the air into his lungs to shout any louder. As his mind raced, he quickly tried to assess the situation; the Kursk was still afloat that much was clear and from what he could feel she was horizontally balanced. Furthermore there was no movement beyond the shocked bodies of men slowly coming round to the disaster that had befallen them. Kuznetsov shook his head and glanced behind him where he caught sight of Bodrov. The young officer was lying on the ground next to Wang who lay face down in some 25 centimeters of water. The Captain's heart jumped to his mouth at the sight and he let go of the bulkhead he had been leaning on for support to get to the two men, stepping over debris and the still warm corpses of boys he had been tasked to take care of. How many dead –he silently screamed to himself – at least half the compartment gone and now, dear God, no, Bodrov.

Kuznetsov felt the tears begging to be released as he neared the staring soulless eyes of his second-in-command. Within his right hand Bodrov still gripped the microphone he had used to guide the crew; fulfilling his orders to the very last breath. Kuznetsov took the microphone from Bodrov's grasp and checked his pulse. Nothing. The young officer from Ukraine had gone and the pain Kuznetsov felt was

140

surprising and immediate. As he battled to contain the grief sweeping up from his gut, he bent forward to close the first officer's eyes.

Raising his head, Kuznetsov caught sight of the steel door to the torpedo room which had been bent out of shape yet remained closed. He also noticed the water level had stopped rising, at least in his compartment. The point of impact had to have been to the front, he concluded. He then noticed the equipment that had managed to more or less retain its position, but knew that it would be a minor miracle if even one of the systems had survived the explosion. And yet the 1MC on the wall next to him was still showing lights. Hardly willing to believe it, Kuznetsov picked up the microphone and pushed the talk button. The pressure of his fingers echoed through the loudspeakers throughout what was left of the command center.

"Torpedo room, respond. Vitaliy, are you there?" Kuznetsov waited for a few seconds. "Anyone? Please respond, this is your captain speaking."

The sea seeped through every crack of the torpedo compartment, starboard wall, raising the water level by the minute to slowly cover the lifeless bodies of the men who had died on impact. Small fires had broken out as loose wires connected and a single burst of flash flare had blackened the walls as well as singing the hair and eyebrows of men who realized they were lucky to be alive. Stuck between heavy machinery and debris, the shock of the surviving crew members was complete and for a while there was nothing to hear but the slap of the water hitting the charred walls and bellies of the torpedoes that fallen from their trestles to stack like a pile of Mikado sticks.

Underneath Hatch Four lay Lieutenant Vitaliy Polyakov. The man in charge of firing the Kursk's torpedoes lay fatally wounded by another firing officer's launch and the shock was all too clear to see in his open, lifeless eyes. If he had remained alive, maybe he would have noticed what those who were left didn't, but he had died and over at the hatch holding the Shkval nobody registered how the bolts on the locks of the tube had been loosened enough to create an opening for the clear fluid dripping from the torpedo to escape into the chamber where it gradually snaked its way towards a rusty weld.

In contrast to the torpedo room, the propulsion compartment looked relatively undamaged with only some loose papers and a few work tools upon the floor to suggest anything untoward had occurred. Beyond the bruises and shocked expressions, the sailors looked more or less unharmed, but they were scared and they expressed that fear to their immediate commander Mischa. They wanted to know if the Kursk was sinking, what had happened, and whether they would die.

"Stop! Calm down and just listen for a moment," Mischa implored, stretching his arms out in front of him. "I know as much as you do, but I'm sure we're going to be fine as long as you all keep your heads. I'll try to find out what's going on, but give me the time to do this."

Mischa looked around the room, taking in the nervous faces of each and every one of his men knowing that internally he shared every one of their concerns. If ever he needed a drink, it was right now. Shaking his head, he straightened his shoulders and headed for the 1MC only to reach it as the frantic voice of the young nuclear engineer Bogdan Polakov sounded through the speakers.

"Is anyone receiving me? Hello?"

Mischa almost ran to pick up the microphone.

"Kastamarov here. How are you doing, Vitaliy?"

"There's no one left, Sir," the younger man cried. "I'm alone. I don't know what to do!"

"OK, OK, stay calm son. I need you to stay focused. Are you injured?"

"No, I don't think so, Sir. I don't know. There's no one left, Sir. There were four of us and now I'm the only one and I don't know what to do, Sir."

"It's OK Vitaliy, this is why I'm here; I'm here to help you. Now let's try and get through this together. Is the compartment dry?"

"Yes, Sir."

"Are the reactors still functioning?"

Polakov glanced through the small window. "The reactors look OK, Sir. I know what to do to shut them down. Should I shut them down? Are we sinking?"

"Take it easy, Vitaliy. No one said anything about sinking, but I need you to be ready to shut down the reactors when needed. Don't do anything until I give the order. Now stay close to the radio and I'll come back to you shortly."

"Will do, Sir. Thank you, Sir."

As Mischa was about to replace the microphone he heard a faint, but familiar voice. "Captain, is that you?" he asked. "Kastamarov here. Please respond. Captain, are you there?" Mischa flipped a lever on the radio and tried again. "Captain, are you there?"

"Kastamarov, is that you?" Kuznetsov's voice sounded through the loudspeakers and relief flooded the faces of every man in the compartment

"Kastamarov here, Sir. Good to hear your voice. Can you tell us what's going on?"

Kuznetsov paused before replying. When the answer came it was shocking in its honesty. "There's not much left up here," he admitted. "We've lost most of our systems, but though it's unclear what has exactly happened, for now we seem to have stabilized."

Back in the torpedo compartment, the Shkval continued to leak fluid in Tube Number Four. As it touched the rust of the weld a spark ignited a small fire in the tube. Within a fraction of a second it transformed into a flash fire that charged through the tube from one end to the other, further heating up the torpedo's HTP fuel mix of hydrogen peroxide and kerosene. As the HTP reached its auto-ignition temperature the torpedo exploded. And with the waterside door closed, the pressure buildup forced its way through the unlocked torpedo hatch on the inside blowing out a large part of the torpedo's tail into what was left of the compartment. In an instant, the temperature increased within the room to more than 4500°F. The first torpedo to reach its critical temperature exploded in a burst of yellow and orange flames that quickly engulfed every corner of the room igniting the compartment's remaining arsenal of weapons. The blast was so enormous it took out the entire bulkhead dividing the torpedo room from the command center. As fire ripped through the floundering Kursk a large portion of her nose blew off and she rapidly began to sink; falling to the bottom of the Barents Sea killing all left alive in Kursk's nose.

James and Anders listened carefully to what Coleman had to say, but the picture wasn't getting any clearer.

"We're receiving all kinds of contradictory readings and cannot yet distinguish between exercise maneuvers or the Baltimore and our target. Have you heard from Norsar yet?"

Located north of Oslo, Norsar, originally monitored earthquakes but now also kept an eye on the any seismic activity in the region, particularly of the nuclear kind. Though they were mainly tasked with monitoring violations of the Nuclear Test Ban Treaty, they also watched for anomalous readings during Russian exercises in the Barents Sea

"Actually, Sir, we've got Norsar on line now," one of the officers called to Anders and the Norwegian immediately flipped a switch on his radio to speak. "This is Admiral Fredrik Anders of the Marjata alongside Commander Mitchel James of the United States Navy. Over."

144

"Good day, Admiral. My name is Ludvig Holberg and I'm here with Petter Dass. We're monitoring activities in your region and we're getting some notable and disturbing readings."

"Such as?"

"Sir, we measured two outstanding seismic events near your location. The explosions were registered in the deep which is unusual because practice explosions during an exercise are expected to be surface-based."

Anders glanced at James. "So what can you tell us about the explosions, Mr. Holberg?"

"Well Sir, we fixed the first event with a magnitude of 1.5 on the Richter scale at coordinates 69°38′North 37°19′ East, which is roughly 120 miles north of you. The second event happened exactly two minutes forty seconds later some 400 meters from the first at: 69°36′North 37°34′East. That measured just over 4.2 on the Richter scale. That's a pretty big shake, Sir and I'll assume you wouldn't want to be in the epicenter of such an earthquake."

"You assume correctly," Anders responded. "And you're sure they aren't seismic disturbances from the naval exercise?"

"I've measured a lot of exercises, Sir, but I've never seen anything of this magnitude and never this far below the surface."

"All right. Thank you. Please keep a close eye on the area and get back to me when something out of the ordinary happens."

"Aye, Admiral. Norsar, out."

As the intercom fell quiet, James and Anders exchanged another glance. They had no way of knowing what state the Kursk was in, but the damage inflicted on her by the Baltimore could have made her vulnerable in a quake and if she had been caught in it things could get very messy very quickly.

From the moment Mischa lost contact with Kuznetsov he felt the Kursk fall; taking any hope that they were not in fact sinking with it.

Every man in the room knew exactly what was going on and they raised their eyes to the ceiling as if to say goodbye to the world above before grabbing hold of anything they could find that was bolted down. After that, they could only brace themselves for the landing.

It took ten seconds to reach the bottom, ten seconds for the surface light to fade and cloak the Kursk in a veil of black. At 100 meters below, 15,000 tons of steel slammed 5 meters into the sand and clay bottom sending a mushroom cloud of dust and debris surging through the water to encompass the stricken submarine.

At the brutal landing, the crew was thrown around their compartments like marbles rattling in a tin. Men collided with machinery; bodies were bruised; skin was cut open; and bones were broken. The screams of the injured and the hopeless filled every part of the Kursk.

As the sub stilled, Mischa found himself lying against one of the driving shafts. He checked himself over to discover blood lightly seeping from a head wound. Clearly the cut was shallow and he felt no pain for which he was more grateful than he would acknowledge. Looking around his compartment, the men scattered about the floor were hard to distinguish from the debris of furniture and machine. Some sailors immediately tried to get to their feet, others lay lifeless in pools of their own blood. About 3 meters away he spotted Grisha and his heart leapt to his mouth. His friend was leaning against the bulkhead, his chin on his chest, his eyes closed.

"Grisha!" Mischa yelled, and to his great relief his friend slowly lifted his chin and opened his eyes. "Grisha!" Mischa shouted again. "Talk to me, man!"

Grisha opened his mouth to find the words to speak, but Mischa couldn't hear him over the groans of the injured. Pushing himself onto his knees he crawled over the floor. As he reached Grisha he took hold of both his hands and looked him straight in the eyes.

"Are you all right? Can you move?"

146

Grisha's eyes began to focus on Mischa. "I-I believe I'm OK," he stammered. "What happened?"

"I don't know for sure, but we took a very bad hit and we went down fast. We're at the bottom, Grisha."

"At the bottom? What does that mean? What do we do now?" his friend asked, his eyes widening in disbelief and panic.

"I don't know yet," Mischa replied honestly. "I really don't know."

18 The Second Aftermath

Saturday, August 12, 2000: 12:31 pm

IT WAS NIGHT and the Baltimore sat still in the quiet shallow waters, submerged to only periscope depth. In the command center, there was no visible damage other than some loose materials lying around. As the men quickly tidied the place up, Cook pulled himself together to take command of the situation.

"Damage report!" he ordered in a voice that was firm and calculated to give nothing away.

Eric Sanders paced behind the bank of specialists' desks. "Reports coming in from all decks, Sir. It seems we remain fully dry, but we have other problems."

"Like what?" Cook demanded.

"Propulsion is damaged, Sir. We are still assessing the exact damage, but it looks we have only one fifth speed."

"Sonar?"

"Sonar's back up and functioning at one hundred percent, but we have lost our bogey, Sir."

"Damn it, is it going to be one of those days?" Cook asked, exasperation creeping slowly into his voice. "All right, keep all eyes on the lookout for that bogey. Until definitive orders are received we need to be extra vigilant. Get me a full damage assessment on our propulsion in fifteen minutes."

"Aye Captain," Sanders answered.

Cook picked up the radio and looked around. All the men were focused on the tasks at hand; no one was panicking or looking lost and Cook felt his chest swell with pride at the crew's inherent professionalism. They must all be worried, he thought; the adrenaline racing through his own body was proof enough of the gravity of the situation. They were in new territory that was for certain, and in many respects it felt like being at war. "One Control this is Listener One do you read?" Cook waited and though the silence only lasted seconds it felt like minutes

"One Control here, Captain," came James's voice over the crackle of the intercom. "How are you doing out there?"

"All crew accounted for and no casualties, Commander. We suspect we took some damage on the hull, but on the inside we're pretty much OK except for the fact we seem to have some propulsion problems. For now we have limited power so it seems we are not going anywhere fast. Do you have any news on our bogey?"

"Nothing definitive. We lost contact shortly after the collision, but Norsar reported some disturbing seismic readings that we are still awaiting confirmation on. I'm sure you must have noticed something too?"

"Yes, we were also a little shook up, but we didn't have any sonar capabilities at the time so we couldn't pinpoint the origin."

At the revelation, James backed off from the microphone to throw a questioning look at Anders. The Norwegian's face tensed as he reached for the intercom.

"Admiral Anders here, Captain. Is your position compromised?" he asked Cook.

"I don't think so, Admiral. We are at periscope depth and we have only about one fifth power. The advantage, if there is one to be had, is that we can still run silent."

"Any chance you'll be able to fix the damage yourselves?" James asked.

Cook looked around the room to try and gauge the general view of his men. The room remained silent until Sanders rushed to his side to hand him a piece of paper. Cook took a moment to read the message understanding at once that the prognosis was far from good. Taking a second to rub at the frown creasing his forehead, he hit the 'talk' button on the intercom to relay the bad news to James. "It seems we have serious propeller damage," he said. "In fact it's so serious it can only be fixed in dry dock. We need new orders, Commander."

Cook's request was met with silence. In his mind's eye he imagined the scene in the Marjata, picturing the discussion taking place between the American and Norwegian heads of the mission. Eventually Anders's voice sounded again to confirm Cook's suspicions regarding the complexity of their situation. "Hang in there, Captain. We need some time, but we'll get back to you as soon as possible."

Anders noticed the beads of sweat forming under James's nose. "Hot?" he asked.

"What do you think, Admiral?" James shot back, unable to hide his nerves or indeed his irritation. Frantically pacing the room, his mind whirring with a million possibilities, consequences and unfolding tragedies, he finally stopped at the end of the conference table and poured himself a coffee from the coffee-maker. He lifted his cup towards Anders. "You want some?" he asked, hoping the apology would be clear in the offer.

"No, thank you," Anders replied, "and by the way you've been pacing around I'd advise you to hold back on the caffeine."

"It's decaf," James answered tersely, before adding with a smile, "I switched to decaf about an hour ago; after my tenth cup."

Anders returned the smile. "Did you get in touch with Washington?"

"Yes, a few minutes ago and I was told the chiefs of staff were gathering. I guess they're now trying to decide whether to fight or take flight."

"We have no choice," Anders firmly stated. "There isn't a cause to fight for and any admission of guilt will only lead to a confrontation politically, giving the president some valuable points in his new job. Furthermore, should things escalate to the point of response it could very easily lead to the next Cold War. No, our only choice is to flee!"

James scratched at his temple, buying time to think things through, but time was something they simply didn't have enough of. "All right, I understand, but how?"

"OK, it's not the best time to sound sentimental, but I remember that as a child we used to play uh… '*gjemsel…*' what do you call it in English when a child needs to go searching for another one?"

"Hide and seek."

"That's it, hide and seek, *gjemsel* we call it. You see, when we played it I was at a slight disadvantage because of my weight back then so I knew that without an accomplice I wouldn't stand a chance. So I made a deal with one of my friends that one of us would show ourselves and while he was hunted I would be home free. So…"

"Do I understand you correctly and are you suggesting we 'sacrifice' one sub on behalf of the other?" James asked, scarcely believing the Norwegian could be so callous.

"Well, in this case it would not really be a sacrifice, but more of a decoy. We have two subs in the area, one of them severely damaged. So if we allow the Detroit to show herself the Russians are bound to

152

follow her, creating space for the Baltimore to limp away to a safe location."

"They probably don't know we have two subs in the game," James admitted, his eyes catching fire as Anders's idea took hold. "So that way, the focus will be on the Detroit and should anyone start to ask questions we can show them the sub to deny there was any collision. Of course, we'll need approval from Washington, but the idea seems sound."

"What's the position of the Detroit now?" Anders asked.

"I've ordered her further into international waters awaiting orders. She's fine. I'll contact Washington and inform them of our plan."

On Peter the Great's bridge balcony Petrov and Junping looked tiny against the huge rising windows. The Barents Sea was calm, but against the morning sun the sky slowly darkened signaling the weather was about to take a turn for the worse.

"Still no sign of the Kursk?" Junping asked.

Petrov slowly put down the binoculars that had been practically glued to his face up to that point. Before he could answer Junping the bridge door opened and an officer appeared.

"Any news?" Petrov asked, the impatience clear in his voice.

"Sir, we detected a hydro-acoustic signal characteristic of an underwater explosion that seems to account for what we felt."

"Is it related to the demonstration?" Junping asked, hoping that the reason he was there might finally get underway.

Petrov curled his mustache, a personal tic that most of his men had come to read as a sign of indecision. In truth, Petrov dearly wanted to order the Chinaman off his bridge, but protocol advised him to proceed with tact. "At this moment we can't be sure about anything," he finally replied, as calmly as he was able. "However, I'm afraid I'll have to ask you to return to your quarters, as procedure dictates in this type of situation."

"This type of situation?" Junping asked. He knew what answer to expect, but he had picked up on the Russian's irritation and he had decided he wouldn't make it easy for the man.

"Surely you have similar procedures regarding guests in your own navy during uncertain circumstances?" Petrov replied courteously. "We'll call you when procedure allows. I suspect this won't take long."

Before Junping could question the request Petrov straightened his hat and threw an order over his shoulder to report the incident to headquarters, he then marched briskly from the balcony. The next time the Chinaman saw him, he was ducking under the rotating blades of a waiting helicopter on the flight deck below. Within minutes he was gone.

Bogdan Polakov looked around him as the alarms rang in his ears. The nuclear reactor compartment was lit up with amber lights and he found himself blinking, unable to believe he was the last man alive. Ahead of him the door leading to the front of the sub appeared to be bulging under some kind of heavy pressure. Instinctively he stepped backwards and into the door protecting the reactor. *'The reactor?'* Turning to the small window at his shoulder he was almost too afraid to look through it, uncertain of what he might do should things turn even worse than they were already. It took a few seconds for him to muster the courage to look, but when he did he exhaled heavily as relief swept through his body. The cooling rods were still positioned down into the reactor. "It's still working," he spoke aloud even as he noticed his hand had come to rest on the red emergency shutdown button next to the window. Frowning, he removed his hand form the button and walked carefully to the bulging front door. Coming to a stop one meter away, he stretched out his arm so he might feel the temperature with the flat of his hand. Nothing. Feeling braver, he inched closer to touch the door. Though it felt warm it wasn't hot. Taking a deep breath, Polakov placed both hands around the steel of the door lever. Pulling gently at first, he soon had to apply more force as the door remained jammed shut. Panic began to grip at his chest again as he realized this was his way out. With increasing desperation he pulled and pushed at the lever, at first grunting with the effort and then screaming as he gave it all he had and came away with nothing. The door wouldn't budge. Polakov fell to his knees and faced the warm steel door as a tear rolled down his cheeks.

"*Otche nash, izhe yesi na nyebesyekh*, Our Father, who art in heaven..."

As his lips ran through the Lord's Prayer his mind raced through every aspect of his training, and by the time he reached 'Amen' he knew what he had to do. Polakov, got up from his knees and walked purposefully the reactor control panel then, without any further thought, he pressed the emergency button. Through the windows, he saw the cooling rods immediately respond, retracting from the reactors and effectively shutting them down. He may not have been the most experienced sailor on the Kursk, but he was fully aware of procedure, and given the circumstances he felt this was the only possible thing to do.

Mischa walked up to the 1MC only to find it smashed into pieces. In the dim light, the moans of his men reached his ears before his eyes picked out the injured and he briefly watched the more able-bodied members of the crew tend to the wounds of their comrades, pulling bandages and pads from medical kits whilst trying to calm fears with assurances they didn't believe in.

"What do we do?" Grisha asked him.

"Well, we have no way of knowing what's going on elsewhere."

"So what do we do?"

Mischa looked at him and with a smile that didn't reach his eyes he said, "I don't know, this is my first disaster so I guess I might need to improvise."

Grisha shook his head. "How do you keep so calm?"

"I don't know," Mischa admitted honestly. "I just have a feeling we're all going to be OK as long as we keep our heads."

"Do you think we're the only ones left? Will anyone know we're down here? Shouldn't we move to the front and check it out?"

As Grisha fired questions at him his voice grew ever higher and Mischa tried to calm his friend's panic because such emotions were contagious.

"Hey, slow down, cowboy, one question at a time. Look, there's no way of knowing what's behind that door so let's try and find out everything there is to find out before we start exploring. Actually, wait."

Mischa climbed onto a chest in the middle of the room. "Friends! Friends!" he called out. He tried to keep his tone affable and the room responded in an instant "Look, please, I need all of you to stay calm. I don't know what happened, but I promise you I am going to find out. So if all of you who can still walk could gather in front of me we can start to take stock of the situation and discuss what to do next."

As Mischa finished, anyone who could walk did so, and a few who could only crawl dragged themselves forward to be counted. The number of casualties was overwhelming and Mischa felt a knot tie in his stomach as he saw how badly beaten most of the men were. For the first time in his career he felt the weight of expectation land on his chest as he realized how much the future of his men relied on his leadership. "Let us first do a headcount," he said gently, feeling an uncommon fear of the unknown flutter in his chest as he began taking names. All in all, there were 22 of them, including him, still fit for purpose.

"And what do we do next?" Grisha asked again. As Mischa struggled to find an answer, a door suddenly opened and Bogdan Polakov all but fell into the room.

The men reacted with shock, disbelief, relief and in some cases tears. They had assumed they were the last men standing given the force of the blast. Now knowing they weren't they directed all their questions at an increasingly bewildered Polakov.

"Come on, give the man some room!" Mischa yelled as Polakov slowly backed up against the wall. "Ivchenko will you get some water, please? Someone close the door behind him, but keep listening for anyone else who may want to enter." The sailor closest to the door lifted his hand to silently acknowledge the order. "Boga, what happened? What did you see?" Mischa then asked while everyone gathered around to hear what the younger man had to say.

"Oh my God, my friends, am I glad to see you all," he said, seemingly oblivious to Mischa's questions and still struggling to catch his breath.

"Please," Mischa demanded loudly and the room turned quiet. "Sit," Mischa ordered, placing a chair in front of Polakov. "So, again. It's very good to see you alive, but can you tell us anything about what happened out there?"

For a second, the young sailor's eyes worked to focus on Mischa's face. He so wanted to relay good news, but there was none that he could tell. "I don't know what happened," he replied honestly. "One minute we we're talking to each other and the next things started flying around. I've never seen someone die. Now all my comrades are dead. You are all that's left."

"How can you be sure?" Ivchenko asked the tone of his voice tight with both anxiety and fear.

"When I left the reactor room the doors to central command were ready to give in from the other side. I don't know what went on there, but I don't believe anyone could have survived that. So I figured the only way to go was astern. I locked down the reactors to safe mode and came up here."

"What did you see on your way up here?" Grisha interjected though he could already guess at the answer seeing as Polakov had turned up alone. "Nothing but death," Polakov revealed. "And I don't understand it. I don't understand why I'm still alive. I mean, all I have are a few cuts and bruises, but other than that I'm fine. Yet they are all dead."

"We're also still here. You are not alone." Mischa placed a hand on Polakov's shoulder. "And the reactors, they are OK?"

"I believe so. The emergency shutdown hadn't kicked in, but I was able to shut them down manually. What do we do now?"

Once again, Mischa felt all eyes on him, warming the back of his neck as the pressure of leadership returned. He climbed on the chair next to Polakov and raised his arms. "All right, listen men. Now before anything else I need everyone who's able to move to gather everything we might need like food, water, blankets, flashlights and batteries. Also we need to gather all the CO2 scrubbers we can find and bring them here to the back. Got it?"

"Got it!" came the reply from a dozen or more lips, and the men dispersed to scavenge through the wreckage of the compartment. As Grisha, Polakov, and Ivchenko also moved to gather what they could, Mischa asked them to stay. "Not you my friends, I need to ask you to help me collect the dead bodies and bring them to the front of the compartment. Grisha you're with me. Polakov you work with Ivchenko."

Although it was the grimmest of possible jobs to be assigned to, none of them disagreed.

As Mischa and his friends positioned the last body at the front of the compartment, they covered their fallen comrades with a tablecloth. The four of them then stood, motionless and speechless, as the stack of dead bodies revealed the full horror of their situation. When Polakov crossed himself the others followed his example.

"I didn't know you believed," Polakov said to Mischa.

"I don't. But today is different. We could all use a little faith today."

As if hit by inspiration Grisha looked upwards; perhaps seeking God and finding a glimmer of hope. "What about the escape hatch?" he asked, pointing at the ceiling. We cannot reach the escape pod in the front but the hatch should be OK. Right?"

"Yes that should work!" Ivchenko added, nodding his head eagerly. "Let's try the escape hatch."

"Hold on, hold on," Mischa said quietly. "Let's not rush into anything. It looks like we have enough oxygen for a while and we need to think about our next step carefully." He paused to look around before pointing to a lever on the side of the room. "First, let's try to release the emergency buoy. You never know."

"What do you mean, 'you never know'?" Ivchenko asked.

"In my training days I worked three months at the shipyard in Polyarny. Out there most of the buoys on the submarines are welded to the hull because off construction problems they got lost all the time."

"Let's try it anyway," Grisha said as he walked up to the red lever on the side. As he pulled it down the men anxiously watched the red light above them to see what might happen. A second later the red light turned to green and all the men cheered.

"Take it easy men, take it easy," Mischa ordered. "The only thing we know for sure is that the release clamps let go. It would look the same if it was welded down. So we cannot assume that the buoy has floated to the surface. Therefore we need to act as if we are on our own and make our plans."

As the helicopter neared the Peter the Great, heavy rain and fierce winds caused a headache for the pilot as he battled to land on the flight deck, and once the chopper was down Petrov almost ran from the exit.

As he raced through the ship's narrow corridors and up her staircases he passed a number of sailors and failed to salute any of them. The men were not unused to the temper of their captain and none of them dared say anything as they watched him head to his cabin and slam the door shut behind him. Once inside his room, he sat down at his desk, opened the paper log he kept and started writing:

August 12 2000, 1100 hours. No sign of Kursk. We're operating under the assumption that something is wrong. Sent a helicopter to search the last known grid, but nothing reported so far.

Petrov closed the book and picked up the telephone.

"Give me the head of search and rescue services."

19. Severomorsk

Day 1 - Saturday, August 12, 2000: 16.45 pm

ARKADY BEREZIN was dressed in a thick sweater and jeans. Pushing forty, his face was prematurely lined and partly hidden by a short, salt and pepper beard. The look he went for was one of rugged charm. The flat, wide forehead and twinkle in his eyes had more to do with nature than design, but they suggested an honest character, and in fact Anatoly was a straightforward guy with nothing to hide. As was his habit, he walked along the piers of Severomorsk at sundown before heading home. He liked this time of day, the light was more forgiving on the antiquated equipment his men had to deal with and it helped him believe that all would be well once he had gone and the night shift took over.

As he came to the end of the last pier on his daily ritual, a young man came running from the small, cabin-like office ahead of him, shouting and waving his arms.

"Captain, phone call for you!"

Knowing the phone call wouldn't be going anywhere, Berezin waved in reply to show he had heard and continued walking back at a leisurely pace. When he reached the cabin, the young man passed him the phone.

"Arkady Berezin here." To his surprise, the voice on the end began barking orders, catching him unawares. "Yes, Admiral. Yes, I heard," he confirmed and continued listening to the officer with increasing exasperation. Berezin had never signed up to the military because he knew that sooner or later they would screw up and when they did they would need to call on men like him to clean up the mess. But even so, he wasn't a miracle worker. "Sorry to interrupt," he finally interjected, "but you must be aware of our situation here, Admiral, and you'll therefore know we're nowhere close to being equipped for such a mission. You'd be better off contacting your colleagues in the Atlantic Ocean, after all for $35,000 a day they can take you to see the wreckage of the Titanic. Meanwhile I'm stuck up here with a 20-year-old converted lumber carrier and two training rescue subs."

As the line went quiet, Berezin waited. Gradually he started nodding as the commands began again. "Uh-huh, yes, that we can do, but we still have limited resources. We'll have to scrape together all the bits and pieces we can find and even then. Yes. Sure. Of course, we will. As you wish, I'll set everything in motion. Let us know when and where and we'll meet you there."

As he put the phone down, he paused to mutter about the absolute madness of the situation before picking up the receiver and dialing. "It's me and we have orders," he stated with no preamble. "It looks like we're sailing on short notice. I need you to muster all the crew you can find and have them load the AS34 and AS32 onto the Rudnitsky. Include all the submarine rescue materials you have. Regarding the crew; I don't care if you have to find them at a bar or whether they're sober or not, just get me the best men for the job."

On the Peter the Great, Petrov paused to collect his thoughts before picking up the phone again and dialing the Captain. In a voice weighted by the gravity of the situation he told his officer to load their Smerch-3 rocket launchers and then fire them close to the surface in the last known position of the Kursk. "If there's any problem with communications I'm sure that will bring her up to the surface," he explained before adding, "I'll make my way up to you."

After the order was relayed down the ranks, almost to a man the crew looked out over the Barents Sea. The night was nearly upon them, thick cloud darkened the sky, and as the rockets were fired they lit a trail of light over the water before hitting their target with a splash, sending a fountain of fiery water into the air.

"Anything?" Petrov asked while entering the bridge.

"Nothing, Sir."

Petrov winced at the news.

Mischa, Grisha, Ivchenko and Polakov sat on the floor watching the pile of supplies that the men gathered grow in front of them.

"Now, what about the escape hatch?" Grisha asked impatiently.

"You want to swim up?" Mischa asked, starting to get irritated with his friend's incessant demands for action when he hadn't even begun to think through the consequences. To his surprise and further frustration Ivchenko then joined in.

"Why not swim up? The air in here is already starting to get thin."

"For crying out loud, we have no idea how deep we are so how can we know if we would survive the trip up?"

"We know we are in shallow water. How deep can it be?" Grisha insisted.

"And risk the bends?" Mischa asked. "That's if you even make it alive to the surface. The chances are you'll die from decompression or undercooling before then; the water temperature even in this season is very low in this area. Should we make it to the surface and have to wait to be rescued we would likely die within an hour."

"Perhaps. but that has to be better than suffocating in here; dying in the fresh air instead of the dark. We have some IDA-59 rebreathers to get us up." Grisha pointed towards the stack OF red life jackets. Each one had a cylinder attached to the front and two black hoses ending in a mouthpiece. Mischa picked one up.

"These things?" he asked. He then tore the safety lid off. "You know what the 59 stands for? Look! Look what it says under here."

Grisha inched forward to read the small black imprint on the red. "1959."

"Indeed. 1959; that's the date these rebreathers were manufactured. But besides the question of whether they will work after more than forty years we only have a dozen of them. So who gets to go and who has to stay?"

"We'll all die here," Ivchenko said with a sigh.

"Nobody dies here," Mischa corrected him angrily. "Can we at least agree for now that we wait, we prepare and we see what happens?"

Despite their fears, the men nodded in agreement just as Polakov came to grab Mischa by the arm and pull him towards the stern. Instinctively, all the men turned to look and what they saw stole their breath.

"We're making water," Polakov said, his own terror reducing his voice to a whisper. Mischa saw the danger of rising panic in the eyes of his crew.

"What do you expect?" he asked easily. "With no propeller motion at this depth it's perfectly normal to take in water through the shafts. We simply need to wrap it. Boga, you take Ivchenko and find all the towels and any other cloth we've got and wrap it all as tight as you can around the shafts. Let's makes as little room for the water to get in as possible. Grisha, will you please keep an eye on them and help them. Though this is nothing unusual we do need to stop the water."

"Of course we need to stop the water if we don't want to drown," Grisha replied testily.

Mischa came to his friend's side and whispered harshly in his ear. "Let me tell you something. When the water level rises, the pressure in the boat will significantly increase. With everyone breathing out carbon dioxide the oxygen level is going to deplete fast so we'll suffocate long before we drown. Now, when you get the chance start separating the CO_2 scrubbers from the supplies. If we can't stop the water we're going to need them."

As Grisha walked away to help the men plug the leaks at the stern, Mischa walked to the furthest corner of the compartment away from the other sailors. Sitting down, he took the pen from his breast pocket and, after finding a blank page towards the back of a nearby 'greasing manual' he started writing though he could barely make out his own words in the dim light.

'*My dear Sophia, it's getting late and I miss you so much. I'm not sure but I think we are the only survivors. The carbon dioxide increases the pressure in the compartment. We cannot swim to the surface as we will die from the decompression. Some of us wanted to swim to the surface but we have made the decision to stay. There's still hope*'

Mischa blinked and tried to rub the life back into his tired eyes before ripping the note from the manual. He then carefully folded it and walked to a table at the side of the room where he found some plastic sheeting in one of the drawers. Carefully wrapping his letter in the plastic he placed it in his inside pocket with a pat. He then returned his attention to his colleagues who were busy gathering supplies and wrapping the sub's leaking shafts.

Above the Barents Sea a helicopter with Russian markings hovered above the surface. Searchlights bounced off the waves below as well as the lone form of a marine dangling on the end of a rope frantically trying to get hold of a red, spherical object being tossed on the waves. As the wind whipped up the water, the marine reached out to grab the object for the umpteenth time only to have it snatched from his grasp by the angry sea. When it reappears the marine tries again only to have it disappear altogether beneath the surface. For a while, the helicopter tries to retain its position as the marine scours the waters, but the weather is getting worse and when there is no sign of the ball he signals to the crew above him and they steadily reel him upwards. Minutes later, the helicopter swings away from the scene and the sea turns black.

Petrov sat alone in his quarters pouring over charts on his computer. It was his way of dealing with the situation. He needed to be alone. He couldn't cope with the distractions of men firing their theories and calculations in his ears. His orders were to continue with the exercise in as normal a manner as possible while the search for the Kursk continued with as few people as possible knowing about the disappearance. What better way to do that than to withdraw to his own quarters and his own thoughts? Finally turning off his computer, the welcome silence of his cabin was abruptly ended by the ringing of the phone. The voice on the line came from the bridge and revealed a barely controlled excitement.

"We've found what we think is a rescue buoy. We couldn't bring it in, but it was red and it was sphere shaped. According to the marines that discovered it, it wasn't one of ours."

"I see. Anything else?"

"Not now, Sir."

"Thank you."

Petrov closed the line, took a deep breath and then tilted his head up before pushing a button on his phone. "Put me through to Defense

166

minister Federov." It took more than a minute before there was any reaction from the other side and Petrov could feel his temper rising in his chest. He hated being made to wait. It was such an unnecessary ploy of politicians to bolster their own sense of power and self-worth. He assumed it stemmed from a feeling of inferiority when dealing with the military, and this sham of superiority made him hate politicians even more. "Comrade, Petrov, what can I do for you at this late hour?"

Biting his lip so as not to suggest the minister might want to answer his phone more sharply in future, Petrov kept his call to the point. "Comrade Minister, you know why I call. I think it's time we alert him."

"Why now?"

"We can't put it off any longer. We found a buoy."

"What kind of buoy?"

"A rescue buoy. According to the marines it was possibly American."

"So you didn't recover it?"

"No. The weather was too bad, but the fact is that if the Americans are involved we cannot keep him uninformed. I will not be held responsible if he finds out any other way – via the Press for example."

Petrov paused, almost feeling the ice travel through the phone line. "This is my call, Admiral," came the minister's frosty reply. "For now I want you to continue searching before I decide it's time to inform our president. I trust you can do that?"

"What do you think we'll do; stop the search and tuck ourselves into our warm and cozy bunks for the night?" Petrov retorted, finally losing his temper in the face of the minister's stupidity. "For now, I'll let this be your call, but if you haven't informed the president before midnight, I will."

Petrov then slammed the phone down, not waiting for an answer.

20. The Search

Day 2 - Sunday - August 13, 00:30

IN KURSK'S PROPULSION control compartment Mischa and his comrades gathered around the propeller shafts and sat down on the floor. Their breathing had become labored and they were beginning to find it difficult to speak. The temperature had dropped to around 50 degrees Fahrenheit yet because of the nitrogen buildup in their blood their faces look sweaty. Even though the propeller shaft was swaddled in yards of cloth, water continued to seep in.

Ivchenko wiped the sweat from his forehead, smearing black grease over his face in the process. "It won't close completely, but we did the best we could," he said with a sigh while nodding towards the main source of the leaks.

"It's OK. It will do for now," Mischa replied, trying to sound confident even as his body succumbed to another coughing fit.

"It's getting harder to breathe," Grisha said. "Isn't it time again to consider the escape hatch?"

"If we wait any longer the oxygen levels in our blood will become dangerously low," Polakov added.

The men looked at each other, reading their own fears in the other's eyes, before turning to Mischa willing him to make the decision for them. Feeling the weight of everyone's expectations land on his shoulders, Mischa was overwhelmed by a sudden compunction to run; to escape the responsibility, to flee the madness of a situation he felt ill-equipped to deal with. 'How did I get here?' his mind demanded to know. 'And who am I to make these kinds of decisions for these men? Was this his fate? And what if Sophia could see him now, would she be proud, would she be scared?' But of course there were no answers to his questions because there was no one other than him qualified to lead the men. For many years he had enjoyed their company and respect and it was now time to earn it. As much as he may have wanted it to be different, there was no one he could contact or even left alive who could help him make the necessary decisions. There was only him.

"Look, as long as we keep most of the water out I think we should be all right for at least a day or so. All our comrades on the surface must be looking for us now. They must have known where we were at the time of the incident, so they cannot be far away."

"And if they're not near?" Ivchenko asked, and the fear was evident in his voice. "What if they don't know where we are? Or what if they don't want to find us, have you ever thought about that?"

"Yes, what if they don't want to find us?" Polakov repeated.

"Why wouldn't they want to find us?" Mischa challenged, taken aback by the sudden onset of paranoia. "This is just an exercise. We are not at war. Trust me. This isn't you, this isn't what you think, this is the low oxygen speaking."

Ivchenko stood up from the floor and raised his arms defiantly. "We have breathing masks and I say we use the hatch, three men at a time, and take our chances at swimming up. What's the worst that can happen? We might die? If we stay down here we'll die for sure!"

"You have to calm down, my friend." Mischa stood up and put his arm around Ivchenko's shoulder. "Look, I don't have all the answers, but you know as well as I do that we don't have enough breathing masks. Look around you, most of us are too weak to stand let alone swim to the surface and survive. And what will you do should you reach the surface? It's night up there, who will find you?"

"So what do we do then?" Ivchenko cried in panic, grabbing Mischa at the shoulders and shaking him hard. Grisha and Polakov immediately stepped forward to intervene, wrestling Ivchenko away until Mischa gestured they should let him. As they released their grip, Ivchenko slumped forward. His face landed softly on Mischa's chest and he started to cry.

"I want to go home,' he sobbed.

"I know," Mischa said gently, and he put his hand on the back of Ivchenko's head to try and comfort him. "I promise you I will do everything in my power to get us out of here. In fact, I'm still certain that we have every chance of being rescued. So please, calm down a little and conserve your energy so we may fully discuss our options."

As Ivchenko removed his head from Mischa's chest he wiped the tears from his cheeks and gave his comrades a sheepish smile. "So what are our options?"

Mischa pressed the younger man gently on the shoulder before turning to the rest of the crew. "It is clear that I cannot make the decision for all of you, but I still feel we stand a better chance of surviving if we stay where we are. Down here we have enough oxygen to last us another day. After that we have the CO_2 scrubbers, which will give us an extra source of oxygen."

"And how long can the scrubbers give us extra oxygen for?" Ivchenko asked, glancing at the large stack of devices by the wall which looked like brown office envelopes covered in plastic.

"I truly cannot say with any certainty. If we seal off this compartment from the rest of the sub it might buy us another day, possibly two."

Mischa lowered his eyes. He was damned if he was going to lie to his men. Sometimes the truth wasn't pretty, but he knew better than most people about the consequences of denying the truth, after all it was the constant drinking and the lies that caused his own father to get demoted to a teaching job at the naval academy. Right now, this moment was his moment to do things differently, to show he was different.

"So, if we stay we've got a maximum of three, possibly four days?" Grisha asked, having quickly done the math.

"That sounds about right, Einstein." Mischa smiled at his own joke and while there was no debating the gravity of the situation everyone who was able to laugh, laughed. "But seriously, we have to make a decision," Mischa insisted, his tone turning serious as he looked everyone in the eyes for a second or more to convey the fact that this would be their collective decision and not his alone. "Therefore I think it only fair that we put it to a vote; staying or going. For the record, if you decide to go we will need to figure out who gets to go. So, please raise your hand if you want to stay."

Mischa and his friends looked around the room as the men started to raise their hands. Although a few remained unsure within a few seconds everyone who could raise their hand had done so. "And you my friends?" Mischa said, turning to Grisha, Polakov and Ivchenko.

"I really don't know what's best to do next," Grisha admitted before raising his hand. "However, I trust you my friend. If there's anyone left who can bring us back to our wives it will be you."

As Grisha finished, Polakov also raised his hand. "It's not just a matter of trust; I'm an engineer and to me staying looks like the most logical option with the highest probability of survival. I trust God, Mischa and my own engineering skills on this one."

172

The three friends now turned to Ivchenko. Mischa placed his hand on the younger man's shoulder. "My dear friend, I know it's difficult but I'm sure it's the right decision to make. Do you remember the time we got into that bar fight? You trusted me back then when I said it was time to leave and I now ask you to trust me in staying."

"But can you promise me it's going to be OK this time?" Ivchenko said with a small smile. He wanted it to sound like a joke, but both he and Mischa knew he couldn't be more serious.

"I can promise you that staying gives us the best chance of survival," Mischa told him. "There are no guarantees that can be given here, but I think comrade Polakov said it like it is. We need to trust in God and everything we know to be true about each other."

Though Ivchenko had been hoping for more, he kept silent, closed his eyes for a second, and finally nodded to show his agreement.

The Marjata danced on the waves of the Barents Sea and Admiral Fredrik Anders held firmly onto the handrail on the bridge. This was his place; the place he felt most comfortable. In the dark night every wave that hit the bough of the ship came as a surprise, capable as it was of tossing the vessel 35 meters in any direction it wanted. This was the true nature of the sea; huge and unpredictable. One moment the waters could be as smooth as silk and the next a crew could be fighting for their lives upon waves as high as the Norwegian Fjords. Yes, it was just the way he liked it.

As the bridge door swung open James called out to him. Though it was impossible to hear anything over the roar of the wind and the crash of the waves, Anders understood James's arm signals and with some regret he turned his back on the black sea to go and speak with the American.

"We have contact with Washington," James shouted as the admiral neared.

"What's the plan?"

"They want you present, on the radio, for the verdict."

"Then lead the way."

As the two men entered the conference room Anders looked at James who hurriedly cleared the table of candy wraps, plastic coffee cups and loose papers.

"Sorry; waiting has never been my strong suit. I have to be doing something."

"No problem," Anders said easily, "As long as you clean up your own mess."

James nodded and smiled before reaching for the radio. "This is Commander James together with Admiral Anders on the Marjata, do you read?"

Almost immediately, a clipped American accent broke through the crackle. "Marjata; Charles Turner here."

"Good to hear your voice, Sir," James answered. "What news do you have for us?"

"We've discussed your proposal in the Security Council and though we're not keen on using the Detroit as a decoy we don't see any viable alternative. You are hereby cleared to order the Detroit to set sail to Bergen, Norway, keeping her detectable on the surface at low speed."

"Perfect, Sir. We can do that."

Almost immediately James felt relief flood through his sugar-fueled system. Now he had the backing of Washington, any future decisions he might have to make would be a hell of a lot easier without the fear of them wrecking his career should they backfire.

"Any orders that we can give the Detroit in case the Russians contact them?" Anders asked Turner, who appeared to have been prepared for such a question.

"The Detroit is in no way to divert from course. In an emergency situation they are allowed to be halted, but under no circumstances will any foreigners be permitted on board, military or otherwise."

"Anything else, Sir?" James asked.

"Only that from here on in, we will take over the conversation with the Baltimore. You don't need to worry about her from now on. That's it for the time being, gentlemen. We wish you all the best of luck and please contact us when required or if anything changes."

"Thank you, Marjata out."

As he put the microphone back on the table James looked at Anders and shrugged his shoulders. "So, that's it?"

"For now," Anders replied, clearly believing this was only the start of things. "Let's wait and see."

"And in the meantime, have you received any news about what might have happened to the Russian sub – officially or unofficially for that matter?"

"Amazingly little," Anders answered, unable to hide the disappointment he felt. "One would expect scattered messages on all channels, but it's as if nothing has happened."

"I guess the Russians would prefer to keep it that way as long as possible, at least until they know who to blame. By all accounts, the new leadership must have wanted to show the strength of his navy, now he may have a disaster on his hands. What he chooses to do next will be telling; it might also bring about another Cold War, or something worse."

Hearing the words said aloud, struck James in a way his own private thoughts hadn't and Anders couldn't help but notice the shadow creep over the American's face.

"Anyway, for now let's start relaying those orders and see what happens," he said.

Michail Federov's office in the Ministry of Defense building in Moscow looked out onto Arbat Street, the place where the country's youth, hippies and punks had largely chosen to hang out since the 1980s. Federov was not a fan of the view from his window; for him it symbolized everything that was wrong with the Russian republic. Not that he would be taking in the view much today. No, his ear would no doubt be glued to the phone as he gathered every last stitch of information about the incident in the Barents Sea before deciding whether or not to inform his president.

"Comrade Petrov, what's your latest?" On the other end of the line, the head of the Northern Fleet tried to sound helpful, but that fact was there was little he could supply in the way of fresh information. "Sir, we still don't know for sure what happened, but we are sure that she's in trouble. We have some twenty-five vessels searching for the Kursk, but for now we have no idea where to look so we continue to circle her last known location."

"And what will you do once you find her?"

"We can only take it one step at a time, Sir." Petrov tried to keep his voice level even as he fought an overriding urge to shout 'do I look like a damned fortune teller?' Politicians were all the same and Federov was no exception; searching for quick answers and explanations to save his own skin from the wrath of his superiors. He didn't know why he was even surprised anymore; it was the Russian way after all "While we are doing all that we can here, we also have the search and rescue vessel Rudnitsky on its way. However, in my experience, I would say that it is highly unlikely we'll be able to keep this a secret for much longer. Therefore, I would advise declaring an emergency."

At the advice, Federov stood up from his desk and with the phone still in his hand he turned to the window, lost for words as his brain tried to register the full repercussions of such an action.

"Are you still there sir?" Petrov asked.

"Still here, Admiral." For a second, the minister felt something close to envy as he watched the hippies below; assuming their most pressing decisions would revolve around which beaded bracelets to sell. They had no idea how easy they had it. "OK Admiral, I think you're right. We'll declare an internal emergency. No press. I'll conduct the politics from here, you command the search and rescue. Contact me if anything changes."

"Will do, Comrade Minister."

As soon as he put the phone down, Petrov walked out of his cabin with a sense of renewed purpose. It took him only two minutes to navigate the immense corridors of the Peter the Great and reach the helicopter deck where some 20 members of the Press were gathered. Petrov went to stand behind a small lector. "People of the Russian and International Press I'm proud to stand here before you as commander of this year's Northern Fleet summer exercise. Since the exercise is still in progress I cannot give much in the way of detail other than to tell you that the drills we have so far carried out have been a great success."

"So can we say that the exercise has shown the Russian Navy is once again a force to be reckoned with?" asked a journalist in the front row.

Petrov smiled. "No. The Russian Navy never went away; we simply chose not to reveal so much of ourselves in the past few years." Petrov pointed to another journalist who had raised a hand.

"There were rumors about the test of a new and revolutionary weapon. Can you comment on that?"

"Sorry, I cannot comment on that at this time. However, what I can say is that our newly-elected leader has a stable and forceful Navy at his disposal armed with the newest and best equipment available."

As the morning sun rose above the horizon the Rudnitsky arrived at its destination. Below two large cranes were two orange and white striped rescue submersibles, the AS32 and AS34; their bright colors making them stand out against the grey of the ship. As Berezin walked the deck he noticed that despite the predictions the weather wasn't too bad and though the waves were fairly high they wouldn't give the ship any problems with regard to holding her position after anchoring.

"Drop the anchor!" Berezin shouted across the deck and almost immediately the first anchor dropped into the water, sinking more than 100 yards before reaching the sea bottom. Berezin glanced at his watch; it would take an hour and three anchors to get the Rudnitsky into position. So while he continued to oversee the operation, he also made time for a call.

"We're securing our position, Sir, at the place where the Kursk was last known to be.

"Thank you, Captain," Petrov replied. "You're about 16 miles south of us. We're staying away in order to prevent any attention diverting to you. Did you encounter any problems at the start of your operation?"

"No problems, Sir. The weather works for us, for now, though I would feel more comfortable if we had at least some proof of her location. It's a big sea bottom to search."

"We've two reported, but unaccounted for, explosions. The second one occurred straight below your bow. I'd say that there's a pretty big chance that if she isn't able to sail you'll find her there."

"If she's there we'll find her, Sir. What happens then, well, I'm not so sure yet."

"Well, I'm sure you'll do everything you can, Captain," replied Petrov before his tone turned darker and more authoritative. "Of course it may come to the point where I will need even more than your everything – and I'll expect you to deliver."

Berezin bristled slightly at the comment. He wasn't a kid, he knew his job, and he wasn't in the habit of not rescuing men when he could. "I'll get back to you when we have news," he said. He then hung up the phone and glanced once more across the deck to see how the anchoring was progressing. When he was satisfied everything was fine he walked up the stairs and onto the bridge.

The Rudnitsky was a 21-year-old converted lumber ship and though she was a tough old girl it was clear from the narrow, small bridge that she had never been designed to carry as much equipment as she did. On all sides, heaps of electronic devices seemed to be randomly stacked on top of each other. Keyboards, microphones and large manuals cluttered the table space. In fact, the room was so piled high with equipment it left little room for the four men in civilian clothing who were employed to operate it and as a result they frequently bumped into each other, apologizing as they did so.

"How are we doing?" Berezin asked as he came to join them.

"We're steady on the water, Captain" one of the engineers immediately answered.

"How long till we are ready to take our first look?"

"The crane with the camera just swung from deck onto the water and is lowering as we speak."

"Image?"

"It will take up to another minute or two to reach any significant depth, but when it comes it will appear on Monitor Four."

"Are we talking one minute or two?" Berezin asked, raising his eyebrows to show his displeasure at the imprecision of the engineer's answer.

"Sorry, Captain, it's honestly hard to say when the equipment is this old."

Berezin shook his head, but he let the matter drop because ultimately he knew the engineer was right, and so he waited – for a minute that felt like an hour.

"Pictures coming up, Sir," Orlov Volodin called and Berezin came to join him at Monitor Four. Though the engineer was relatively young he had served as Berezin's second for some years. As a result, the men knew each other well. "There we are," he said pointing to a static image that resembled little more than grey clouds in the sky. "Depth reading; 65 meters and descending."

As the camera continued to drop, small particles of what looked like dust broke through the grey cloud, passing from view to reveal the direction the camera was heading in. Next to the screen a counter signaled the meters covered – 72,73,74 – and with every meter that went by the image became clearer yet darker. At 104 meters the camera movement stopped to reveal the sandy bottom of the sea almost too dark to be recognizable. "We appear to have reached the bottom, Sir. Visibility can't be much more than 5 to 10 meters, depth 108 meters."

"All right, let's take her back up to 20 meters above the seabed and hold at that height."

"At that distance the bottom will be barely identifiable, Sir," Volodin advised Berezin.

"Perhaps so, but at this height we can cover a greater area and we get more, besides, we don't need to see the bottom; we are looking out for a sub that's going to be sticking out of the seabed by at least 18 meters." Berezin couldn't disguise the pleasure he felt in teaching the younger engineer a little commonsense and to his credit the younger man took the lesson with a smile. "Now," Berezin continued, "are you able to get me a 45-degree angle and still rotate?"

Volodin nodded and got to work. The camera was little more than a square box with large white lights at every corner dangling in the water from tiny steel cables. After tilting it started to slowly turn clockwise. The beams of light cut through the dust clouding the water. It always reminded Berezin of the old news reels that showed beams of light cutting through the sky in the hunt for enemy bombers during the Second World War.

"Camera angle is in position, Sir. Rotating now," Volodin said and every one watched the screen which was mainly picking up dust and the occasional fish tail. "I suspect the image isn't going to be any better soon."

Berezin waited until the camera had fully rotated twice more. "That's OK. Get another panorama at eight meters on video. At least we now know what to expect down there with regard to the view, image quality and light. After the image is complete bring her back up."

180

Berezin moved to a table and picked up a large standing microphone. "Crew your attention, please."

At the captain's voice, every member of crew stopped what they were doing and looked towards the bridge.

"This is the moment we came for. You all know your job. Let's ready the AS34 for immediate diving. Be ready to launch in one hour."

From the bridge, Berezin watched the men below salute him before returning to their work. It was a habit they had picked up that left him quite baffled. They weren't military after all. He turned his attention to the rescue subs, waiting side by side. The AS34 looked somewhat smaller than the AS32, but Berezin realized that was only because it wasn't fitted with the robot-like arms at the front. The AS34 was the reconnaissance vessel. Once something was found the AS32 would then be launched. In truth, Berezin admired the Priz class submarines; coming in at only 13 meters long and 5 meters high they were the unsung heroes of the sea world. The rescue sub was equipped with a round skirt on its belly that would be placed over the escape hatch of a sunken sub. After being pressurized any stricken sailors would then be able to escape. These were actually the same submarines used to hunt the Titanic with one vital difference; the one's used at the Titanic possessed a new battery system that was ten times more efficient. His batteries only had a life span of 3 hours before they needed recharging, which could take up to ten hours. The search and rescue business was not the quickest of pursuits, which was ironic because time was something most sunken subs did not have. Therefore, Berezin knew he had to be thrifty with his subs and use them as economically as possible. Another thing he insisted on was that a three-man crew should drive the boat rather than rely on the more power-efficient method of remote control. He insisted on this because he knew beyond doubt that more could be seen from the portholes under water than on a computer screen above water. It was a belief that may have marked him out as a traditionalist, if not a relic from the past, but the day had not arrived when he would trust a computer over his men, though he had to admit that day would come the way technology was progressing. But that day wasn't here yet, and he was the man in charge.

At the Zapadnaya Litsa dockyard in Vidyayevo naval base almost all of the buildings looked empty and quiet, all that is apart from the "cantina".

The building was less than impressive to look at and not any better on the inside as it was merely a large open space filled with 26 steel tables each with six chairs. The concrete floor was a carpet of dust. And yet, that day the venue was packed to the rafters. At the end of the room a small stage had been set and most of the tables were occupied by women chatting loudly amongst themselves. Although it was customary for the wives and families to gather every Sunday morning when their husbands and fathers were at sea, today was different and the few sailors in uniform that where present and armed watched the crowd with expressions that were blank and yet somehow tense. At one of the tables sat Mischa's mother Elena, listening to Sophia and Galina talking.

"I don't think they really know anything," Sophia stated firmly.

"Even if they did I very much doubt they would tell us the truth," Elena interrupted.

Galina leaned over the table to whisper. "I've talked to just about everyone here and they all keep telling me the same thing; about some rumor that one of the submarines is in trouble."

"So what exactly did you hear?" Sophia asked impatiently.

"The mother of a receptionist at the base said her daughter had overheard a conversation that a submarine was laying at the bottom of the sea. But that was all she knew."

"Well, all this can't be just about the exercise," Mischa's mother said as she waved a hand towards the stage. "Do you think it could still be about the exercise?"

"I don't know, *Mama*. I never heard of submarines lying at the bottom of the sea, but who knows. The only thing we know is what they tell us and that's always that the exercise is going well."

"Mika often told me about the problems they had with their communication systems," Elena said. "I'm sure there's nothing to worry about. You know how sailors' wives like to scheme and imagine all kinds of horror stories. Let's just wait and believe the official announcements before jumping to any conclusions."

The Rudnitsky bobbed upon the ever-growing waves as the large steel cranes swung the AS34 from the deck above the sea. Berezin walked towards the sub carefully holding onto the rail. He always made it is his job to direct every launch and as he glanced through the porthole of the small sub he noticed Lieutenant Antonov inside, his head not much bigger than the window. As Antonov saw Berezin he stuck his thumb up and Berezin smiled and returned the gesture before turning to the crane operator, still holding his thumb up.

"OK, let her go!" he shouted across the deck.

The crane lowered the AS34 gently into the waves before automatically unhooking the sub. As the vessel hit the water Antonov officially took over command of the mini sub and looked to his left and right to see whether his fellow engineers were good to go. Both men nodded and Antonov pushed two levers into the dashboard. Immediately the submarine began to sink. From the Rudnitsky, Berezin watched the AS34 slowly disappear below the waves until there was nothing left but an orange glow in the water, rather like a goldfish swimming in the deep. Silently wishing the sub luck, Berezin then returned to the bridge where an engineer was constantly repeating a message into a microphone.

"Kursk. This is search and rescue ship Rudnitsky searching for K-one-four-one, Kursk. Can you please respond?"

Berezin made his way towards Volodin. "OK, so what are we looking at?"

Pointing at the banks of monitors in front of him the engineer started his explanations. "These two monitors show the front view from the AS34, this third one is from the rear at a closer angle to the sea bottom in case we missed something, and the fourth and last one shows the inside of the mini-sub from rear to front. Not much to see yet I guess, but they're still descending." Berezin looked at the fourth screen, seeing three men of the crew lying down behind their dashboards while Antonov sat upright in the middle steering the sub with what looked like two large joysticks. Volodin turned his eyes from the screens and pointed at the men with the microphone.

"Our friend in the corner here is trying to reach Kursk by radio on all known frequencies. To be honest, my money is on the mini sub."

"Why would you say that?" Berezin asked.

"I just think that if they could they would have responded by now."

"Yes," Berezin admitted. "I'm afraid I agree with you, but who knows; maybe someone down there is fixing a radio right now so please keep trying. Do we have audio?"

Volodin flicked a switch and pointed at the microphone on the desk.

"Go ahead, Captain."

Berezin sat down behind the desk and pushed the button on the microphone. "Gentlemen, how's it going down there?"

"Captain we are sailing smoothly," Antonov replied, looking into the camera on board for a second. "As you can see from the empty benches behind me we haven't picked up any passengers yet."

184

"Let's hope it doesn't come to that, Captain. And all of this turns out to be a misunderstanding."

"We're coming up to our planned cruising depth about 15 meters above the sea bed. All cameras work fine, but the image is unclear on all angles. There's a lot of dust in the water reflecting our searchlights. I don't know what you see on your monitors, but the visibility is minimal."

On the bridge monitors grey areas interspersed with vague dark shadows were the common picture. "I believe we see the same thing," Berezin answered. "Will you be able to identify the target under these circumstances?"

"Hard to say, Sir. I estimate visibility is between five or ten meters. It's a bit like searching for a 118-meter-long cigar in these kinds of waters. My guess would be that if we were to miss her visually she would still create a large enough reflection to give a positive echo on the screen. Unfortunately, getting closer to the bottom isn't going to fix our problems so..."

"All right, then," Berezin interrupted. Keep your depth and start your course heading two-three-seven, speed zero-point-two knots. What's your estimated distance to her last known coordinates?"

"Nearing fast, Sir. Estimated time of arrival within the minute. Please stand by."

"Standing by," Berezin replied even as he tapped his fingers on the desk impatiently."

"OK, we're there," Antonov informed the bridge.

"We read you, Captain," Berezin answered, stroking his beard while watching the monitors impatiently. "Can you give us a full three-sixty from your perspective?"

"That shouldn't be a problem, Sir. Starting our rotation now."

"Thank you, Captain. Keep your eyes on the lookout through those portholes." Berezin turned to the bridge. "Men record all angles and keep your eyes pinned on the screens. Let's see what we can find."

Despite the intensity of the men's gazes, the screens remained grey with flecks of dusty bouncing the camera's light back as it rotated. "Rotation complete, Captain," Antonov said. "No visible leads or echoes to go on. What are your orders?"

Berezin thought for a second before pressing the mic. "Alright, this is what I want you to do. Keep your course, heading two-three-seven. That way you will keep going downstream the same way any uncontrollable object would travel."

"Confirming course two-three-seven at zero-point-two knots speed."

"Comrade Antonov," Volodin interjected "we are reading a more than 50% in battery power drop on the 34. Can you confirm?"

Antonov checked the meters on the dashboard tapping his fingers a couple of times on the glass that showed 48. "That is correct. We have the same reading down here. It was only at 85% when we left so..."

"Thank you, gentlemen we'll get back to you on the battery issue as soon as possible," Berezin interrupted. "Keep your eyes and ears open." As he let go of the microphone he turned to Volodin. The young man had joined the team at the last minute and though Berezin was grateful he still felt the need to somehow apologize. "You must know these subs, well, unfortunately they are not the best Russia has to offer. However, they are the only thing Russia has to offer at this place and time."

"I know," Volodin nodded. "I've worked with them before and I know they'll do for now. Fortunately, we can, at least in part, counter the age of the equipment with the expertise of your men."

"If only our batteries could match the stamina of my men," Berezin said with a smile, appreciating the younger man's easy understanding of the situation before his eyes were drawn to a change

186

between dark and light on one of the screens. "Did you see that?" he asked. "Did anyone see that?"

The men on the bridge shrugged their shoulders.

"AS34, Antonov, did you notice something on your starboard side?" Berezin asked over the mic. "From here, it looked like some kind of a shadow."

"Not to me," Antonov replied before turning to look at his colleagues"

"Nothing here."

"Sorry."

"Could have been a shadow from something caught up in our lights," Antonov said. "Do you want us to go back?"

Volodin and his coworkers looked to Berezin. It was a difficult call to make given the fading battery life and the lives at stake and Berezin knew that the decision he made now could be the difference between life and death. Had he seen something? Were his eyes deceiving him? Wasn't the best view to be had from the sub? And yet...

"Turn 180 degrees and reverse heading for about 75 meters and watch your port side carefully," he instructed. "After 75 meters set course North-West, three-one-five at one quarter speed. That way, if there's anything there you should run right into it."

With little visibility the AS34 turned to go back the way it had come. Antonov and his men watched like hawks through their portholes, but as they neared the 75 meters point the view didn't change; there were no distinguishable contours and yet it felt like they were moving toward the cast of a shadow.

"Rudnitsky, are you getting this?" Antonov asked. "We are at the point of changing our heading to North-West, three-one-five."

"We're definitely getting something out here," Berezin said as his eyes grew bigger to match the intensity of his gaze concentrated on the screens before him. "Yet it's just color without pattern. Continue with your course change, please."

"Course laid in and turning now," Antonov responded. "Visibility is none. Permission to slow down further in this soup?"

"Take every precaution you think is necessary for a safe ride, Captain. We'll also be on the lookout for anything strange from here."

As the AS34 completed her turn she slowly picked up speed. Under water the bright orange color of the mini sub was hardly distinguishable more than a few meters away. The view from the front portholes turned ever darker as she continued until suddenly the shadows seemed to move upwards before the image on their screens turned brighter for a second. Before Antonov and his men even had time to consider what that meant a screeching sound filled their ears and the crew felt the nose of their sub dip, as though it had been pushed down towards to the seabed. On the Rudnitsky's monitors the sudden movement was seen by everyone as the dust swirled before their eyes. Antonov reacted swiftly, instinctively steering hard to starboard and away from whatever obstacle they had encountered. As the AS34 moved, one of the search lights attached to the sub's side seemed to snag in something before breaking.

"What happened?" Berezin called out.

"We don't know, Sir. It looks and feels like we hit, or rather scratched, some hard surface. Strange thing is that the obstruction was not below us but somewhat above us. We are free now but we took some damage on the portside destroying one of the searchlights. We are trying to determine if we have any other damage, but for now I think we're OK."

As Antonov spoke, the crew with him began to busily check their instruments; pushing buttons, pulling levers and reading meters.

"Did we get all that on video?" Berezin asked Volodin.

"We did, Captain. Ready for viewing."

"What's the status on their batteries?"

188

"Drained by 85%, Sir. They cannot stay down there much longer."

"All right. Let's get them out of there. And as we don't know the extent of the damage yet, give the order to get the AS32 to prepare to crane out."

"Will do, Sir," Volodin replied.

"Antonov, what's your status?" Berezin asked, turning back to the microphone.

"Were fine, Sir. Just a broken headlight, nothing else. We're good to go on your orders."

"I want you and your men back up here. Your battery power is low. So get back here and in the mean time we'll start analyzing the data and get the AS32 ready for deployment."

"On our way, Captain."

"Volodin, when she gets back immediately start recharging the batteries and personally take a closer look at the damage. I don't want to take any unnecessary risks if we need to back into the sea." Berezin then turned to the rest of the crew on the bridge. "All right men, while we wait for them to return can we get all the camera footage on the screens here?"

"How far back do you want to go?" One of the engineers asked.

"Just give me the last minute, from all available angles, please."

The engineer turned to his screen, pushed a few buttons and beckoned to Berezin. "Playing now," he said.

As he watched, Berezin could feel his heart pounding with hope in his chest. He didn't want to voice his opinion, but what else could the sub have hit? He gazed at the screen, willing it to supply the confirmation of the very thing they all wanted to see, but for the first thirty seconds there was nothing but grey, until suddenly on the center screen the light changed for about a second followed by the sudden movement of the sub they had witnessed earlier.

"Anyone have any idea what we've just seen?" Berezin asked looking around only to have everyone reply with a shake of their head. "OK, let's slow it down, starting from two seconds before the color change." On the monitors the requested image played frame by frame. "Is this the best quality we can get?"

"These are the old analog low resolution cameras, Captain," the engineer half-apologized. "Unfortunately, we don't have any image enhancement capabilities either."

"That's it! Stop!" Berezin shouted pointing excitedly at the screen, in front of them. "Go back image by image and freeze frame. Great. OK. Right, stop here, freeze and look!"

Crowding around the screen to look, Berezin began to draw his finger on the computer screen, outlining the area that had caught his attention. "You see?" he asked. "To me, this light area looks like a possible part propeller blade. This darker side could be part of the stern stabilizer."

"This would mean that…" Volodin started but was immediately interrupted by Berezin.

"Yes, this would mean we're probably looking at the back of a submarine sticking out above the sand. The AS34 must have grazed her bottom before sailing away to starboard from under the tail." Berezin took a deep breath and turned to face his men. "I think it's safe to say, we've found her."

21. Hope

Day 2 - Sunday - August 13, 09:30

"DID YOU HEAR THAT?" Grisha asked.

"I heard something too," Ivchenko quickly added.

"It sounded like a bump of some kind from the outside," Polakov said.

Refusing to be drawn into pointless speculation, Mischa stayed still, sitting on the floor, looking at the ceiling waiting for some kind of confirmation that would allow him to offer the hope the other men so desperately needed. When nothing further happened he lowered his head knowing he had to give them something. "I heard a noise and yes, it did sound like something or someone on the outside bumped into us."

"You see!" Ivchenko cried out and turned to face the other crewmembers. "They are coming to rescue us." Ivchenko walked up to the bulkhead and picked up a large steel pipe that had fallen from the ceiling after the first explosion. "We must make as much noise as possible to let them know were here. Come on, pick up something heavy, all of you, and make as much noise as possible."

Ivchenko started to bang the walls as loudly as he could and within seconds some twenty crewmembers found the strength to join him.

"*Po-masch*! Help! -- *Pa-ma-gee-tye*! Help us!"

As the desperate cries for help grew in strength, even the men who didn't have the strength to get up and bang the walls joined in, shouting for all their worth.

Grisha and Polakov looked to Mischa, not sure what to do, if anything.

"Let them try, just for a little while," he said, loud enough to be heard over the screams and clatter of their crewmates. In a way he was glad of the distraction. He looked around him saw energy where seconds before there had been only silence and sadness. "They need to regain their confidence in hope of a rescue."

"For a while at least," Grisha said.

Mischa sighed. "It makes me think of when I was a child, when my father was still at home. Throughout the week my father and mother would argue and, sometimes when he drank, my father would hit my mother. Except for Sunday afternoons. On Sunday afternoons, the entire family, including uncles and aunts gathered at my grandmother's. There the men would exchange their latest stories and watch sports on TV while the women, well, I don't know exactly what they did, but they talked with each other. Man and woman separated. No quarrels, fighting or whatever and as a result I would have a great time with my cousins. You know what, those Sunday afternoons would always give me hope; hope that things would be better afterwards. And because of those afternoons I found the strength to go on, to forget everything for a while and be a child again, as it should be. That's why I recognize hope when I see it."

Grisha and Polakov looked at Mischa who had closed his eyes. Neither man was quite sure how to react and for a moment they sat with their mouths a little open wondering who should be first to break the

192

silence caused by their friend's confession. Before things grew awkward, Mischa opened his eyes, exhaled deeply and shook his head, as though he was working himself out of a trance. "And we're back!" he cried and both men started laughing.

"You were pulling our leg!" Grisha shouted.

"Playing with us!" Polakov accused, and Mischa smiled.

"Well my friends, whether or not I told you a true story you will find out when we are back on dry land. For now..." Mischa stood up from the floor and with the loudest voice he could muster he yelled out to silence the yelling and banging. "Comrades, please stop for a moment and listen to me, Comrades!" It took a while, but the room fell silent. "Thank you, thank you for helping. I think that you're right and there is or was someone out there looking for us. So if that's true we must assume that they found us and that a rescue attempt is now just a matter of time so we probably don't need to keep on with all the noise."

As Ivchenko walked back to his friends he threw down his pipe, put his arms around the shoulders of Grisha and Polakov and looked at them one after the other with a big smile on his face.

"However we are not out of the woods yet," Mischa continued. "Assuming they have found us it is imperative that we stay calm and rest. We need to preserve our oxygen and in so doing create more time for whoever is out there looking to rescue us."

The men nodded and gave Mischa a soft cheer before they settled down, spreading themselves over the room, crawling under their blankets.

The waves were growing larger and they pummeled the side of the Rudnitsky as the AS34, hanging from the crane, rose above the surface. Berezin and Volodin watched from the deck waiting to see the extent of the damage.

"What do you think?" Berezin asked.

"The light fixture and arm are heavily damaged, Sir, but it's nothing we cannot fix in a relatively short time. We have all the spare parts on board."

"That's good news."

"But it's not our biggest problem!" Antonov called out from the sub, his head sticking out from the hatch of the AS34 as he prepared to climb out. As he stepped onto the ladder that had been placed against the sub, Berezin and Volodin walked up to him. Berezin simply frowned. He didn't like vague statements though he respected a certain directness from his men. In his line of business there was no time for small talk.

"The batteries on the 34 are almost drained and we'll need to recharge," Antonov explained.

"How long will that take?" Berezin asked hardly able to disguise his irritation. Berezin and Antonov looked at Volodin who knew the most about the outdated batteries.

"Up to ten hours," he replied. Thinking that a few years ago it was about half of that but now, with the maintenance state everything was in.

Of course, Berezin already knew how long it would take to recharge the batteries, but he always lived in hope that someone might offer him a more palatable answer. But the trouble was the equipment was old and getting older, and even as little as a few years ago the batteries could be charged within five hours. He didn't dare to think how much further they would deteriorate within the coming years. "Did we find any spare batteries before we left?"

"I'm afraid not, Captain," Volodin answered, sorry to disappoint his commander. "You made the right decision on preparing the AS32 to go and get a better look. I expect the AS32 to have even less stamina than the 34 but she has her arms and winches to clear anything we need to clear and give us the image we need to proceed while charging the 34."

194

"All right, worst case scenario," Berezin started to summarize, "both mini-subs can carry about 20 guests, so if we need to extract the entire Kursk crew we will need six runs to do so. Assuming each attempt takes up one battery charge, the whole process, including recharging, will take up to about 30 hours."

"Once we have found a way in," Antonov added, throwing yet another difficulty into the equation. Volodin and Berezin looked at him. "We don't know her condition yet," Antonov clarified. "The hard part will be making a watertight connection once we locate an entry point."

"You're right, of course," Berezin admitted. "But first things first; Captain, are you ready to go back down with your crew in the AS32 and assess the situation further?"

"We have the backup crew standing by, but me and my men have been doing this for a very long time, Sir. We won't be the ones to cause you any problems."

"All right then. Transfer yourselves to the 32 and lower yourselves as soon as possible."

"Aye, Captain."

Antonov saluted Berezin and Volodin before walking up to the second mini-sub. Berezin merely grunted at the gesture.

In the dark the Marjata appeared to be lit up like a Christmas tree in the Barents Sea, albeit a Christmas tree tossed about on choppy waters.

"How are we doing in here?" Anders asked James as he walked into the conference room, startling the American who had been so engrossed in trying to keep his dinner down he hadn't heard the admiral enter. "To be quite honest, I figured this ship would be a bit more stable on the water."

"Well, she's a small ship but I hope we'll be safe enough."

James looked at Anders to see whether he was joking.

"Of course I'm joking!" The Norwegian laughed, surprised by the American's gullibility. "The Marjata is a super stable ship. It has to be in order to deliver a stable sensor platform. Any news from your end of things?"

"I've monitored most of our known unscrambled communications lines, but so far there's little to nothing to suggest that the exercise is in any kind trouble. Any news from the Norwegian side?"

Anders shook his head. "The only news we have is that the president left his vacation spot earlier than planned and is on his way back to the Kremlin. No reason given."

"I guess that's never a good thing."

"What about your subs, any news from them?"

"I've been in regular contact with the Detroit. She is, as her Captain calls it 'sight-sailing', but she hasn't had any contact, visual or otherwise with any Russians."

"That we can call a good thing, I guess."

James frowned. In his current disposition he was finding it increasingly hard to tap into the European sense of humor. "So, what now; we just sit tight and wait?" he asked, tapping his fingers on the table to illustrate his impatience.

"Well, either this thing will blow over soon or we will hear that it hasn't shortly. Don't worry, in my experience these kinds of situations tend to reach their peak within the first 48 hours."

"I don't know what worries me more; the fact that we don't know anything or the fact that you have experience of these kinds of situations." James joked and Anders awarded the effort with a small smile.

The AS32 followed the previous course of the 34, its searchlights scouring the sandy bottom of the sea that looked like an underwater beach. There was little vegetation to be seen and, as a result, very few fish although occasionally a shellfish was sighted scavenging for food on the seabed. "Coming up to the designated area, Captain."

Antonov's voice sounded from the speakers of the Rudnitsky's bridge.

"We read you loud and clear," Volodin replied. "What's your status down there?"

"Visibility has diminished further and the current is stronger meaning we'll lose power quicker than the last expedition."

Berezin pinched the bridge of his nose before pacing along the small pathway between the chairs and the back wall. After a few seconds he returned to the microphone. "Do you see anything yet?"

"Give us a minute. We're just slowing down now at the location... Wow, did you get that? Did you get that?" Antonov yelled with some excitement. "Stopping now!"

On the bridge monitor the image in front of them grew ever clearer as the particles of sand began to settle revealing the clear contours of the starboard propeller hanging some 10 meters above the sand.

"We see it. It looks like you found her again. Thank you for that, Captain." Although Berezin kept his voice emotionless he felt his heart pounding. "Can you get a wider shot?"

"Sorry, Sir. We would need to more distance between us and even then we would probably lose the picture because of the dust reflecting off the lights."

"Antonov? Do you think you can follow the hull up to the front?"

"No problem. Follow us on the screen, please."

In front of their eyes, the propeller disappeared from their screens as the AS32 maneuvered above the tail of the Kursk.

"Look at the distance between the sand and the propeller," Berezin instructed his crew. "From the height we can calculate the angle at which the nose must be embedded in the sand."

At about five meters above the Kursk's rear deck Antonov stopped in order to give the Rudnitsky a clear view of the stern.

"She seems intact," Volodin said softly.

"Moving to the front," Antonov informed them.

"She looks absolutely intact," Berezin said as the camera panned over the huge sub. "Antonov, what does your Geiger counter read?"

Antonov looked at the meter and out of habit tapped it a few times with his fingers. "Thirty microRem, Captain, way below the threshold."

"Look!" Berezin called out, reaching forwards to point at the monitor screen. "There's a distress buoy."

"How many do they have on board? One?" Volodin asked with a frown.

"Correct," Berezin confirmed.

"So what does that mean?" Volodin asked.

"It could mean they weren't able to release the buoy or that they tried to release it but it was welded to the hull. It wouldn't be the first time. One thing is for sure though nobody has found a buoy from *this* boat."

"They found a buoy?" Volodin asked.

"The report said one was found but that they couldn't recover it. So if the report is correct the buoy didn't come from this boat."

"Correcting our course some ten meters to starboard; coming up to the conning tower."

As the view on the monitors shifted from the upper deck to the side of the conning the huge red Tsar's seal filled the screen. The image clearly revealed that all the windows on top of the tower were smashed and the large antennas and periscopes were gone or broken off. As the mini-sub passed over the destroyed tower everyone in the sub and on Rudnitsky's bridge gasped and held their breath.

"*Bozhe Moy,* oh my God." Berezin whispered as a hole 10x15 meters loomed into sight allowing them to see into the nose of the stricken sub.

"Stop here," Berezin ordered.

As the image froze Antonov neared the gaping hole, and the sheer size of it dwarfed the AS32. Now they were close, they could see the debris of twisted metal and broken equipment scattered across the seabed.

The spotlights from the AS32 beamed into the hole partially lighting what was once the outer hull. Bordering the hole, two missile tube lids could also be seen, torn off to reveal the red missile-heads intact.

"It looks like her entire nose has been blown off," Antonov commented.

"Something massive must have happened," Volodin said quietly, struggling to find his breath. "Could anyone have survived?"

"That depends," Berezin replied calmly. "All the hatches appear to be closed, including the one from the escape vessel in the top of the tower, so no one got out. Therefore, our only hope is that they had time to get to the rear and seal themselves in. If they managed that, there will be survivors."

"The part of the periscope that's left shows the periscope was up so the Kursk must have been close to the surface when whatever happened, happened." Volodin concluded as Berezin picked up the microphone.

"Antonov, can you please take all the readings and images you can and turn back over port, taking video over the long hull from the other side. There's nothing more you can do out there. We'll analyze the video from here and devise a plan."

22. Scrubbers

Day 3 - Monday - August 14, 06.00

O N MONDAYS, the Zapadnaya Litsa cantina was usually a desolate place, especially when the men were at sea. However, this particular Monday the cantina was brimming with parents, wives, sisters, brothers and friends of the Kursk crew. The sailors' immediate families had received a call in the night simply asking them to come to the dockyard at 6am. Such a call could only signal bad news and the message spread like wildfire among the small community so that, come dawn, anyone with even the slightest connection to the crew came running.

"No explanations, nothing! It is unheard of," Grisha's mother Valeria railed as she slammed her hands on the table in front of her. Valeria was a big woman with short bleached hair and a fearsome temper that she sometimes found hard to control.

"*Mama,*" Galina warned quietly, while Elena and Sophia each placed a hand on top of Valeria's tight fists. "I know you are very emotional right now, but we need to stay calm and wait a little longer."

Turning to Elena and Sophia, Galina explained how her Mum hadn't slept since receiving the call at 2am.

"I don't think any of us slept after the call," Valeria accurately replied before impatiently twisting her head around to look at the main entrance. "What's keeping them so long?"

By now there wasn't an empty chair in the hall and the standing room was filling up fast. On the stage before them, in front of a bank of cameras, were a number of tables covered in white linen on top of which carafes of water had been placed. Clearly, whatever was coming was going to be thirsty work, thought Elena, though she didn't express her concerns; there were enough people starting to do that already.

As the crowd began to grow increasingly restless, they suddenly hushed as a number of uniformed officials entered the room to take their positions on the stage. There were no name tags present, only a small cardboard sign placed in front of a slight man in a badly-fitting suit that read 'Press Officer'.

"This is something you don't see every day," Elena eventually said.

"What do you mean, *Mama*?"

"I mean the Press, all those cameras... I've been to press conferences before, during my days with your father-in-law, but I never saw any cameras present. Must be the new breeze; transparency."

"Or covering their asses," Valeria sneered and despite, or maybe because of the gravity of the situation, they all started laughing.

The Press Officer stood up from behind his table and pulled a microphone towards him. "If I can have your attention, please. I have a statement to read so your cooperation would be appreciated." The Press Officer paused and the room stilled. "Before I begin I must make it clear that we will only be issuing this statement; we will not be taking questions. Following the statement you will all be asked to approach the table in order to tell us how you wish to be kept informed. So, without further ado and if you're ready," the Press Officer looked towards the

TV cameras and after receiving several nods, continued. "The submarine K one-four-one, Kursk, has experienced minor technical difficulties during an exercise in the Barents Sea. Because of those difficulties the submarine has descended to the sea floor so that repairs can be carried out. We are in contact with the crew and we are pumping air and power to the boat. Everyone on board is accounted for and well. For the record, we would also like to state that there were no nuclear arms on board. We expect all of your fathers, brothers and friends to be returned to you within days. And this is all we have to tell you at this moment."

Naturally, and despite the Press Officer's requests, questions immediately began to be fired towards the stage, not only from the journalists, but the families of the crew. Ignoring them all, the officials left their seats and exited the stage to be replaced by civilians tasked with gathering the contact details of relatives.

"They must be lying," Elena stated, not even bothering to move from her seat until the crush was over.

"Why would you say that?" Sophia asked.

"Don't you know when a Russian official is lying?"

"No," Sophia, Galina and Valeria replied in unison.

"He opens his mouth," Elena told them, and she was only half-joking.

"*Mama,*" Sophia softly scolded.

"OK, but in all seriousness, Mika told me that whenever a Russian ship sails out to sea it always carries nuclear arms on board, in case of an emergency."

"Well, even if that's true it doesn't mean they are lying about everything else," Galina said, more in hope than conviction.

"The fact of the matter is, we know nothing more now than when we first came here. They could have told us this over the phone."

"My little Grisha," Valeria said with a sob, unable to control the emotion rising in her chest a second longer. "It's his first trip and I was so frightened something might happen to him that I made him promise ten times or more to come back to me safe and sound."

"He better come back quickly and in one piece or he'll have me to answer to," Galina said loudly, putting her arm around her mother-in-law as she did so. Sophia smiled, but when she looked into her friend's eyes she saw they didn't match the bravery of her words.

Inside the Kursk's propulsion compartment, the crew were largely silent, save for the moans of the injured. The water was rising, making it no longer possible to lie on the floor and the air was getting thin. Mischa sat alongside Grisha, Polakov and Ivchenko, propping themselves up against a stack of 'envelopes' of CO_2 scrubbers. "How are you feeling?" Mischa.

"Light headed and I'm finding it hard to breathe," Admitted Grisha.

"Nobody's coming," Ivchenko mumbled, his voice barely rose above a whisper.

"Nonsense! And speak up, man!" Polakov demanded, trying to reignite the spirit in his friend.

"Nobody is coming to our rescue. We are dead," Ivchenko said a little more forcefully.

"Now why would you say that?" Mischa asked softly. "We are not dead. We're very much alive and awaiting our rescue."

"Then why haven't we heard anything? Not a single sign. They aren't coming for us!"

Mischa could feel his patience wearing thin. He really needed Ivchenko to calm down before his pessimism infected them all like a virus, but just as he was about to advise his friend to keep his own counsel the lights in the compartment dimmed once again. The light that remained was barely the glow of a single candle. "What now?" Polakov moaned.

"I told you, we weren't going to make it," Ivchenko muttered.

"Oh come on! You know as well as I do that this is normal procedure," Mischa said as loudly as his own energy levels would allow. "The batteries will have shut down to minimal usage to conserve energy."

Polakov looked around the room, finding it hard to distinguish his crewmates from the furniture. "Great, we can barely see each other."

"Which is kind of a blessing when I remember your ugly face," Grisha managed to joke.

Mischa felt for the sealed packs behind him. "The light's not our problem, but oxygen will be if we don't do something about it. I believe it's time we put the CO2 Scrubbers to good use."

"For what?" Ivchenko asked, the roundness of his shoulders already revealing how far the will to live had deserted him. "So we can buy ourselves a few more minutes before we die?"

"So these will help?" Grisha asked, plaintively ignoring Ivchenko.

"I told you before; trust me. They will absolutely help. The scrubbers will buy us precious extra time, not minutes, but hours and maybe even days."

Polakov immediately dragged himself to his knees, anxious to get going. "So, what do we do?"

Mischa picked up a scrubber pack. "The main point is we have to be completely careful when handling these," he warned. "Find pieces of wire or something similar, gently unpack the scrubbers and hang them from the ceiling. But make sure you don't hang them anywhere near or in contact with oil."

"Why's that?" Polakov asked.

"Oil and water can cause enough of a chemical reaction to start a fire when it in contact with an open scrubber. Here, let me show you how to do it."

Mischa stood up, picked up a package, tore the lid off and took out a flat square plate that looked a little like the honey frame of a bee hive. He pointed to an opening at the top of the plate.

"Put the wire through here and hang it from the ceiling like this," he instructed and climbed onto a chair in order to tie the scrubber he held onto a pipe attached to the ceiling. "That's it."

"Don't we need to switch it on or something?" Polakov asked.

"It works all by itself. There's nothing to it."

Grisha stood up to show he was ready to start working. "How many do we need to hang up?"

"About half of the stockpile should do for now. We'll see how that goes and work from there."

Grisha and Polakov each picked up a package and waded through the rising water to look for wires and places to hang the scrubbers. As Ivchenko picked up a package Mischa noticed his body shivering and his hands shaking. He came over to him and removed the scrubber from his fingers. "Are you all right?

"I don't think so," Ivchenko stammered honestly. Despite his efforts he couldn't stop his body from shaking. "I don't think I can do this anymore. I can't stop thinking about whether I will see my family ever again."

"OK, sit back down for a second," Mischa ordered gently. After Ivchenko crouched down to sit on his heels, Mischa joined him. "I know it's hard but you're not alone. I too can't stop thinking about my wife and family."

"So how do you do it? How do you stay so calm?"

"Trust and confidence, I guess. I trust our comrades on the outside to come and save us and therefore I'm confident I will see my family again. Besides, it has to be harder on them than us. At least we know what's going on. They can only speculate."

"You think they don't know?"

"Who knows, but as we're dealing with military officials I'm sure they've come up with some cockamamie story hoping to ease our families' worries and instead only increasing them. So, in a way, we have it easy. We know."

"I wish I had your confidence."

"You can; just stay calm and save your energy for when the rescue starts. In the meantime, Grisha, Polakov and I will take care of the scrubbers. You stay put and let us do the work for now."

Ivchenko leaned back as he watched Mischa rise to his feet. "Thank you."

"You can thank me later when we get out of here."

A small fleet of ships had come to surround the Peter the Great. Admiral Petrov paced the bridge, looking at the clock every 30 seconds or so. The time was 12:15. Visibly agitated he picked up a telephone.

"Get me Berezin on the phone right now!"

As he waited for the operator to carry out his order, he glanced through the window at the fleet of ships. "What's going on out there?" he questioning mumbled, seconds before Berezin came on the line.

"Captain, you promised to get back to me at noon. What happened and what's your status?"

"What's happening here is that we are trying to set up a rescue with antiquated materials and that takes time, Admiral. We're almost ready to relaunch the AS34, but the weather and the undercurrents are making it more challenging by the hour."

"So what's you plan."

"Our plan is the same as it ever was. We've deployed the skirt to the AS34 with the objective being to connect it to the rear escape hatch. For that we need to stabilize the 34 in the heavy current down there. If there are any survivors, that's where they'll be; at the rear. But it's like I told you, it's going to be very difficult to reach them."

"You are our only hope, Captain," Petrov said in an intentionally emotive call for the younger man to take on the responsibility. But Berezin was wise to the tricks of authority. He could only do the best he could with the equipment he had. "With all due respect, Sir, it's like I said; it will take time, possibly more time than we have. We don't have all the necessary equipment and what we have got is not really up to the task. As you know, the Norwegians or even the British are far better equipped to the task and more than that it is known they are in the region. If you want my advice, you should consider external help."

"Well, I didn't ask for your advice, Captain, so why don't you do your job and I'll do mine. Worry about your own task for now."

"I'm just saying, if you want to get the survivors out alive..."

"Thank you, Captain. Now when exactly will you be ready to go back in?"

"We're ready now," Berezin replied tersely. "We're just waiting for a break in the weather and a few seconds of clear sky, then we'll take our chances."

"I trust you'll do the right thing, Captain."

"Likewise, Admiral."

23. In A Cat's Eye

Day 4 - Tuesday - August 15, 00.30

WITH THE LIGHTS DIMMED and the curtains closed, Elena found it hard to tell day from night. At the kitchen table, Sophia read a newspaper while Elena scoured the news channels looking for something, anything, about the Kursk. Neither of them had slept since the previous day's press conference because the officials' claim that everyone was alive and well had been turned on its head within 24 hours. Now, no one knew who to believe.

"The Kursk, one of the country's most modern nuclear submarines, exploded and sank on August 12 during naval maneuvers, possibly killing its entire crew of 118 men. In an unofficial statement, Deputy Prime minister Korsak said the submarine may have hit an old World War II mine. He also said that probably all of the sailors died before the vessel hit bottom..."

"...Admiral Vladimir Polanski stated the accident had been caused by a serious collision, although he couldn't say what the Kursk had hit ..."

"-...Eyewitness reports claim that the command vessel of the exercise, the Peter the Great, fired a missile at the submarine accidently sinking it..."

"...Vice Admiral Valery Rakovski said that it wouldn't surprise him if inadequate training and poor maintenance would have caused a serious incident aboard the submarine..."

"...No one seems to know the truth. However, all the reports seem to agree that a submarine belonging to the Russian Navy sank in the Barents Sea during an exercise. Admiral Mikhail Medved, chief of staff of the Northern Fleet, told the Press that 'a mass of indirect indications had shown there was another underwater object in the immediate vicinity of the accident-stricken Kursk..."

Elena flicked the remote control again, hardly able to contain her rage and desperation, until she came across the Kremlin's Press Secretary addressing journalists. Standing behind him was the new president. Elena turned up the volume causing Sophia to look to the television. She immediately put her newspaper down.

"...It is true. One of our submarines is having trouble in the Barents Sea. The situation is critical, but well under control. We have no indication of casualties and are doing everything to save the crew. For now there's no reason for concern. We have all our best materials and men at the site to help. The president will leave here soon to go to the location to oversee the rescue operation personally. Therefore, if you will excuse us...".

"Sophia, why didn't they call us?" Elena asked.

"I don't know. They told us they would get back to us if they had any news. So there can't be anything further to say."

"Nothing further to say? It's all over the television!"

"What's all over the television? Rumors and speculation, that's all. Once one TV station picks on something it's followed up by the next channel until they begin creating their own rumors in order to have their own experts testify to something they know nothing about. I know it's hard, but I think it would be a good idea to try and get some sleep."

Elena looked at her daughter-in-law. The dark circles under her eyes were testament to the girl's own fears about what had happened and what was happening, despite her brave words. She was coping in the best way she knew how; by hoping for the best.

"You get some sleep, dear," Elena said softly. "At my age you don't need so much. I'll wake you when there's news."

"You promise?"

"I promise."

Ten meter waves and heavy rain beat the Marjata throughout the night, tossing her like a lost toy on the sea. On the bridge, James and Anders looked at the radar screen that stood next to a monitor showing a press conference about the Kursk.

"It's real news now," James said and Anders thought he detected an air of disappointment in his voice.

"Forget the news. This is what's really going on down there. The Russians appear to be concentrated here," Anders said pointing at the radar screen, "about 75 kilometers due east."

"But what are they doing? Our intel says the Rudnitsky is at the scene to perform the rescue."

"We have the same intel," Anders confirmed. "And we also know that the Rudnitsky is little more than an old lumber ship that has been decommissioned already. Which begs the question, what chance do they have?"

"If the men aboard that sub have to depend on Russian fleet materials, I fear the worst. Do you have the means to contact your old pal Petrov directly?"

"I wouldn't call him an 'old pal'." Anders replied with a frown. "Why?"

"Well, don't you think it's time to offer some assistance?"

"Both of our countries have offered assistance already; it's standard procedure."

"I know about standard procedure," James replied icily. "But isn't it also standard procedure for the Russians to decline help, for several obvious reasons."

Anders thought for a moment. "Of course you're right," he said. "In the old days we had a landline that ran all the way up from Bergen to the, then, head of the Northern fleet in Severomorsk. I assume Petrov also operates from there and if that's the case perhaps they will know of a way to reach him directly."

"If it still works."

"It's low-tech so I think there's a real chance. The question is whether there is someone still listening at the other side of the line after all these years. I suppose I can give it a go."

As Anders finished, James looked pleased. For him, any kind of action beat the waiting and if they could do some good, why, all the better. He watched Anders pick up the phone. "Get me someone on the other end of the old DCL to Severomorsk," he ordered. "…It doesn't matter, anyone will do." As he waited, Anders turned to James with a smile. "I don't think this line has been used in, like, a decade. If there is someone on the other line they will be really surprised."

Then, to both men's surprise the radio crackled with static before an indistinct female voice was heard.

"Hello…who is this?" Anders asked. "This is Rear Admiral Anders calling from Norway."

"I speak little English, Sir. You are connected with the Severomorsk base reception."

"I'm trying to get a message through to Fleet Admiral Petrov?" The line stayed quiet for a few seconds and Anders folded his hand over the microphone to speak to James. "So, they rerouted that old line to the base receptionist, which could be interesting." Anders shrugged feeling like a child playing a prank in spite of the severity of the occasion.

"Sir, Admiral Petrov is not on the base and cannot be reached."

"I understand. Can you help me get a message through to him? It's regarding the accident with the submarine. Get him the message that I can help him and that he can reach me on the old DCL line. He'll know."

"I have family on that submarine Sir, I'll see what I can do but no promise."

"My sincere commiserations, and I understand; no promises. Thank you, thank you so much. Please do your best."

Anders hung up the radio.

"And?"

"Well, she was distant at first, but when I mentioned the accident and being able to help she also became more helpful. She told me Petrov wasn't there, but as she has family aboard Kursk she would do everything possible to get the message to him."

"Small world," James replied before turning towards the conference room. "So, back to the waiting room for now."

The crew tried to lower the AS34 back into the water, but the heavy rain and huge waves crashing against the boat was causing the min-sub to swing wildly on its chains, endangering all on the deck. An officer dressed in a yellow poncho screamed into his radio, hardly able to be heard over the roar of the wind.

"We are trying, Sir, but we're having trouble getting her out far enough without her hitting our bow."

As the Rudnitsky slammed into a coming wave, the AS34 disappeared from view, almost fully under water.

Berezin and his men watched the scene and though they could barely stand with the force of the sea, and the ship struggled to keep steady in the storm, there was no other way to get to the doomed Kursk – the AS34 had to go in.

"Lieutenant, I don't care how you do it. We have been at sea for almost a day now; we must go in, and we have to do that now! Try releasing her in the swing at the furthest point from the ship. She'll get beaten up a little in the fall, but I'm sure she can handle it."

"We'll try, Sir," the deck officer yelled in reply. "Men, at the lowest point on the third wave I want you to release all lines and drop her into the sea."

"Antonov, did you hear that? Brace yourselves. You're going in," Berezin hastily informed the sub captain.

"Anything has to be better than forever rocking in the wind, Captain," Antonov replied. "We're turning pretty green in here. Don't worry about us, we'll hang on tight."

As the AS34 hit the lowest point for the first time, the deck officer started counting: "One... two... three ... now! Let her go!"

The AS34 dropped into the sea with a mighty slap on the waves before disappearing from view almost immediately. The deck officer picked up the radio to admit, "It must have been a bit messy inside, but she's down, Sir."

"Thank you, Lieutenant. May I suggest you come inside and warm up before she returns," Berezin replied. "Lieutenant Antonov, are you and your men OK? The landing looked pretty heavy from up here."

"You wouldn't be wrong, Sir. I'm simply glad there aren't any mirrors on board because a) they would be broken by now and b) we're all looking a little rough. Even so, better in the deep than flying above it."

"And how's the going down below."

"Not easy," Antonov admitted. "We're about 30 meters down and I'm having a hard time keeping her on course, Captain. There are a lot of corrections going on."

"Let's hope it gets better when you're deeper."

"Sure hope so, Sir, otherwise we're going to have a really hard time connecting."

With careful and skillful steering, the AS34 descended to the middle of the Kursk's tail. Below the mini-sub's hull a large white chute, like a veil, hung down from the center.

"Try to keep her straight, men!" Antonov ordered as the AS34 threatened to veer off course again. He then called in to Berezin.

"We're as straight as we're ever likely to be above the rear hatch," Antonov informed him. "From five to fifteen meters the visibility is fine, but we are constantly battling to keep our position in the current. If you ask me, we're going to need more than skill and experience to get this job done. We'll need all the luck in the world."

"We now have you on video," Volodin interrupted, offering the only support he could to the men below.

"We're all with you down there, Lieutenant," Berezin added.

On the center screen Berezin and his men were given a view straight down from the chute onto the Kursk's deck. From the shifting image it was clear that the AS34 was struggling to hold her position in the strong current as the view of the escape hatch kept disappearing from the screen.

"What do you think their chances are, Captain?" Volodin asked quietly.

"Slim to none," Berezin answered bluntly, "but if we don't try…
Anyway, firstly we have to ensure we create a watertight connection
between the two vessels or those men down there are dead for sure."

"Setting down for the first run," Antonov announced over the
speakers.

Berezin moved closer to the center screen which was now
focused on the escape hatch to watch the skirt of the AS34 lower on to
it.

"Forty, thirty, twenty, ten, contact," Antonov reported as the
chute tapped onto the Kursk's deck. "Keep her here, Comrades. Now
let's put some pressure on that connection."

As the crew of the AS34 got to work, there wasn't a man on the
Rudnitsky not holding his breath. They had all done what they could,
but now it was up to the men below.

"How's that connection coming on?" Antonov called out to his
colleagues in the sub just as an explosion of mud and debris wiped the
escape hatch from the screen monitors aboard the Rudnitsky.

"What happened?" Berezin shouted into the microphone.

"*Eto piz`det* – this is fucked up!" Antonov cursed though the
speakers before apologizing for the outburst. "Sorry, Sir, we did have a
connection, but we weren't stable enough to get the water out, get the
tube in and make the permanent connection manually. We'll need at
least three steady minutes to do all that, Sir. To be honest, I don't see
that happening any time soon."

"Thank you, Lieutenant. Do you have enough power for another
attempt?"

"Power is not the problem this time, Captain. I can easily try
another three or four times, but if the current continues to be this strong,
well…"

"I hear you. Please keep trying. Once you're up here there's no
telling when we can get you down there again."

"What is the weather forecast?" Berezin asked Volodin who turned to a different computer screen. Without saying anything Volodin looked back at Berezin and shook his head.

"Get me Petrov," Berezin demanded with some agitation. As he waited the tension on the Rudnitsky's bridge rose as they all watched the screen to see another failed connection.

"Admiral Petrov, Captain. "Volodin said as he handed Berezin the phone."

"Admiral," Berezin greeted, his voice firm and less than friendly.

"Captain," Petrov returned calmly, "you sound uh, let's say, disturbed."

"That's probably because I am, Admiral. Things are not going well out here."

"Tell me, what's wrong?"

Berezin felt the hair rise on the back of his neck at the fact that Petrov could remain so calm and detached during such a crisis. "With all due respect, everything's wrong," he told the senior officer. "This whole mission is doomed to failure. We will not succeed and all the surviving men down there, if there are any, will die if we don't come up with another plan."

As he spoke, Berezin paced along the small space of the cabin.

"But you are the plan, Captain," Petrov said dispassionately.

"And I'm telling you we are failing and when I say 'we' need to come up with a new plan I mean 'you'! Our attempts to connect are failing and they are failing because we cannot get a stable connection because of the strong underwater current which is only going to get worse in the coming hours!"

"I don't think I like your tone, Captain."

"Then I'm glad I'm not one of your men so I don't have to care about what you think and I can care instead about the life of whoever is down there." For a few seconds there was silence on the line, and Berezin tried to regain his composure. "Listen," he said, "all I'm asking for is that you consider calling in outside help to give those men a fighting chance of survival. I'm not a sailor in your navy, Admiral, but those men are."

"It's not up to me," Petrov finally replied. "I'll make some calls." He then hung up the phone, leaving Berezin to gaze at his while wondering how far he had overstepped the line.

"How did it go?" Volodin asked before just as Berezin smashed the phone on the table. "That good huh."

Inside the Kursk's propulsion control center the water had risen to the men's crotches, many of whom were now clambering on top of crates, tables and closets in order to stay dry.

"We've stacked everything we can find. We should all be able to stay dry for a while longer," Grisha informed Mischa with heavy, labored breaths.

"How are the rest of them holding up?" he asked.

"Not good. We dragged another two to the pile of bodies. There are only fifteen left, including us, and I'm worried about four of them." As Grisha finished his voice cracked with emotion. He was trying to stay calm, official even, like he imagined a good military man should respond at such a time, but he knew the men who had died, he knew them all and his brain was filled with images of them lying with their mouths slack and their eyes open as the fight left their bodies.

"What do you think they are doing out there?" Polakov asked restlessly.

"We can hear them so they must be doing something out there," Ivchenko added hastily.

"I'm sure they are," Mischa replied.

"Is it me or is it getting harder to breathe again? Are the scrubbers gone?" Polakov asked.

218

"You're probably right," Mischa admitted. "I feel it too. It is getting harder to breathe. It's probably time to unpack the second lot of scrubbers we have, but I'm afraid that's not our only problem because it's not so much the oxygen, but the pressure build up. The rising water is displacing the air, crushing it in a way. And we are now breathing that crushed air."

"How long have we got?" Grisha asked.

"I don't know, but we need the scrubbers anyway otherwise we'll suffocate."

"No problem," Polakov responded with something close to enthusiasm before jumping into the water. "I'm going crazy doing nothing so I'll do this."

Before anyone could react he picked up a scrubber and waded into the compartment.

"All the same places?" he asked while walking towards the bulkhead just as a loud thump sounded from somewhere close to the wall. The sound was so loud that every sailor immediately looked up as Polakov took two steps back from the wall and glanced at Mischa.

"What is it?" Ivchenko asked.

"Sh. Keep quiet." Mischa ordered as he climbed off his table to wade up to the wall. As he reached it the sound came again.

"It's coming from over there," Grisha called out, pointing at some clothing lockers against the back bulkhead. Mischa moved up to the closed lockers and stopped in front of them. Slowly, he reached out a hand to open one of them. "Are you sure you want to do that?" Polakov asked nervously.

Of course Mischa didn't want to do it, but he had to, and because he was not a little frightened he didn't give Polakov an answer.

"The right, one," someone shouted out as the sound came again and Mischa calmly moved his attention two doors across. As everyone held their breath he then reached out to firmly pull at the locker door only to have a streak of fur jump passed his face and land in the water with a mighty splash. Toma!

"*Derr`mo*, shit!" The men cried out as the cat clawed its way up Polakov's clothes.

"Got him!" Polakov called out, holding a soaking wet Toma in his arms.

As they all recovered from the shock, the men started breathing again and laughing.

"You gave us quite a scare there, little one," Polakov told Toma as he tried to stroke the water from the cat's fur. "Can you take him from me?" he asked Mischa who walked up to him.

"Sure." Mischa spread out his arms to get the cat, but retracted them immediately. "One moment," he said and started to search his pockets. From a pocket he took a five-ruble coin, gave it a kiss and handed it to Polakov.

"You know, for luck," Mischa said, acting out the old superstition of paying someone who gives you an animal, before taking Toma onto his arms

"Thanks, we could use some."

24. Fire

Day 5 - Wednesday - August 16, 6.30am

On the Marjata's bridge balcony Anders looked over the waters of the Barents Sea through his binoculars. The morning sun warmed his back and his attention was so focused on what appeared to be black dots in the distance that he didn't realize James had come to join him until the American coughed.

"Did you manage to get a few hours sleep?" Anders asked, without setting down his binoculars.

"A few," James answered, his eyes little more than slits as he peered into the distance to try and see what the Norwegian was seeing. "It's still bugging me not knowing what's going on. Anything new?"

"The weather has cleared up. That's the good news. The other news is that last night I gave the order to sail us into visual range. They're all still out there. Look!" Anders handed James the binoculars.

As he adjusted his eyes, James moved the binoculars left and right before settling on the scene that had held the Norwegian's attention since first light – a few kilometers ahead was a field of grey ships dead in the water.

"There must be dozens of ships out there," James said.

"I counted seventy-five."

"Any idea what that means?"

"Not entirely sure yet. Look about two-thirds from the left. Do you see the big one with two massive cranes on deck? That's the Rudnitsky we talked about – sitting almost exactly on top of the location Norsar reported for the second seismic disturbance."

"Doesn't leave much to the imagination," James responded as he handed the binoculars back. "They haven't responded to us being here, then?"

"No, they don't seem to be bothered by us just yet. We are in international waters, of course, but you never know, the Russians might yet take offence. It wouldn't be the first time." Anders grinned grimly.

"You care to share?"

"Let's just say that in 1995 we were studying the Aurora Borealis when we fired a rocket some 1.5 kilometers into the sky that got confused for a Trident nuclear missile. The story goes that the nuclear weapons command suitcase was brought to Boris Yeltsin and it took quite a few phone calls to convince them they were not under attack. As the story goes that is."

James looked deep into Anders's eyes unsure whether the big Norwegian was playing with him. He'd not heard of the incident, but that meant little – problematic international incidents were rarely shouted about.

"Well I guess that, for today, it means that whatever they are doing they have not finished yet," James said. "They can't have succeeded in any way otherwise half of the ships would be long gone. They must have the entire Northern Fleet out there. Any new plan?"

"As ever we wait. About half the world has offered assistance by now, but officially there hasn't been any reaction, as far as I know." As Anders finished one of the bridge officers approached.

"Sorry Sir, we have a phone call for you."

"Who is it?"

"It's hard to tell, Sir, other than she's a Russian woman speaking very bad English." Anders and James looked at each other, the hope animating their eyes.

"I'll take it in the conference room," Anders informed the officer and as he turned to go, James followed.

"Rear Admiral Fredrik Anders here. Yes, I'll hold."

After a few clicks, there was a moment of quiet as the other person on the line either paused to catch breath or thought. Eventually a man's voice broke the silence, speaking English in a heavy Russian accent.

"Fleet Admiral Nikolai Leonid Petrov here, Admiral. You called?"

At the greeting, Anders covered the mouthpiece of his phone and nodded enthusiastically at James before answering. "Yes, I called, and it's good of you to call back. It's been a long time, Admiral."

"It must be ten years at least. How are you doing?" Although Petrov kept his tone light, both men were acutely conscious of the moment of history they were in, and of their roles in it – and the pleasantries, nice as they were, did little to ease the tension.

"I'm doing OK, thank you Admiral. I guess I don't have to ask how you are doing."

"I got your message and as you obviously understand, I've been better. Before we discuss anything you have to understand that I'm calling you without any form of formal support. For now, nobody here or in Moscow knows or wants me to speak to you."

"I understand, Admiral. I'm simply glad we can have this unofficial conversation. The bottom line is I'm calling to see if there's anything I can unofficially help you with."

The Kursk lay alone on the seabed while the rescue crew changed shifts following the tenth failed attempt. Wrapped in blankets against the cold, the survivors were constantly on the search for ever higher ground in order to stay dry. Struggling for breath and shivering, they could barely speak.

Watching Polakov hang CO_2 scrubbers in positions high above the water level, Grisha and Mischa sat back to back, sharing a single blanket.

"I tell you, I haven't heard anything f-f-for a while now," Grisha stammered to Mischa, unable able to control the tremors racking his body from taking over his speech.

"And I tell you; stop shaking for a moment because you're starting to give me the shakes."

"Ha." Grisha attempted to laugh, but could do little better than offer a small smile.

"Well, where are they then?" Ivchenko asked, sitting one table away from his comrades and separated by two meters of water. "What if they've given up or they've run into some kind of problem?"

"Do you really think they would leave a billion-dollar submarine lying on the seabed?" Mischa scoffed, mainly in an effort to reassure his friend rather than out of any great conviction. "I don't think so. They are still with us and I'm sure they're doing all they can. We really must stay calm and try to preserve our oxygen, just for a little longer."

Ivchenko turned on the table he was sat on and suddenly jumped into the water. With his hands high in the air, and with the water reaching his waist, he tried to run towards the ladder leading to the inner escape hatch. Despite the lack of air crushing his lungs, panic powered his voice as he shouted o the rest of the crew. "I'm going out! I'm going out now! Maybe they will come back for the sub, but what about its crew?" As a very real and raw fear ripped at his throat, Ivchenko let out an anguished howl before beating his fists against the walls. "We're here! We're here! Help us!"

As he stepped onto the first rung of the ladder, Mischa, Polakov and Grisha rushed forward to stop him.

"Ivchenko, wait! Calm down." Mischa yelled.

"Get back here and save your oxygen," Polakov ordered before tripping on something underfoot and plunging headfirst into the icy water. Grisha leapt to his friend's side and grabbed hold of the back of his shirt, pulling him above the water. Polakov gasped for the thin air and coughed the water back up from his lungs.

Mischa was roughly three meters from Ivchenko when he was stopped in his tracks by the sight of a CO_2 scrubber hanging on the stairs two rungs above his friend.

"Vladimir Ivchenko, stop right there! That's an order!"

Sensing the urgency, both Grisha and Polakov also yelled at their friend until Mischa ordered them to shut up, pointing to the scrubber above Ivchenko as he did so.

Slowly, Mischa approached the ladder and took a few steps towards Ivchenko who bursts into tears. "I can't take this anymore," he admitted. "It's OK, I understand," Mischa tried to assure him as he inched his way further up the ladder.

"Stop right there," Ivchenko warned as he guessed at Mischa's motives. "Don't come any nearer. I don't want you here. We should have gone out long ago. You are taking us all to the grave. You hear me, everyone? Mischa's taking us all to the grave!"

"Get down from that ladder, you lunatic, and sit down. You're putting us all in danger," Grisha cried out as next to him, Polakov started to pray.

"I will not get back down! I don't want to die. I am 22 years old. My parents, my sister, they all depend on me to provide for them." As he spoke, Ivchenko waved an arm in desperation, hitting the CO2 scrubber immediately above him. Instinctively, everyone held their breath as the scrubber swung wildly on the rung before unhooking and falling towards the water.

"No!" Mischa's cry echoed through the compartment as the scrubber fell into the oil-stained water instantly igniting a flash fire around Ivchenko. As the flames engulfed him, his wet clothes at first offered some protection from the intense heat, but within seconds he was also alight, and his blood-curdling screams tore through the heads and hearts of the remaining crew as his hands let go of the ladder and he fell into the water below. The flames died on impact and Ivchenko's screams were taken up by all who had witnessed the horror. Mischa raced to pull his friend from the water, but Ivchenko was face down and when Mischa turned him over he recoiled in horror at the burns that had eaten his friend's face.

"Ivchenko!" he cried, shaking the younger man's lifeless body, determined to force him to live again. "Please, please."

As Mischa sobbed, Grisha and Polakov arrived at his side to help keep Ivchenko's body above water. Mischa felt his wrist for a pulse, but there was nothing.

"Is he?" Polakov asked, and Mischa could only nod as the tears rolled down his cheeks.

"The fire? Mischa managed to ask after the first tears had been shed.

"It went out as fast as it started," Grisha told him.

Mischa wiped at his face and sniffed loudly before nodding towards the front of the compartment where the rest of the crew's deceased had been laid to rest. "Let's get him up there," he said and with little more said, both Grisha and Polakov began to pull Ivchenko's body towards the pile of corpses that had once been colleagues and friends. After placing Ivchenko's badly charred and dripping body at the top of the pile they covered him with a blanket.

"What now?" Polakov asked after they returned to their own spots in the compartment, well away from the dead, towards the back. At first nobody replied because they were too busy trying to regain their breath.

"We must have lost more oxygen in the fire," Grisha said, hoping someone would tell him he was wrong. Shivering, he took his place back on the table, well above the water.

"There's no way of telling how much we lost or how much is left," Mischa told him, even though the effort it took was monumental and made him sound defeated.

Polakov searched his pockets, took out his rosary and started to quietly pray.

"Save your breath," Grisha told him. "You're on your own kid."

"Leave him be," Mischa softly admonished his friend, but Grisha was no longer in the mood for orders.

"You know what?" he asked. "I should never have tried to please my father."

"What are you talking about?"

"Well, he's the reason I'm here, in this shithole, isn't he? If it wasn't for him I would now be selling someone a pound of nails or a hammer. But no, I wanted to please him and so I joined the navy. Of course, I also wanted to be with you, my friend."

Mischa was at a loss for words, having had no idea that his friend felt that way, and because he was sorry Grisha had been pushed into a profession he had no passion for he stayed silent.

"My mother... my mother and Galina," Grisha continued, "they will be crazy worried by now. You know, I have a hard time seeing them in my mind? I miss them so much." As Mischa reached out a hand to comfort his friend, Grisha's bottom lip began to tremble and with no warning he suddenly cried out for his *Mama*, his grief pressing out what little air he had left in his lungs."

"What's wrong with him?" Polakov asked as he came to stand by the two of them.

"Oxygen deprivation – hypoxia – it's the same thing mountain climbers get in thin air. They become disoriented and can even start hallucinating."

Mischa abruptly stopped talking. What was the use, he thought – all that information he had gathered over the years, all the pointless knowledge he could reel off at a seconds notice that always seemed to impress his men – what was the use when it couldn't save them from dying. Yet unbeknown to him, for some of the men, Mischa's expertise was actually a lifeline that kept their minds occupied, and when Polakov wasn't praying he continued to question Mischa simply to keep the fear from overwhelming him.

"We know help is near so shouldn't we get out now? You know, try something?" he asked.

Mischa glanced around him, taking in the seemingly lifeless forms of the remaining crew while wondering how many of them were actually dead rather than stilled by exhaustion. Deep in his heart, he wished he could go and check on each and every one of them, to make sure they were alright, to offer words of encouragement that might keep their hope alive, but he was finished; he simply hadn't the energy anymore.

"I am so sorry," he told Polakov. "Getting out is no longer an option. Our lungs are already being crushed by the compressed air caused by the rising water. If we were to exit now our lungs would explode on the way up and we would be dead before reaching the surface."

Mischa dipped his head into his hands. The decision he had taken to stay where they were had always been a gamble and now it was a gamble he appeared to have lost. Not only that, it was a gamble that could have cost his men their lives, and that killed him more than any fear of his own death ever could.

Anders and James walked the gangways of the Marjata on their way to the conference room. The sea had calmed, the wind was no more than a gentle breeze and the sun shone brightly, at its highest point, making the Barents Sea sparkle "So what do you think?" Anders asked.

"I think it's a plan," James answered, "a plan with a very uncertain outcome. Personally I prefer my operations to be a bit more predictable."

"I'm afraid it doesn't get any better than this," Anders told him bluntly, and knowing it was the truth, James kept his mouth shut.

As the two of them walked into the conference room, four sailors quickly stood up to salute their admiral.

"Please sit down," Anders said, waving his hand to indicate they should retake their seats as he and James joined them at the table. "Gentleman, thank you all for being here. We, Lieutenant Commander Mitchel James and I, asked you, my senior officers, here to discuss a new mission. This undertaking involves the rescue coordination of a Russian submarine in these waters. Now before I can tell you anything else I need to inform you that this mission at this time isn't officially sanctioned by either of our governments. So we don't know what the final outcome will be at this moment. Our only goal is to rescue the survivors, if any exist, from that sub. Suffice to say, this is the point, the only point where you'll get the choice to participate or not. Anders looked around the table. Not one of the four officers moved. "Great," he said with a firm nod. "That being settled we can share some of our more privileged information with you. You already know why Commander James was here."

James looked up and nodded to everyone in the room.

"His presence also means that at the press of a button, if all goes well, we'll have contact with the United States." Anders pressed the button on the hands free phone in the middle of the table.

"Mr. Turner are you there?" James asked as he leaned across the table.

"I'm here, gentleman, thanks for having me."

"Mr. Turner is Security Advisor to the White House in this matter," Anders explained. "And now that we are all here, so to speak, you can open up the folder in front of you. In the folder you'll find all the information we have up till now, which as you can see is not very much. While you read, Mr. Turner, can you tell us about the position of your government in this matter?"

"I can. Twelve hours ago the White House officially offered the Kremlin our support in the rescue of a submarine that sank during an exercise. Our support was declined and a statement was made saying that they couldn't confirm any incident having happened. That's everything official I have."

"Well we thought as much," Anders replied.

"Unofficially," Turner continued, "there's a huge amount of chatter that has been intercepted on the radio channels. Our firm belief is that the Kursk has definitely sunk to the bottom and they're now trying to rescue survivors from the boat using old Priz Class rescue submarines. Those rescue submarines are the exact reason we're here. We believe that though the weather topside looks OK with the undercurrents and the age of the equipment the Russians don't have a hope of rescuing anyone. Now, in Washington there has been some debate as to whether we are entirely without guilt in this matter. So needless to say, when your Admiral called us with his unusual request we were not completely unwillingly to cooperate. And that's all I have for now."

When the speaker fell silent, Anders moved to the head of the table where he took up position behind a stand.

"What did he mean by 'unusual request'?" One of the officers asked.

"All right, people. Listen up," ordered Anders, choosing to ignore the question. "This morning I had an interesting, and unofficial, conversation with Admiral Petrov, the boss of the exercise in our neighborhood. Apparently they have indeed had some trouble with a submarine and he could use our help. Though officially he didn't have permission to contact us, he did. As you heard Mr. Turner say, we are inclined to help, but since the call was unofficial we cannot ask our NATO friends for help. So we have to rely on our contacts and allies to devise a plan, and that's where you all come in. You officers," Anders paused to point at the four Norwegians in front of him, "will be the only ones, besides us, on board that know what our mission actually is. Therefore, we need you to relay our orders to the crew as though this were merely an exercise, keeping everyone else in the dark for now. I assume that's not going to be a problem?"

"No sir," the officers all replied, shaking their heads.

"All right, then onto our plan. Do you want to take over?" Anders asked turning to James.

"Sure." James got to his feet, thankful for the opportunity to be of assistance for once, rather than a third wheel. "Admiral Petrov informed us that they have a nuclear submarine lying about 300 feet, 100 meters below. He also revealed that the two Priz subs working at the accident site are experiencing difficulties."

"What kind of problems?" one of the officers asked.

"We're not entirely sure, but it seems that only the rear escape hatch is accessible and that the hatch has some kind of crack in it, which is making it difficult to connect. Also, they are experiencing bad visibility under water as well as undercurrent speeds of more than two knots. He wasn't able to give many more specifics, but he did tell us that they had made 14 attempts to connect to the hatch so far without success."

"What do we know about the crew?"

"Nothing," James admitted. "They gave us no information about the crew, but be sure that Petrov wouldn't call for our help if he thought there was no one left alive. Unfortunately there's no more information than that. All we know for sure is that they need our help. So we have come up with a plan."

James pushed a button on the laptop in front of him and the lights dimmed to reveal a picture of the Kursk sailing on the waterline on the wall behind him. "This is our goal everyone," he said, pointing to the Russian sub. "We must find her and rescue whoever's still alive. In order to do this we need to first find a rescue sub able to connect to a Russian submarine hatch." James pushed another button on his laptop and the Kursk disappeared from the wall to be replaced by a slender rescue sub painted orange and white and clearly a generation or more up to date than anything the Russians could call on. "This is the British LR-5 DSAR class submarine rescue vehicle," James told the room. "At 10 meters it can carry up to 16 persons and with its state-of-the-art equipment it can find just about anything that's lost in the ocean. As we speak, one of these subs is currently at Norway's Trondheim base. In order to get it here I've contacted my British Colleague Commodore Hugh Foster who has agreed to load the LR-5 onto the Normand Pioneer, a private tug and supply vessel, and then sail it near to the Norwegian-Russian border and into international waters."

Behind James, the Normand Pioneer appeared on the wall – a 100-meters long ship painted bright red. It also looked brand new.

"The Normand Pioneer is a new vessel filled with cranes and winches that can support just about anything in any kind of weather," James continued. "It will be good to have her on site. And last but not least, Petrov requested divers that can operate at a depth of 100 meters. For this, Admiral Anders called in a favor from some friends at Stolt Offshore, a Norwegian private contractor who have kindly volunteered to send another tug and supply vessel, The Seaway Eagle."

The next ship to appear on the wall was painted yellow. The forked nose also revealed her main purpose was to lay communication cables between continents.

"I must admit I've never understood the fascination with such bright colors," James joked, "but I do know the Seaway Eagle will be a valuable addition to our mission. She will also be accompanied by twelve saturation divers and a diving bell to work from. We hope to have everyone and everything gathered here by Saturday night at the latest."

"Wouldn't it be faster to fly the LR-5 to Murmansk and sail from there?" one of the officers asked and both James and Anders sighed before the Norwegian decided to answer.

"Yes, it would," he admitted "It would be up to two days faster, but our Russian friends will not give us permission to fly to Murmansk so this is the next best we can do." Although he didn't say as much, the tone of Anders's voice betrayed his irritation at the irrationality of playing political games when lives were on the line and time was of the essence. "Please continue," he said to James.

"I'm afraid we'll all have to deal with some frustration on this mission sooner or later so we better get used to it sooner," the American told the room "So basically the plan is simple. We gather everything and everyone on site and load everything onto the Seaway Eagle and she will become the base of operations. The Marjata will stay as the command and communications ship. In the meantime we will work out the finer details of our plan and gather all the necessary data to try and make this mission a successful one. We asked for all the specifics about the accident, as well as the schematics of the Kursk. Our Russian friends were very reluctant, but we expect to have everything we need before everyone arrives. Admiral, do you have anything to add at this time?"

Anders stood up from his chair. "Thank you for the update, Commander. So, one last time; your job is to tell everyone this is an exercise and relay your orders as such. Let this be our little secret and ours alone. Oh and before I forget, I have one more thing. You might have noticed the Russian planes are dropping buoys in the water. These are sonar buoys. Admiral Petrov explained to me that they think there's a possibility that another sub was responsible for the sinking of the Kursk and that this sub was heavily damaged when it happened. They believe it's a possibility she's still in the area so they are basically sub hunting. I must emphasize here that this is none of our business. We are here on a rescue mission and nothing more. So now you know what's at stake, I expect every one of you to do more than your best to make this mission a success. Any questions?" Anders gave the room a cursory glance that wasn't intended to prolong the meeting. "Dismissed," he said.

25. Drugged

Day 6 - Thursday - August 17, 2.00pm

T HE RUDNITSKY LOOKED CLOSE TO PEACEFUL as she sat quietly on the calm Barents Sea. After four days and nights with men constantly running around, launching and retrieving rescue submarines, the deck appeared eerily empty save for a few man gathering tools and cleaning equipment. Below deck, attempting to find some much needed rest in his cabin, Berezin watched the international news on his TV.

"...There are conflicting reports about the incident being given by Russian officials. Fleet Admiral Petrov was reported as saying that there had been no explosions aboard the Kursk, that the sub was still intact on the seafloor, and that an 'external influence' may have been to blame for a leak that has appeared between the first and second compartments of the submarine. However, Russian Defense Minister Michail Federov has gone further in his official statement claiming that the vessel most likely collided with a foreign submarine that was monitoring the Russian fleet's exercises. He said this theory was more

credible than reports of an on-board explosion. Meanwhile concerned mothers and other family members of Kursk's crew continue to gather at a cantina in Zapadnaya Litsa, looking for explanations for what happened and what to expect. We have some rare footage picturing the scene near the submarine's home base...."

The camera cut from the reporter to show a group of women gathered in front of a large, non-descript concrete building yelling and crying in desperation.

"...Why was our president on holiday? Our children are dying here. Why are we in this trouble?...-"

"...Why are we being kept in the dark? The headquarters are right behind us and there's a TV station right here. Why isn't there any news?..."

"...Why don't we know anything and why is everyone saying something different?...-"

"...All news goes to Moscow first to get censored."

After a woman is shown shaking her fists in anger, the reporter cuts into the report, pressing at her earpiece, as she begins to speak.

"We have breaking news about the situation in the Barents Sea. In a short statement today officials stated that at 1400 hours our president accepted the British and Norwegian governments' offer of assistance...."

There was a knock at the cabin door and Berezin turned off the TV as Antonov and Volodin walked in.

"You wanted to see us, Captain?" Volodin asked.

"Please sit down, men."

Berezin sighed heavily unsure how badly the men would take it when he thanked them for doing their jobs while ultimately revealing they had failed in their mission. Hell, he didn't how he would ever live with the failure himself. During the past days he had done everything in his power to rescue the men waiting for help some 100 meters below the surface, but it hadn't been enough. He had failed them, he had failed his men and he had failed himself – and now he had to admit that truth Antonov and Volodin.

"I called you to tell you that an hour ago I talked to Admiral Petrov and officially resigned our mission," he stated flatly.

Volodin and Antonov looked at each other, their eyes registering shock, disappointment and anger before settling on sad resignation.

"I think I speak for both of us when I say we expected as much," Volodin said.

"Are you sure you want to do this, Sir? Are you sure we've explored every option?" Antonov asked because they had never failed a mission before; they had always found a way. Yet even as he spoke the words he knew what the answer would be. The team had made 30 attempts and each time they came away more frustrated than the last attempt. At some point someone had to be man enough to say 'enough'.

"You have to know," Berezin continued, "that this is the hardest decision I've had to make, ever. Unfortunately, I've played out every possible scenario in my mind, over and over again, and I see no possibilities left. With our equipment the task would be near to impossible even under ideal conditions, but with the underwater currents being so strong at this time of year we could keep trying for months, which of course would be fruitless. We don't have months. Anyway, what is done is done and I simply want you to know that the blame here lies with the Russian military cutbacks over the past decades. Nothing else."

"We know that, Captain," Volodin confirmed. "What will happen now?"

"We've accepted outside help from Norway and Great Britain who are on their way here as we speak. They are due to arrive Saturday night and they will take over the rescue."

"Do you think they will be up to the task?" Antonov asked somewhat skeptical.

"I think they are. They have materials equal to our best in the Atlantic and they will be eager to show us how it's done. So yes, they might not be coming for the right reasons, who knows, but right now they are the best chance those poor souls below have."

"But the earliest they will be able to do anything will be on Sunday. That's eight days after the disaster," stated Antonov.

"I know." Berezin said quietly. "Like you I have questions and doubts about the government's chosen path. But there's nothing to be done now but wait and see what happens."

"So we do nothing more?" Volodin asked.

"No more than gather every scrap of information we have and give it to Admiral Petrov who will then share it with the new rescue party, probably after censoring it, of course."

"Probably," Volodin and Antonov said together.

The air in the Kursk's propulsion compartment was stale and heavy with the stench of blood and death. The last men left alive were more or less motionless, occasionally murmuring, or crying, sometimes verging on delirious due to oxygen deprivation. With every breath he took Mischa also felt the oxygen fleeing his lungs, leaving in its wake the feeling of a heavy weight landing on his chest time and again. Every move caused his entire body to ache. Only Toma seemed to be taking the catastrophe in his stride, managing to purr every time Mischa's hand vaguely stroked his back. To his left, right next to him, Grisha lay motionless on a table in fetal position. Mischa reached out to check on him, but it took about ten seconds before his fingers connected with his friend's shoulder and he winced as he shook him. Though there was no response, Mischa saw Grisha's body move ever so slightly with each shallow breath he took. In some ways, Mischa was relieved Grisha had lost consciousness; at least he would be saved from the pain and misery around them. On his other side sat Polakov, straight up, with his eyes closed and his chin resting on his chest. He was mumbling something and although Mischa couldn't distinguish the words, from the rhythm of them he knew it was a prayer. Even Mischa had to admit only a miracle could save them now.

Mischa knew it wouldn't be long before the last vestiges of rational thought left his mind, and he could feel panic and desperation waiting in the wings to seize their moment. He knew he should keep on hoping, but it was getting close to impossible and before he gave up entirely there was something he needed to do. So rallying every last ounce of strength he reached into his breast pocket and took out a paper and pen. Even though he could no longer even see what he was writing, he continued anyway because he needed to say goodbye – goodbye to Sophia, to his mother, to his family and friends.

'Without light it's hard to write to you., Sorry if you cannot read my writing. We cannot escape. I think our chances of survival are getting slimmer every moment. If you read this, I've added a list of the men that joined me in the aft compartment. I don't know if there's anyone left alive in the front. I just want to say I love you. And who knows, as long as we're alive there's hope. Mischa Kastamarov.'

The Zapadnaya Litsa's cantina was packed with family members and friends of the Kursk's crew. Many of them were crying, some of them were shouting, all of them were concerned. On the stage were some Russian officials ready to field questions from the bank of reporters below. By now, the local and national media had been joined by the international giants and maybe because of their presence, Elena, Valeria, Sophia and Galina were more hopeful of getting some real news for once. Taking center stage was a man who clearly stood out from the rest due to his lack of uniform. Elena squinted as she stared at him, hardly believing her eyes.

"Is that Deputy Prime Minister Igor Borodin?" she asked.

"I think so," Sophia replied, also surprised to see him on stage. It also made her even more nervous because the presence of such a high-ranking official couldn't be a good thing.

"What do you make of it?" Valeria asked, her face etched with a pain that mirrored the despair in her heart.

Galina wrapped an arm around her mother-in-law's shoulders. "*Mama*, please take it easy. We just have to wait a few minutes more. I'm sure we're worrying for nothing. Just…"

At that moment Borodin's voice boomed through the speakers to steal everyone's attention. "*Tovarisch po neschast'yu*, fellow sufferers," he started. "If I could have a moment of your attention please. I regret to inform you that as of yet we still haven't been able to resolve the issues with our troubled submarine in the Barents Sea. We are still working on the problem using all our available resources, but for now I can only give you a short outline of what we know and what we are doing."

Quickly coming to the conclusion that they were once again being fobbed off, the crowd started to grow restless.

"What are you doing to help our boys?" Valeria demanded. "Why won't you tell us what really happened?"

"If you'll please let me finish I'll give you all the information I have," Borodin said, raising his hands to calm the room. "And if you have any questions afterwards, I and my colleagues will be happy to answer them."

The minister glanced at the military guards watching the scene from both sides of the room, finding assurance in their steady gaze and professional manner and though the room had not entirely quietened down he decided to proceed.

"After losing contact on Saturday we discovered the submarine at 11.00 hours on Sunday lying on the bottom of the sea. We tried to establish contact with the crew, but there was nothing. Unsure as to what had happened we immediately sent two rescue submarines to the location of the Kursk to take a look, make contact, and if necessary rescue the sailors. Unfortunately, so far we have been unable to either make contact or rescue any of our comrades."

Unable to control herself any longer Valeria almost screamed as she got to her feet, demanding more from the minister.

"You know nothing!" she yelled. "Your rescue? I heard you're using a never-used mini-sub from 1968? Why won't you really help them?"

Sophia and Galina both reached out to try and calm her, knowing how unwise it might be to confront a senior politician, especially in front of the world's Press.

"I will not shush anymore!" Valeria furiously told them, wrenching her arms from their grip. "I want to know what happened. Why won't you be honest with us?"

"What's your name, madam?" Borodin asked, fully aware of the reporters' interest in his reaction at such a moment.

"My name is Valeria Sokolov and my son is Lieutenant Grisha Sokolov who is aboard your boat for his first trip." As she spoke the words, Valeria burst into tears and Elena gestured to Sophia and Galina to leave the woman alone.

"There's nothing you can do now. Let her get it out," she ordered them softly.

"I'm really sorry," Borodin said from his place on the stage, and the calmness of his voice only seemed to agitate Valeria further. "However, I told you everything there is to know at this moment. I understand your…"

"We haven't got anything," Valeria screamed at him. "We live in intolerable conditions. We barely have enough money to feed our families. And now this! You are all bastards, and I want the whole world to know that. Fifty dollars, that's all my boy earned to end up in that grave under the sea. Tell me, why does Russia do this to her children? Don't you have children of your own? Don't you understand anything of what we are going through? Why?"

All eyes, including those of the Press were now focused on the furious form of Grisha's mother. As Borodin felt himself losing control of the situation he nodded to an officer at the front of the stage and two men in uniform walked up to Valeria to try and calm her down. When their words didn't work, a woman appeared and quickly administered an injection in the woman's thigh.

"You don't understand anything," Valeria continued, oblivious to what had happened even as her words began to lose their power and she grew increasingly drowsy. Sophia and Galina did their best to support her legs, but Valeria was growing heavier by the minute.

"My husband was in the navy for twenty years," she slurred. "And for what? To see our son get killed? You all sit up there, your belly's filled. You don't care about us. Not even a shred of remorse. You are doing nothing to help our children." Valeria sank to her knees. "I will never forgive you," she spat at them. "You're not even qualified to speak to us. You're a disgrace to the Russian people. Our people will not take any more of this."

Unable to utter another word, Valeria collapsed into her friends' arms and they tried to seat her on a nearby chair. At the front of the stage, the Press was already being told to pack up ready to be escorted off the premises while Borodin placed a hand on top of his microphone to whisper to the colleague next to him.

"This is a disaster. We need to go."

242

26. Schematics

Day 8 - Saturday - August 19, 12.15 pm

'*T*HAT'S ONE BIG UGLY YELLOW PIECE OF TUGBOAT,*' James thought as he watched the Seaway Eagle arriving. Anders caught him looking and maybe because they had grown accustomed to each other he accurately read the American's mind.

"Built in 1997, she's a state-of-the-art 10,000-ton big multipurpose ship. I'll admit she's not much to look at but…"

"I'll give you that one," James interjected.

"You better watch what you say in the presence of Seaway Eagle's sailors, Commander. She's Norway's pride and insulting her could get you into serious trouble."

James looked Anders in the eyes to ascertain how serious he was, but he knew there were very few people as easily offended as sailors when it came to their ships. Thankfully, Anders couldn't keep a straight face and James knew his off the cuff remark would go no further. "What's next?" he asked when a bridge officer approached them.

"Sorry, Sir," he said before turning to Anders and handing him a radio. "It's for you; Admiral Petrov."

Anders raised his eyebrows at James before taking the call. "Anders here. Any news? Yes, Admiral … I heard … I can imagine, but I doubt they'll listen to me … I'll make one phone call and that's all I can do... The Seaway Eagle just arrived and we expect the Normand Pioneer to be here in a few hours. I'll let you know and see you then."

Anders frowned as he handed the radio back to the officer and rubbed his temples to better help him think.

"Trouble?" James asked.

"I am not sure yet," Anders admitted. "Yesterday the Detroit arrived in Norway at Haakonsvern submarine base. We didn't see them, but it seems the Russians followed her there and are now demanding to inspect her. The Norwegian government has refused."

"And Petrov wants you to put in a good word for him," James smiled. "It sounds to me like everything is going as planned. We always knew this could happen, so we only need to hold out long enough for the right amount of pressure to be seen to be applied before we simply grant them leave to make their inspection."

"True," Anders replied, but his face didn't look convinced. "I just don't like the idea of Russians inspecting an American sub on Norwegian ground. But you're right; it's all going to plan. Did you receive any news regarding the Baltimore?"

"Nothing, but even if there was any I doubt they would tell me. The Baltimore is probably half way across the Atlantic by now. But hey, what's bothering you? You look lost all of a sudden."

Anders didn't even blink at the question, keeping his eyes focused instead at a point in the distance. "I was just thinking," he answered quietly. "Tell me, what do you see when you look at the scene of the incident?"

James glanced at the vast and seemingly empty waters. "Nothing much," he concluded.

"Precisely. Nothing much. So what worries me is the fact that another day has gone by without any activity taking place in the area. Most of the ships have left the scene. Therefore it looks like they are either stalling or they have given up on the rescue. So, isn't it strange that they refused to give us permission to fly in rescue materials, claiming that they wanted to continue the rescue mission themselves using the resources at their disposal, and then, well, simply stop trying?"

Anders rubbed at his temple again. Having made his career in the navy he had spent much of his years as a sailor trying to second guess the motives of the Russians both during the Cold War and after. Yet every time he thought he was on the brink of understanding them they always managed to surprise him. However, one thing he knew for sure was that in Russia there was no reward for bringing home bad news so every decision made was usually based on efforts to avoid being the bearer of such. In contrast, James understood the Russians were different to him and he'd never made any effort to understand them.

"Can't help you with that one, Admiral. Though I must admit it is strange."

Anders shook his head, snapping out of the trance-like state he had fallen into before turning to James. "Before I forget," he said. "I think it's best that once the operation is underway we keep you out of sight. We don't want to give the Russians the wrong impression or the idea that there is official American involvement in our offer of assistance."

"That's OK, I understand," James said easily. "Let's just hope everybody gets here soon so we can finally get going on this."

At sunset the Marjata and the Seaway Eagle were joined by the bright red form of the Normand Pioneer. On its rear deck sat the LR-5 rescue sub waiting below a big yellow crane. Above the nose of the ship, a helicopter took off only to land minutes later on the deck of the Seaway Eagle. Ducking below the chopper's blades, British Commodore Hugh Foster scuttled towards Anders who was waiting on deck to greet him. A slender, grey-haired man in his 50s, the British officer warmly shook hands with the Norwegian.

"Welcome to the Seaway Eagle, Commodore," Anders shouted in greeting, but his words were pretty much drowned out by the noise of the departing helicopter. The Norwegian turned his hands palm up to convey his dilemma and the Brit laughed and gestured for him to lead the way.

After making their way to the conference room, passing pleasantries about the weather on the way and the coming forecast, they joined the table in the center of the room where a loud discussion was already taking place among the officers and technicians gathered there. Naturally, their appearance caused a pause in the conversation and Anders half-jokingly told them not to stop on his account. Although a few men did continue to talk, they soon stopped as it became increasingly apparent that two men of far greater rank were waiting for them to shut up.

"Thank you, gentlemen," Anders said, his voice dripping with sarcasm. "Well, now that we are all here I believe we can start. I'm glad to hear you're already up to date on events because as you know we have little time to spare. Therefore, as most of you only know each other either by name or reputation I suggest you introduce yourself when you have something to say."

"If I may start," Petrov immediately jumped in, lifting himself from his chair.

"Please do," Anders replied.

"Before we begin I would like to address the fact that I'm having difficulty with a group of civilian divers conducting this operation."

At the Russian's words, a somewhat rugged and handsome man sitting at the far end of the table laughed loudly and with little mirth.

246

"And what's that supposed to mean?" he shouted before remembering to introduce himself. "Gibson Harper, manager of the civilian divers you're not happy with."

"As I told you earlier it's nothing personal Mr. Harper," Petrov said, trying to sound affable despite his inherent distrust of anyone not in the military. "However, I think military personnel are a better psychological match for this task. Furthermore, you have no submarine experience and if everything goes bad and dead bodies are involved I would rather not put our faith in emotionally unstable and undisciplined men."

"Let me remain polite, but be blunt," Harper replied though his face was red with rage. "My men are experts in their profession who have operated all over the world, in many and varied situations, including the retrieval of dead bodies from the Piper Alpha. Furthermore, I'm assuming the only reason we are here is because your military personnel have been unable to do the job themselves."

"Gentlemen," Anders intervened, holding up a hand as he spoke. "We are not here to fall out, we are here to work together and plan the rescue of a number of sailors trapped below these waters. So, let's get on with the job we've come here to do. Now, first and foremost, do we have everything we need to get a rescue operation underway?"

The men around the table all looked at each other and after a moment of discussion they all nodded.

"Actually, there's one more thing you should know, Admiral," Petrov said. "I had to promise my superiors that we would continue our own rescue operation until Sunday, which means you are not permitted to enter the site until midnight tonight."

"I don't understand," Commodore Foster said bluntly before remembering the rules and introducing himself. "We noticed the Rudnitsky leave the area yesterday. So what are you doing up there? What are we waiting for?"

"Commodore, I know the British are known for speaking their minds, and from your reputation I understand you are a fair if outspoken man, but how we conduct our business and what we are doing to save our men should be of no concern to you right now. We are a proud people. If we think that we can do it on our own we will do just that."

"And it's just that, which will get your men killed, Admiral," the British officer retorted, and Anders quickly jumped in to stop the discussion from getting out of hand.

"Gentlemen, even if we go in at midnight, we still have a limited time to make our preparations, so let's settle down. Admiral Petrov, can you tell us anything about what we can expect that may influence our plan?"

Before answering the Russian man sucked at his teeth before shooting a frosty look at Commodore Foster. "The front of the sub is strictly prohibited," he said. "For this reason you will not be allowed to bring in or use your LR-5 until we are absolutely sure that there are actually any survivors to rescue. This is why we also requested divers."

"This keeps getting better and better," Harper piped up. "How to trust the military in five easy steps!"

"Why did you think you were here, Mr. Harper?" Petrov sneered. "Your men will first go down above the tail of the boat and you are to stay at the rear and not go to the front."

"Great. You're sure you want us to rescue people?" before Harper's sarcasm could be challenged Anders intervened.

Anders shook his head and turned to a civilian in his 30s sitting next to Harper. He had been a professional diver since leaving high school, but after helping to retrieve more than 100 bodies from the Piper Alpha wreckage in '88 he never did the job again. He now worked as a project supervisor. "Frank Hendrikson, everyone," Anders said loudly, introducing the man with a wave of his hand. "Frank, can you update us on the project?"

The younger man cleared his throat before speaking, wanting to be heard before the conversation erupted again. "The diving plan is relatively simple. Tonight we sail the Seaway Eagle straight above the Kursk. At midnight we lower a camera to get a first-hand look at how the situation is down there. Once we have confirmed everything, we send down the diving bell with Mr. Harper's divers in it. I'll supervise the operation and relay your orders to the divers."

"My divers are already in the pressurization chamber as we speak," Harper informed the group, casting a sly grin at Petrov.

"Isn't that a little premature?" the Russian asked.

"My men can stay under pressure for up to 48 hours, Admiral."

"Wonderful, so they'll be more than ready," Anders interrupted, wresting back control of the discussion. "Once down there the divers will attempt to contact any survivors. Once we have established that there are indeed survivors we can bring in the Normand Pioneer and LR-5 to perform the actual rescue."

"What are our options regarding trying to make contact with the survivors?" Foster asked Petrov.

Petrov shrugged. "The only option available is the old-fashioned one; the divers must bang on the sub's hull with a hammer or something and hope for a reaction. If they get one, you can take over."

"Everything's ready to go at a moment's notice," Foster replied. "The LR-5 can bring up to 15 people at a time and our batteries are good for about 10 runs, which should be more than enough to cope with the 118-man crew."

"There is one problem though," Harper interrupted while keeping his eyes trained on Petrov. "The schematics supplied are nothing more than simple sketches from different angles of the rear hatch. No measurements, no materials or even tool lists – nothing – which is just about the worst preparation my men can get."

"Mr. Harper, I can only take from your words the implication that I don't want to rescue my people," Petrov said icily. "This is deeply insulting to me, but maybe I can help you. The schematics you ask for are secret and I cannot get them from my government officially. Unofficially, however, the Kursk's sister ship, the Voronezh, is docked not so far away and she is virtually identical to the Kursk. So, if you like I can have you flown to the base in my helicopter where you can see the situation with your own eyes and take all the measurements you need."

Somewhat taken aback, Harper stammered his gratitude, much to the Russian's obvious glee.

"I'm afraid there's one more thing," Petrov added. "I will not join you during the rescue. Instead I will monitor the progress from the Peter the Great – this is on orders from Moscow. Vice Admiral Ilya Volkov will take over from me from here on in and supervise the operation."

"Any particular reason?" Anders asked.

"None that I would like to discuss here," Petrov stated firmly and Anders replied by winding up the meeting.

"OK then. I think we all know what to do," he said. "Admiral Petrov, I thank you for your honesty and cooperation. We'll stay in touch. Commodore Foster, I suggest we stay on the Eagle to monitor operations. The rest of you prepare to fulfil your obligations and good luck.

At 8.30pm exactly a helicopter landed at the Bolshaya submarine dockyard and Captain Anatoly Markoff immediately ran over to warmly shake the hands of Gibson Harper and his team.

Though the Russian captain was eager to convey his gratitude to the civilians he kept the chat short and hoped that the warmth of his welcome would give the right impression.

"Here she is," Markoff said pointing at the Voronezh some 50 meters towards the back of the dock. "She's all yours so please send your men in and get to work. However, if you could spare me a minute, Mr. Harper..."

"Gibson."

"Gibson," Markoff replied and he felt his stress levels drop as the three technicians who had also arrived on the helicopter start heading towards the Voronezh. As Harper turned to him, he gave a sheepish smile. Though it felt wrong to ask he was beyond caring right now. "I'd like to ask whether you have received any news from Yaroslav and his crew?"

"Yaroslav?"

"Sorry, the captain – the captain of the Kursk – he's a personal friend of mine, a good man, you know. This was to be his last mission before his retirement. In fact we were talking about it just before he left."

In the background Harper heard his men starting to get to work on the deck of the Voronezh. He knew he should be with them, but he was touched by the Russian captain's request for information – it was the most human reaction he had so far encountered regarding the tragedy.

"I'm very sorry, but in all honesty I don't have any news. All I know so far is that there hasn't been any conclusive sign of life from the Kursk."

Markoff felt his heart miss a beat and Harper couldn't help but notice the tears welling in the officer's eyes.

"If there's anyone alive do you think you will be able to bring them back?" Markoff asked and Harper wasn't deaf to the desperation in his voice. Over the years he too had lost friends, many of them in diving accidents. The sea, as beautiful as she was could also be heartbreakingly cruel.

"If they are alive, we'll bring them back. That I can promise you," Harper told Markoff, and the Russian captain nodded, sucking back the tears at the hope offered.

"Gibson!"

From the desk of the Kursk's sister submarine, a technician shouted for his boss. Markoff saw Harper was conflicted and he patted his arm to reassure him.

"Sure, go," he said. "Please hurry and bring those men back to their families, you hear me? You bring them back!"

Harper nodded before walking away. No pressure then, he thought.

27. Volkov

Day 9 - Sunday - August 20, 00.01 am

The Seaway Eagle's yellow belly was lit by floodlights. In the dense dark of the night a few dozen crew members worked the deck, hauling cables back and forth and shouting instructions to one another. In the center of the deck, nesting in a large three-meter wide hole, the smooth faced diving bell was surrounded by oxygen tanks and diving gear. Anders peered into the hole and then back up to crane above it, holding the bell ready to lower it into the sea.

"Phone call, Admiral."

A sailor stepped forward and handed him a phone.

"Anders."

"How's it going out there, Admiral?"

Anders smiled; they hadn't been long apart but he almost missed James's incessant questioning – almost, but not quite. "We've just arrived at the scene," he said. "I can practically see into Peter the Great's bridge from here we are so close. We've also taken on the man replacing

Petrov, a Russian called Volkov. I was just on my way to meet him when you called."

"Yes, I heard Petrov had been replaced. You know this Volkov?"

"I know of him. He used to be Second-in-Command of the Northern Fleet, behind Petrov, but he disappeared off radar a few years back. We assumed he had resigned, but now it seems more likely that he went off to join the 'political admirals' that frequent the halls of the Kremlin until sensitive situations such as this occur."

"I think you could be right about that. Well, don't let me hold you up any further, but please keep me informed, it's getting pretty lonely up here."

Although James knew Anders would have his hands full and probably had better things to do than keep him informed, he felt he had to ask simply because his own people were mighty keen to know what was going on too.

"I'll do my best," Anders assured him, but James got the impression he was simply being polite.

As Anders walked from the deck towards the bridge he watched a group of sailors lower a one-meter square, yellow box on the side of which was written '**Remotely Operated Vehicle** -- *Eagle*'. Things were finally moving, he thought.

Anders entered the control room to see Harper, Hendrikson and Foster all waiting for him as well as a few officers he didn't know. One of them was a tall, bald man in his early 50s and dressed in uniform. Although Anders didn't know him personally he certainly recognized the man from his old photographs.

"Vice Admiral Ilya Volkov," the Russian said, stepping forward and extending a hand.

Anders greeted him politely, but formally before addressing the rest of the people gathered. In the center of the room, a table was already littered with large maps and drawings as well as pictures of the Kursk, all of which were being energetically discussed as he walked in.

"The ROV is lowered as we speak and should be nearing its target," Hendrikson informed him with a grin. He was standing at the end of the room against a 3x5 meter wall that was blinking like a thousand stars thanks to an array of instruments, switch panels and screens. "Unfortunately, we have no sonar yet."

"Don't be surprised if you don't get any," Anders warned. "The hull is fully covered in thick soft rubber made to absorb most sounds."

In front of Hendrikson a Norwegian engineer steered the ROV using two joysticks. In front of him was a screen showing a 45-degree-angle camera view from the sub. "Visibility is no more than about 3 to 7 meters, Sir," the officer said.

"Depth?" Hendrikson asked.

"88 meters, Sir."

Then, before their eyes, the contours of the Kursk's nose slowly appeared.

As the ROV slowly moved along the Kursk's nose, the officer skillfully maneuvered the camera towards the gaping hole.

"Please direct your camera towards the rear of the boat," Volkov asked politely, though the tone suggested it was not actually a request.

The officer steering the ROV looked over his shoulder at Hendrikson, waiting for confirmation. As Hendrikson nodded he moved the camera away from the hole, passing along the hull, over the coning tower clearly bearing the red emblem of the Tsars seal until it came to a stop at the rear hatch, which stood out in the gloom thanks to the white ring painted on its surface that reflected the ROV's lights.

"There's your hatch, gentlemen," Hendrikson said and for a second or more everyone remained quiet, some of them thinking of the men below, most of them looking for any potential problems that might arise from the image they could now see on screen.

"From here the hatch looks completely intact," Harper told the room, the hope apparent in his voice. "It's also exactly as we saw on the Voronezh."

"What's the reading so far?" Foster asked.

"Visibility more than ten meters," Hendrikson informed him. "the body of the Kursk appears to be fairly level around 8 degrees and the underwater current is weak at five knots."

"Looks like ideal conditions," Harper said and Anders looked at Volkov, noticing for the first time the thin, almost sinister smile that never seemed to change on the Russian's face.

"You told us that the Kursk had listed at an angle of about 30 degrees, the hatch was supposed to be damaged and the conditions were poor?"

"I didn't tell you anything, Commodore," Volkov answered testily. "Therefore, may I suggest we forget what any of my predecessors have claimed and we stay focused on the task at hand? If you want to blame anyone, on either side, for anything – well I should think there will be plenty of time for that later."

Anders wasn't deaf to the accusatory tone in Volkov's voice and he was pretty sure Volkov hadn't been deaf to the theories circulating of western involvement in the disaster, but in at least one respect he was right; the time for blame wasn't now. So instead of taking offence, he asked, "Have we seen enough?"

"I have," Harper said quickly, eager to get on and do something rather than talk about it. As far as he and his team were concerned, they were more than ready for the next stage of the rescue operation.

One level beneath the decks, three men made their way through a tunnel leading from the decompression chamber to the diving bell. Jasper Pearce, Ender Jostein and Leif Alstad were old hands at such missions and were keen to cut through the politics and simply get on with the job they had been hired to do. Through a window cut into the tunnel, Anders and Harper watched the men pass by, dressed in their diving suits and heading for the bell. As they approached the window they each gave the thumbs up. They were more than ready.

"What's the game plan?" Anders asked.

"The team will dive in heated suits to counter the extreme cold in waters this deep. As far as the rest of the plan goes, it's not too dissimilar to the moon landings," Harper said with a grin. "Two divers, Pearce and Jostein will leave the bell for the actual operation. Pearce will do the work while Jostein will keep an eye on things as well as filming and checking security matters. Alstad will stay behind in the bell essentially to keep an eye on things from there and guard their safe return. There are a thousand situations that can occur on dives like these and things can go wrong very fast."

"And communications?"

"Communications between and from all the divers will directly go to Hendrikson in the control room upstairs. OK, they're closing the hatch and locking themselves in. They'll be ready to leave anytime now so I think we should go upstairs and watch from there."

In the control room Volkov joined the rest of the men gathered around the screen to watch Pearce close the bell's hatch from the inside. As Anders and Harper entered the room, the diver's voice sounded through the speakers. "Lock and loaded."

From the camera inside the diving bell it was clear that the chamber was little more than 10ft wide. A curved bench ran around its sides, and in the center was a hole big enough for the divers to enter and exit from.

Pearce looked around, making a last-minute check of the chamber while holding on firmly to the bench. "You ready?" he asked, and everyone heard the nerves creep into his voice. Most of those watching understood why; Pearce suffered from a mild form of claustrophobia and the bell wasn't therefore his most favorite place.

"I don't understand you," Jostein laughed. "You have no problem diving hundreds of meters under water, but you are afraid of a little descent in a diving bell?"

Pearce shrugged. He had worked with both Jostein and Alstad for years and their teasing was nothing new.

"You'll get what's coming to you, boys," he jokingly threatened them. "You know it's coming, when you least expect it, you just wait."

Above the divers, and back on deck, the crane operator looked down the hole containing the bell one more time before picking up a radio. "The bell is loaded and ready to release on your command, Sir."

In the control room the notification couldn't have come soon enough for Harper. Finally they had reached the moment they came for. It wouldn't be long now until they knew for sure what the hell was going on in the Kursk, if anything at all now.

Hendrikson looked at Harper, Anders and Volkov wondering who would give the order to allow the bell to get underway.

"What do you think? Are we ready to do this?" Anders asked.

"Let's get those men out of there," Harper said.

"Yes, let's get this over with," Volkov muttered as though the dive was merely a tiresome exercise rather than a rescue mission."

"All right, let's do this now," Anders told Hendrikson and gifted him a firm nod.

"You have 'Go'," Hendrikson informed the crane operator. "I repeat; you have 'Go'."

At the command, all eyes turned anxiously to the screens monitoring the rescue. One showed the exterior of the hole from which the bell would be lowered. Another gave a wide-angled image from the top of the inside of the bell showing the divers sitting on their benches. As the bell descended, the divers could be seen gripping the seats beneath them in preparation for the moment they would hit the water. Once they plunged under the surface, disappearing from view on the first screen, everyone concentrated on the second screen as Hendrikson started the countdown to the seabed.

"10... 25... 50.... is everything OK down there?"

Pearce gave a clear thumbs up to the camera. "We're good here."

"75, 80, 85," Hendrikson continued. Then, with a small bump, the bell came to a halt some ten meters above the Kursk's hull. "Switching to external camera and lights," he said and another screen in the control room flickered into action to reveal the scene outside the bell.

"Is that her?" Volkov asked, pointing to a large dark shadow.

"It has to be," Harper said and nodded at Hendrikson to give the go ahead.

"All right men, you have arrived at your destination and have 'Go'," Hendrikson told the team and Pearce, Jostein and Alstad all turned to look through the portholes for their first sighting of the Kursk. The bell's floodlights threw beams of light upon the bottom of the sea to reveal the huge shadowy form of the crippled submarine.

"How are you doing and what can you see out there?" Harper asked over the intercom system.

"We're fine," Alstad replied. "Pearce and Jostein are almost ready to leave the bell."

Harper nodded as he watched his divers put on their helmets and conduct a last-minute check of each other's gear.

"Take care of yourself, men. Be wise," Hendrikson cautioned.

"Thanks," Alstad responded for them all. "We'll be fine. The conditions look good." Turning away from the camera he went to stand by the exit. "Opening the hatch," he informed the rescue team above the waves and in the control room of the Seaway Eagle everyone held their breath as they watched the wheel turn to reveal the dark ocean below the bell's floor.

All three divers peered into the dark hole before stepping into the unknown. The scene was almost surreal as the huge form of the Kursk revealed itself in the rippling current ten meters below them.

"We have a visual," Alstad reported, "and we are starting the dive."

With a splash, Jostein was the first to leave the bell. He then filmed Pearce as he plunged into the water. "Do you have the feed from the camera?" he asked.

Anders, Volkov and Harper looked at the picture on the screen that clearly showed Pearce sinking into the sea unwinding the umbilical cable that supplied the power and heat for their dive as he went.

"How's the temperature?" Harper asked.

"Good," Pearce answered. "The warm water system's working fine."

Next to Harper, Volkov strained to follow the conversation before shaking his head. "Do we have a bad connection?" he asked.

"The connection is fine," Hendrikson told him. "Their voices are distorted because they are breathing a mixture of oxygen, helium and nitrogen. It makes it safer to dive for long periods at these depths."

Volkov nodded and turned back to the screen where Jostein's camera was pointed at the large white circle marking the Kursk's escape hatch. This was the divers' focus and the tension in the control room was tangible as they watched Pearce land on the submarine's deck, a little right of the hatch. As the diver bounced a couple of times on the deck, there was a rare sense of unity within the room as everyone allowed a small sigh of relief to escape.

After finding his balance Pearce's voice revealed his excitement over the speakers. "I'm standing on the submarine like I'm standing on a building. It feels unreal. Do you see this too? The hatch looks perfectly intact. From here I can see no sign of damage."

"Even so, please take your readings," Hendrikson instructed.

Pearce reached for the Geiger counter hanging from his suit and held it next to the hatch before pressing a button.

"I've got nothing, it says 'zero'," he informed the control room, which he guessed was more of a relief to him than the men above at that exact time.

"That's good news," Hendrikson replied. "Well, I guess you best get tapping."

"Roger that. Four times four," Pearce responded and Jostein swam over to hand him a fairly large hammer.

"Four times four?" Anders asked and Volkov stepped forward to answer.

"Yes, that's what I advised. Four taps, four times; it's our Russian Morse Code, if you like, to ask if all is all OK."

"Shall I start now?" Pearce asked.

"Roger," Hendrikson confirmed and silence filled the room as they watched Pearce sink to his knees to hit the hatch four times, causing flecks of white paint to come away, like snowflakes in the wind.

Trying to steady the beating of his heart so he might hear a response – should it come – Pearce bent forwards and pushed his helmet firmly to the hull. The disappointment felt heavier than the hammer he held.

"Nothing," he said.

"Hold on," Hendrikson replied. "Give it more time."

"That can't be a good sign," Anders said to no one in particular.

"It doesn't have to mean that they're dead," Harper told him.

"Exactly," Foster confirmed. "They might be incapacitated in some way or simply not able to respond."

"The sound of the hammer would carry throughout the sub," Volkov said flatly, as disappointed as Anders at the result. "Do you want me to try again?" Pearce asked in the doggedly form all actions were confirmed and Hendrikson in his term looked at Volkov who just nodded.

"Yes, try again."

As the hammer crashed against the hull of the Kursk, Anders listened with his eyes closed; his hope diminishing with every bang. "Nothing," he said as the noise stopped, and he shook his head sadly.

"We must not despair yet," Foster said.

"Still nothing," Pearce called out. "What do you want me to do next?"

"Did you bring your wrench and dye?" Harper asked.

"Roger. It's in the bell. Jostein could you go fetch, and check the pressure valve while you're there?"

As Jostein gave the thumbs up, Volkov turned to Harper looking confused again. "Dye?"

"White dye," Harper explained, "also known as milk. It's a simple trick; below the outer hatch is a small tunnel that leads to the lower inner hatch. We need to know if that tunnel is flooded. If it is we can open the outer hatch and enter the tunnel, but if it's dry the inner hatch might be open and if we go in we risk flooding the entire submarine, drowning anyone left alive."

"I see," Volkov said, "But what does the milk do?"

"Pearce's idea," Harper said. "He will open the pressure release valve next to the hatch, just a little, to see if water gets sucked into the tunnel. Of course it's hard to see water moving under water so he'll spill some 'white dye' next to it. If there's air inside, the dye will be sucked in and we can close it fast. Then we plan our next move."

As Harper finished explaining, Jostein returned to Pearce with a net in his hands in which carried a small metal bottle and what looked like a large welded fork. As he put the bottle down he positioned the fork on the knob of the pressure valve.

"It fits," he said with some relief.

Harper seemed pleased. "We took the measurements from the Voronezh," he told the control room. "We then welded the wrench here on the ship."

262

On the screen, Pearce could be seen taking hold of the wrench.

"Turn it counter clockwise," Volkov advised.

"Trying now," Pearce replied and he started to pull, slowly adding more force as the valve refused to budge. Jostein moved forward and placed the camera on the edge of the hatch before adding his own gloved hands to Scots.

"The valve will not open. I cannot open it," Pearce informed the team above. "Could it be we are turning it the wrong way? Please advise?"

"Hold on, Pearce." Hendrikson turned to stare at Volkov.

"I was assured it was counter clockwise," Volkov said. "Anyway, you men looked at the Voronezh yourself. What way did you turn the valve?"

"We took all the measurements we could get in the short time we had," Harper snapped. "Unsurprisingly, we didn't have time to register every thinkable move in this detail. How sure are you? If we apply more force we might break the valve. You need to be really sure on this one."

"Pretty sure," Volkov replied, which wasn't good enough for Harper.

"I need to say this; I don't trust one bit of the information the Russians have given us so what do we do?"

"I say we try the other way," Foster replied.

"Agreed," Anders said in support.

Harper took a deep breath before sighing and turning to Hendrikson. "OK."

Hendrikson nodded. "Pearce, try turning it clockwise."

"Roger."

Pearce repositioned his hands and to a mixture of relief, disbelief and frustration, the valve slowly turned.

"It's opening a little bit now," he confirmed. A second later he stopped and picked up the bottle. "I'm starting to release the milk," he informed them all, and with the bottle next to the valve, he removed the lid to release the milk, which immediately created a white cloud in the water.

"If you get any flow going in you close it, do you understand?" Hendrikson asked nervously.

"Sure."

However, the milk didn't disappear inside. Instead it was slowly swallowed by the sea water outside of the sub. "All right," Pearce said with no triumph in his voice. "The valve is open, but there doesn't seem to be any air inside. Please advise."

Though Pearce sounded calm, his heart hammered for the sailors inside the Kursk, possibly just a few meters away from him, and more than likely drowned as there was no sign of air in the tunnel. To be so close yet so far was like a kind of torture, a very real agony, but there were safety procedures to follow and rushing would help no one.

In the control room, Hendrikson turned to everyone present looking for direction.

"So?" Harper asked.

Foster wiped the sweat from his forehead and looked at Volkov, trying to figure out how the Russian could remain so calm and seemingly disengaged from the events unfolding. He didn't trust the man.

"There's still a slim chance that the tunnel has filled with water from the outside rather than from the inside," Volkov said sounding surprisingly optimistic. "Maybe through some kind of breach in which case the inside of the submarine would remain intact with air inside. I suggest we open the outer hatch to see what the second hatch looks like and make our decisions from there on in."

"Pearce, open the hatch," Hendrikson told him "I repeat, please open the outer hatch."

"Roger," Pearce replied. "Please lower the ROV."

"Will do." Hendrikson replied as Harper explained to Anders what was happening.

"After inspecting the Voronezh we attached a small, but strong motorized robot arm with a claw to the ROV. The claw should have enough power to unlock to outer hatch latch."

"And where is the ROV now?" Anders asked.

"Resting at about 50 meters, just in case, so it should arrive any time now. Well, as you can see on the screen, it is almost upon them."

Harper pointed towards the screen and Anders looked impressed.

Pearce squinted into the bell's floodlights to see the shadow of the ROV appearing. With Jostein, he swam towards it in order to guide it to the target. After positioning it straight above the hatch they directed the claw attached to the robot arm towards the large square holes of the hatch. "We're ready to open the lock," Pearce said. "Please confirm."

"You are authorized to open the lock," Hendrikson replied.

Pearce gave Jostein the thumbs up and he pressed the remote control button, activating the arm which began to slowly rotate. The lock came loose easily, with a loud clicking sound.

"Unlocked," Pearce confirmed as he raised the robot arm back up to the ROV. "Are we sure about the next step guys?"

"Hold on, please." Hendrikson turned and waited.

"What have we got to lose?" Volkov asked.

"I hate to agree, but I'm afraid we have no other choice," Harper answered.

Hendrikson looked around and saw all the men in agreement. "Please open the hatch."

Pearce sat on his knees and pulled at the handle using every ounce of strength he had to lift the hatch, but it refused to budge even a centimeter. Jostein swam over to join him and both men began to pull, grunting into their microphones with the effort.

"Nothing!" Pearce cried in exasperation as he gasped for air. "The hatch is unlocked, but it won't open. I think it's too heavy. It feels like it's loose but… We'll have to use the bag."

"Affirmative," Hendrikson answered.

After quickly swimming back to the ROV, Jostein returned with yet another net this time carrying a very large, but deflated white balloon with ropes attached to it which he handed to Pearce. After fastening them to the hatch, Jostein brought over a hose connected to the ROV.

"Ready?" he asked.

"Fill her up!" Pearce said.

As the balloon slowly started to take shape, Volkov began to grow restless. "How long will this take?"

"Not long," Harper answered, itching to reply that it takes however long it takes. "It's 500 liters at about 75 liters a minute, so you do the math."

"And then? What do you expect will happen?" Anders asked.

"Well I'd guess some 1,500 liters of air should help lift the hatch, but we'll have to wait and see if it's enough."

"And what happens once we succeed in opening the hatch?" Foster asked.

"I don't know yet, but time is starting to take its toll on my men so I'd suggest we open the outer hatch, take a quick look inside the tunnel, and then give my men a few hours rest while we devise a plan for the next step."

Harper looked around the room, and everyone nodded in agreement.

In actual fact, it took only minutes to inflate the large white balloon and once Pearce checked it was securely attached to the hatch he spoke to the control room.

"The bag is in place and we'll try and give it a little help."

As he spoke, Jostein returned to his side and he joined Pearce in pulling at the taut cable between the balloon and the hatch. The two men gave it all they had and though they felt nothing at first they pulled with renewed strength as they saw the hatch cover rise a few centimeters before slamming shut again.

"She's coming," Pearce confirmed over heavy breaths. "Let's give it all we have, one more time, PULL!"

At his shout both he and Jostein pulled at the cable with all their might, finding reserves of strength they didn't know they had until in one swift movement the hatch suddenly opened and both divers fell backwards onto the deck.

In the Seaway Eagle's control room everyone gasped, looking at the screen and expecting the worst and seeing a few small air bubbles rising from the inside of the tunnel.

Pearce crawled back to the open hatch and bent over to look inside, lighting the area with his flashlight while Jostein filmed. "Do you see this?" he asked.

The tunnel was completely filled with water, but both the tunnel and the inner hatch looked OK.

In the control room everyone began to frantically discuss the implications, trying to gauge whether it was good news or bad, and what would be their next step.

"We need some time to think about this!" Anders shouted above the noise.

"I think you're right," Foster confirmed as the room went quiet. "The divers need time off and we need that time to decide what to do."

"I agree," Volkov added.

"Do it," Harper instructed Hendrikson, who then picked up the microphone.

"All right guys. I suggest you get back to the bell and get some rest while we discuss what to do next. We'll alert you when we're ready."

28. Final Chance

Day 10 - Monday - August 21, 07.10 am

At sunrise the Barents Sea was almost without a single wrinkle on it. The absence of wind coupled with the glorious sky colored gold by the ascending sun belied the frantic and increasingly despondent efforts taking place far below the calm surface. The Seaway Eagle and the Peter the Great also looked seemingly peaceful, anchored close to each other with only some 100 meters of water separating them. On their decks there was little to no movement, which again belied the tension below, at least on the Seaway Eagle where military men and rescuers from all over the globe paced the control room exchanging doubtful looks and a very real sense of dread as they tried to formulate their next move.

"If we open the hatch and there's still breathable air inside all our chances are gone," Anders said, knowing he was stating the obvious but feeling the need to at least say something.

"What are our chances?" Foster asked, but again he was merely going over old ground. Furthermore, he knew the answer; he simply had trouble accepting it.

Volkov looked around the room, the exasperation clear on his face as he found it increasingly hard to mask the scorn he felt towards amateurs unwilling to face the inevitable. "We've discussed this over and over again," he said. "The seal on the outer hatch was water tight so the water in the tunnel had to have come from the inside. You all know what that means."

"It means you've given up, nothing more than that," Harper spat back, finally losing patience with the Russian's constant pessimism while the rest of them struggled to find a way to help his countrymen. But Volkov was having none of it.

"It doesn't mean any such thing. However, it seems to me that I'm the only one in the room willing to face the facts. Don't get me wrong. These are our men down there, my men, and if there was anything we could do for them, anything, I would do it but..."

"So you're saying all hope is gone," Anders interrupted, "and short of a miracle we need to face the sad truth."

Harper grabbed a book from the table and flung it against the wall. "So what do we do now?" he shouted. "Nothing? Go home?"

"We can open the inner hatch to see what the inside looks like, but I very much doubt it'll be worth anything more," Volkov answered, his voice cold as ice.

"You arrogant..." Harper roared in frustration and he threw himself at Volkov only to find the sturdy form of Anders step in his way and grab his arms to hold him back. "You know this is your fault," Harper continued to shout. "All of this could have been avoided, but no, you just had to keep on experimenting, trying for yourselves and risking the lives of everyone down there. All of this could have been prevented if only you and your government hadn't been so stubborn and waited for so long."

As Harper finished ranting, Anders relaxed his grip and turned to face the younger man, looking him straight in the eyes, but saying nothing. The message was clear; I'm with you, but this is no way to handle the situation.

As Harper calmed down the room turned quiet and with beaten looks on the men's faces only their heavy breathing filled the silence.

"I think we should do it," Harper finally said. "We've come too far not to know."

"I agree," Foster said. "We need to know for sure."

"All right," Anders said, but he looked at Volkov first before agreeing to the suggested way forward.

"Are you asking me if I agree with my own suggestion?"

Perhaps because of the tension in the room or a shared sense of distrust and anger, no one dignified the Russian's question with a response. Instead, Harper walked over to Hendrikson and placed a hand firmly on his shoulder before nodding. Hendrikson breathed deep and contacted the divers in the bell who were sat leaning against each other as they rested while awaiting their next orders. "Pearce?"

On the screen the three men immediately sat up straight as Pearce reached for the microphone.

"I'm here. Do you have new orders?"

"We do. We want you to go back and open the inner hatch."

Pearce and his men looked at each other and their hearts sank. The order clearly meant that the rescue was over; there was no chance of finding anyone alive inside the Kursk. And maybe because he couldn't bear to believe it, he asked Hendrikson to repeat the order.

"We need you to go back to the Kursk and open the inner hatch. Do you have all the gear you need to open the release?"

After a pause Pearce's voice confirmed, with some hesitation, that they did have the equipment. Rising to their feet to gather all they needed from around the bell, the control room watched the divers on the screen with no word from anyone. What could they say? They had come to rescue the Kursk's trapped sailors only to become spectators at their watery grave.

Pearce and Jostein swam towards the hatch. When they got to the sub the thud of their boots landing on the surface was the first sound to fill the speakers of the control room since the order was given.

"Pearce, Jostein, we have you on screen. Are you ready to do this?" Hendrikson asked.

"We are," Pearce answered, speaking with no hesitation now he was resigned to the new facts of their mission.

Pearce placed himself on the edge of the outer hatch while Jostein filmed the scene, his camera lighting the tunnel into which Pearce lowered a long red metal rod with a T-bar on top and which he positioned inside the release hole on the inner hatch. After connecting, he held on to the rod with one hand and gave the 'OK' signal to Jostein with the other. Jostein lowered the robot arm onto the T-bar and started to rotate it slowly. After turning 45 degrees the release catch gave a small, but recognizable click. Pearce signaled Jostein to stop.

"Release is open. I repeat, the release is open," Pearce informed the control room.

"Roger that," Hendrikson replied. "Give me one second." He looked around the room one more time to allow everyone the chance to change their minds.

"It's your call," Anders said to Volkov, directing the responsibility for what was about to happen to the man who should take it.

For the first time since he had arrived on board the ship, Volkov hesitated. It was a human reaction the other men understood and were relieved to see.

"You are authorized to open the hatch," the Russian finally said.

"Open the inner hatch, Pearce," Hendrikson confirmed. "Please be ready to take water and air samples."

Pearce removed the metal rod from the tunnel and lowered the robot arm attaching it to the hatch. Jostein then used the remote to pull the hatch slowly open. As it lifted a single large air bubble released from the inside, disappearing to the surface. After that, there was nothing left but water in the Kursk's aft compartment. As Pearce and Jostein took their samples the control room remained silent, felled by the sight of the air bubble passing their screens – as though they were witnessing the departing souls of the dead. Anders felt tears stinging the back of his eyes and sniffed loudly before apologizing. Volkov nodded. He wasn't heartless and the moment hadn't passed him by.

"The hatch is open. Please advise," Pearce asked after storing the samples away.

Hendrikson looked to the men in the room. Harper was the first to respond.

"What now? Do we go inside?"

"No," Volkov spoke up. "This was only ever meant to be a rescue mission not a recovery mission. However, I would appreciate it if you could lower a camera into the sub so we could get an idea of what there is to recover."

Harper stepped forward to speak into the microphone, feeling his men might need to hear from him. "Pearce, can you lower your camera into the compartment to give us a look?"

"I believe we can."

"OK then please do so."

Pearce quickly taped the camera to a stick and lowered it into the tunnel and into the compartment below. The image on the control room's screen showed gray, smoke-stained bulkheads and small pieces of debris floating around.

"Can you please rotate slowly?" Harper asked putting one hand on Hendrikson's shoulder while Anders took his other hand.

As the camera turned it suddenly came into contact with something large. After a second of confusion, the shape of a body in overalls could be seen, floating away from the camera.

Everyone bowed their heads, but only Volkov spoke.

"I think we've seen enough," he said quietly. "Clearly, there's nothing more that can be done here."

As Hendrikson relayed the order, every man in the control room sat down, close to devastated, with tears in their eyes.

29. The Tenth Day

Monday - August 21, 08.00 pm

As James played a video game in his cabin aboard the Marjata the phone rang. Instinctively he reached for the receiver only to pause before picking up. He didn't need to hear the confirmation of what he already knew, but neither could he hide from it either. In the end he bowed to the inevitable to find it was Anders on the line. As he listened to the Norwegian's voice James couldn't help thinking that their friendship was the only good thing to come out of the tragedy.

As Anders ran through the details, James closed his eyes, trying to blank out an image of men, not unlike him only different in language and culture, lying dead at the bottom of the sea. All of the men would have had families. Some of them would have had wives and children. And in the pit of his stomach, James could feel the weight of their grief.

"Thank you, Admiral," he said once Anders had finished speaking. "We did everything we could. I will inform Washington."

As James put down the phone, he tasted the lie in his mouth. Maybe they could have done more to save the Russians, but if the US had done less at the start …

The streets of Vidyayevo were eerily quiet; empty of life as the public housing community remembered their dead and battled their grief in the privacy of their homes. Inside Elena's small flat, gathered in the kitchen, were Valeria, Sophia and Galina, all of them crying as they watched a live newscast from the Barents Sea. On the TV, the picture routinely switched between footage from the Seaway Eagle and the Peter the Great. In the background the Normand Pioneer could be seen at the scene; its LR5 rescue submarine sitting unused on the deck.

Aboard the Peter the Great, the ship's crew was lined up on deck, holding their salutes for the entirety of a memorial service while Petrov finished an interview with the Press who had been flown in for the occasion.

"…but life goes on. Bring up your children, bring up your sons and please forgive me for not being able to save our sailors. Thank you."

As the reporters packed up their equipment, none of them followed Petrov as he walked away, and so they missed what might have been a better angle to the story as the Admiral mumbled his intent to spend the rest of his days "finding out who is responsible for this tragedy".

A hundred meters away aboard the Seaway Eagle, Commodore Foster led a smaller, but no less dignified ceremony with the entire crew present, including Anders, Harper and Hendrikson. Afterwards he threw a bouquet of flowers into the sea, honoring those who stayed behind.

In his office Charles Turner sighed as he turned the pages of the dossier on his desk. Every page was clearly stamped 'top secret' in red. Even the touch of the paper made him feel nervous.

With no knock to warn him, the door to his office suddenly swung open and his assistant stepped inside.

"He's on the phone, Sir."

"Thank you," Turner replied with a nod and he waited for his assistant to leave the room before picking up the phone. He then counted to three to steady his breath before speaking.

"It's Turner, Sir," he said. "That's correct, Sir. I have confirmation that our two subs that were in the region are safe and sound in friendly waters. Any official comments made by the Russians before, regarding our involvement have been retracted at the highest level. You are all clear to pay your respects. Yes, thank you, Sir."

As Turner hung up the phone he felt a prickle of sweat at his underarms. He loosened his tie a notch and wiped at his face before reaching for the dossier on his desk. Picking up a rubber stamp he pressed it with purpose and relief onto the cover of the documents. Now designated 'ARCHIVE', he placed the dossier in the filing cabinet where he assumed, and hoped, it would never be looked at again.

Evening had fallen and though it was dark, Michail Federov kept the lights off in his office. Leaning back in his chair his fingers stroked an old Russian-made service revolver he held in his right hand. Outside the window he could hear the heavy rain and he pictured Arbat Street with its empty market stalls drowning under the deluge. 'Even the hippies wouldn't go out in this weather,' he thought. 'If only they knew.'

Lifting the barrel of the gun to his temple, Federov thought grimly of the president and of the inevitable public humiliation he would have devised for him. Federov knew the score; he knew it was simply Russian practice to pass the buck and therefore he knew he would personally be held accountable for everything that had happened. The Chinese deal was in tatters and Russia had been brought to the brink of a diplomatic incident that had the potential to plunge them all back into the dark of the Cold War. 'I could do it,' he thought. 'I could save myself the pain.' He looked at the gun again, almost longing it to make the decision for him because there was also the small matter of the truth.

Federov lowered the revolver and placed it back onto the table unsure whether he was taking the coward's way out by choosing to live or whether the coward's way out was actually choosing to die. In the world of politics nothing was ever simple, not even death. And really, what did it matter? Early on in his life he had made the decision to devote the best part of it to Russia. Perhaps this might be the end of the best part, but he still felt he had more to give.

In Elena's kitchen Sophia switched off the television. She was done with politicians and professional military men offering their condolences and sympathies to families they would forget by tomorrow. Her life was over. Sure, it would continue, but it would never be the same. It would never be complete. The sea had stolen her very heart.

"You know, it seems to me that my husband had a premonition of his death," she told the room. "When I went to see him in the summer, not long before he went to sea, he wrote me a small piece of poetry."

Reaching into her pocket she pulled out a ragged piece of paper that hadn't been out of her sight since the tragedy had started to unfold. Unable to stop her tears, she read the words as best she could through the sobs that racked her body.

"When my time has come my thoughts be for you alone, Softly I would breathe my last breath and I would find the strength to whisper, 'I will always love you'."

30. Afterword

Once all hope had gone, The Russian President finally visited Vidyayevo to address the families and loved ones struggling to come to terms with the Kursk disaster and the loss of all those on board. He promised the bereaved that Russia would support them, for life.

A week later Sophia received a package containing Mischa's dog tags. From that day on, she kept them with the cross her husband had left behind. She never received any of the letters he wrote.

Most of what really happened to the Kursk will probably stay secret forever. However, the one thing everybody agrees on is that all 118 souls aboard the Kursk died in the first week after the disaster. According to the official explanation the tragedy was the result of an accidental explosion of a torpedo in one of the torpedo tubes, which then caused the other torpedoes to explode. The Kursk's hull was salvaged in October 2001 after the nose was sawn off. The nose was later destroyed under water by the Russians. When the rest of the Kursk was finally raised to a dry dock, the Press took photos of the starboard side showing a perfectly round shaped hole. The metal was bent inwards, causing some specialists to claim that this could only have been caused by a torpedo entering the sub from the outside, and then possibly exploding on the inside. The following day the Press was only allowed access to the other side of the wreckage.

Seven days after the incident, the Detroit moored at Bergen, a trip that would normally take two days. The United States and Russia have always denied any American involvement in either the incident or the rescue.

After bowing to severe public pressure the president held to account those leaders who put themselves and their careers in front of swift action. Rear Admiral Volkov was held responsible for not allowing the LR5 rescue sub to enter the area. Admiral Petrov was transferred to another position within the navy. Deputy Prime minister Igor Borodin, who had claimed that a US submarine had been involved in the sinking, was fired as was Michail Federov, Defense Minister of the Russian Federation.

Edward Payne was sentenced to 20 years in prison for espionage. Shortly after his imprisonment he was pardoned on compassionate grounds as the American was said to have a fatal illness. Today Mr. Payne still travels widely giving lectures about his time in Russia.

"Tell me, what happened with the submarine."
"It sank"
Larry King interviewing Vladimir Putin. September 8, 2000

Special Acknowledgement

The Kursk's crewmembers that perished in the incident.

I compartment

1. Senior Midshipman Abdulkadyr M. Il'darov - leading torpedoman (Dagestan Rep.)

2. Midshipman Aleksey V. Zubov - hydroacoustic party technician (Ukraine)

3. Seaman Ivan N. Nefedkov - torpedo compartment commander (Sverdlovsk Reg.)

4. Seaman Maksim N. Borzhov - torpedoman (Vladimir Reg.)

5. Seaman Aleksey V. Shul'gin - bilge artificer (Arkhangelsk Reg.)

6. Senior Lieutenant Arnold Yu. Borisov - attached from OAO "Dagdizel" Plant (Dagestan Rep.)

7. Mamed I. Gadzhiyev - attached from OAO "Dagdizel" Plant (Dagestan Rep.)

II compartment

7-th Submarine Division Headquarters:

1. Captain 1 rank Vladimir T. Bagriantsev - chief of 7-th Submarine Division Staff (Crimea Rep.)

2. Captain 2 rank Yuriy T. Shepetnov - missile flag officer (Crimea Rep.)

3. Captain 2 rank Viktor M. Belogun' - deputy chief of Division Engineering Service (Ukraine)

4. Captain 2 rank Vasiliy S. Isayenko - assistant chief of Division Engineering Service (Crimea Rep.)

5. Captain 3 rank Marat I. Baygarin - acting torpedo flag officer (Saint Petersburg)

Crew:

6. Captain 1 rank Gennadiy P. Liachin - commanding officer (Volgograd Reg.)

7. Captain 2 rank Sergey V. Dudko - first officer (Byelorussia)

8. Captain 2 rank Aleksandr A. Shubin - upbringing officer (Crimea Rep.)

9. Captain-Lieutenant Maksim A. Safonov - navigating officer (Moscow Reg.)

10. Senior Lieutenant Sergey N. Tylik - electric navigation party commander (Murmansk Reg.)

11. Senior Lieutenant Vadim Ya Bubniv - electric navigation party engineer (Ulyanovsk Reg.)

12. Captain 3 rank Andrey B. Silogava - missile officer (Crimea Rep.)

13. Captain-Lieutenant Aleksey V. Shevchuk - commander of control party of missile department (Murmansk Reg.)

14. Senior Lieutenant Andrey V. Panarin - engineer of control party of missile department (Leningrad Reg.)

15. Senior Lieutenant Boris V. Geletin - commander of launch party of missile department (Murmansk Reg.)

16. Senior Leiutenant Sergey V. Uzkiy - commander of target designation party of missile department (Arkhangelsk Reg.)

17. Captain 2 rank Yuriy B. Sablin - engineering officer (Crimea Rep.)

18. Captain 3 rank Andrey V. Miliutin - damage-control assistant (Saint Petersburg)

19. Captain-Lieutenant Sergey S. Kokurin - commander of bilge party of damage-control division (Voronezh Reg.)

20. Midshipman Vladimir V. Khivuk - mustering technician (Kursk Reg.)

21. Captain 3 rank Aleksandr Ye. Sadkov - control officer (Amur Reg.)

22. Captain-Lieutenant Mikhail O. Rodionov - computer party commander (Crimea Rep.)

23. Senior Lieutenant Sergey N. Yerahtin - computer party engineer (Murmansk Reg.)

24. Midshipman Yakov V. Samovarov - chief of sanitary compartment (Arkhangelsk Reg.)

25. Senior Midshipman Aleksandr V. Ruzliov - ship's boatswain (Murmansk Reg.)

26. Midshipman Konstantin V. Kozyrev - electric navigation party first technician (Murmansk Reg.)

27. Senior Midshipman Vladimir V. Fesak - electric navigation party second technician (Ukraine)

28. Midshipman Andrey N. Polianskiy electric navigation party third technician (Krasnodar Reg.)

29. Midshipman Segrey A. Kislinskiy - technician of launch party of missile department (Kostroma Reg.)

30. Midshipman Sergey V. Griaznyh - computer party technician (Arkhangelsk Reg.)

31. Seaman Dmitriy S. Mirtov - steersman-signaller (Komi Rep.)

32. Petty Officer 2 class /under contract/ Dmitriy A. Leonov - steersmen-signallers compartment commander (Moscow Reg.)

33. Senior Lieutenant Maksim A. Rvanin - engineering party engineer (Arkhangelsk Reg.)

34. Seaman Andrey N. Driuchenko - electrician (Arkhangelsk Reg.)

35. Senior Lieutenant Aleksey A. Ivanov-Pavlov - torpedo officer (Ukraine)

36. Midshipman Viktor A. Paramonenko - hydroacoustic party technician (Ukraine)

III compartment

1. Captain-Lieutenant Dmitriy A. Repnikov - assistant commanding officer (Crimea Rep.)

2. Captain 3 rank Andrey A. Rudakov - signal officer (Moscow Reg.)

3. Captain-Lieutenant Sergey G. Fiterer - space communication party commander (Kaliningrad Reg.)

4. Captain-Lieutenant Oleg I. Nosikovskiy - classified automatic communication party commander (Kaliningrad Reg.)

5. Captain-Lieutenant Vitaliy M. Solorev - commander of equipment party of damage-control division (Bryansk Reg.)

6. Captain-Lieutenant Sergey N. Loginov - hydroacoustic party commander (Ukraine)

7. Captain-Lieutenant Andrey V. Koroviakov - hydroacoustic party first engineer (Saint Petersburg)

8. Captain-Lieutenant Aleksey V. Korobkov - hydroacoustic party second engineer (Murmansk Reg.)

9. Captain-Lieutenant Aleksandr V. Gudkov - radio intelligence party commander (Kaliningrad Reg.)

10. Captain 3 rank Viacheslav A. Bezsokirnyy - chief of chemical service (Ukraine)

11. Senior Midshipman Igor' V. Yerasov - crypto operator (Voronezh Reg.)

12. Senior Midshipman Vladimir V. Svechkariov - telegraphy operator of classified automatic communication (Nizhny Novgorod Reg.)

13. Senior Midshipman Sergey A. Kalinin - telegraphy operator of classified automatic communication, missile department (Ukraine)

14. Senior Midshipman Igor' V. Fedorichev - control department technician (Tula Reg.)

15. Midshipman Maksim I. Vishniakov - target designation party technician (Ukraine)

16. Midshipman Segrey S. Chernyshov - space communication party technician (Crimea Rep.)

17. Midshipman Mikhail A. Belov - hydroacoustic party technician (Nizhny Novgorod Reg.)

18. Midshipman Pavel V. Tavolzhanskiy - hydroacoustic party technician (Belgorod Reg.)

19. Senior Midshipman Sergey B. Vlasov - radio intelligence party technician (Murmansk Reg.)

20. Midshipman Sergey A. Rychkov - chemical service technician (Uzbekistan)

21. Petty Officer 2 class /under contract/ Yuriy A. Annenkov - missile department mechanician (Kursk Reg.)

22. Seaman Dmitriy A. Kotkov - missile department mechanician (Vologda Reg.)

23. Dubbing Seaman Nikolay V. Pavlov - missile department mechanician (Voronezh Reg.)

24. Seaman Ruslan V. Trianichev - bilge artificer (Vologda Reg.)

IV compartment

1. Senior Lieutenant Denis S. Kirichenko - damage-control engineer (Ulyanovsk Reg.)

2. Captain of Medical service Aleksey B. Stankevich - medical officer (Ukraine, Saint Petersburg)

3. Midshipman Vitaliy F. Romaniuk - surgeon's assistant (Crimea Rep.)

4. Senior Midshipman Vasiliy V. Kichkiruk - head of sanitary team (Ukraine)

5. Senior Midshipman Anatoliy N. Beliayev - ship's cook (instructor) (Ryazan Reg.)

6. Chief ship's Petty Officer /under contract/ Salovat V. Yasapov - cook (instructor) (Bashkortostan Rep.)

7. Seaman Sergey A. Vitchenko - cook (Leningrad Reg.)

8. Seaman Oleg V. Yevdokimov - cook (Kursk Reg.)

9. Seaman Dmitry V. Starosel'tsev - bilge seaman (Kursk Reg.)

10. Seaman Aleksandr V. Halepo - turbine stand-by operator (Komi Rep.)

11. Seaman Aleksey Yu. Kolomeytsev - turbine stand-by operator (Komi Rep.)

12. Seaman Igor' V. Loginov - turbine stand-by operator (Komi Rep.)

V compartment

1. Captain 3 rank Dmitriy B. Murachiov - party commander of main propulsion division (Crimea Rep.)

2. Captain-Lieutenant Denis S. Pshenichnikov - commander of remote control party (first) (Crimea Rep.)

3. Captain-Lieutenant Sergey N. Liubushkin - commander of remote control party (second) (Nizhny Novgorod Reg.)

4. Captain 3 rank Ilya V. Shchavinskiy - engineering division commander (Saint Petersburg)

5. Captain-Lieutenant Aleksandr Ye. Vasilyev - commander of equipment party of main propulsion division (Crimea Rep.)

6. Captain 3 rank Nikolay A. Beloziorov - engineering party commander (Voronezh Reg.)

7. Senior Midshipman Ivan I. Tsymbal - technician-electrician (Ukraine)

8. Midshipman Oleg V. Troyan - chemical service technician (Azerbaijan)

9. Chief Petty Officer /under contract/ Aleksandr V. Neustroyev - electrician (Tomsk Reg.)

10. Seaman Aleksey A. Larionov - bilge seaman (Komi Rep.)

11. Midshipman Vladimir G. Shablatov - technician-electrician (Mari El Rep.)

V-bis compartment

1. Senior Lieutenant Vitaliy Ye. Kuznetsov - engineering party engineer (first) (Novgorod Reg.)
2. Senior Midshipman Nail' Kh. Khafizov - leading instructor of chemical service (Bashkortostan Rep.)
3. Senior Midshipman Yevgeniy Yu. Gorbunov - diesel operator (Nizhny Novgorod reg.)
4. Midshipman Valeriy A. Baybarin - head of bilge team of damage-control division (Chelyabinsk Reg.)

VI compartment

1. Captain-Lieutenant Rashid R. Ariapov - main propulsion assistant (Uzbekistan)
2. Midshipman Aleksey G. Balanov - head of bilge team of main propulsion division (Chuvash Rep.)
3. Senior Lieutenant Aleksey V. Mitiayev - engineer of equipment party of main propulsion division (Saint Petersburg)
4. Chief Petty Officer /under contract/ Viacheslav V. Maynagashev - bilge specialist (Khakass Rep.)
5. Seaman Aleksey A. Korkin - bilge specialist (Arkhangelsk Reg.)

VII compartment

1. Captain-Lieutenant Dmitriy R. Kolesnikov - commander of technical party of main propulsion division (Saint Petersburg)
2. Midshipman Fanis M. Ishmuradov - technical party technician (Bashkortostan Rep.)
3. Petty Officer 2 class /under contract/ Vladimir S. Sadovoy - turbine compartment commander (Nizhny Novgorod Reg.)
4. Seaman Roman V. Kubikov - turbine operator (Kursk Reg.)

5. Seaman Aleksey N. Nekrasov - turbine operator (Kursk Reg.)

6. Petty Officer 1 class /under contract/ Reshid R. Zubaydullin - electrician (Ulyanovsk Reg.)

7. Seaman Ilya S. Naliotov - turbine operator (Vologda Reg.)

8. Petty Officer 2 class /under contract/ Roman V. Anikiyev - turbine operator (Murmansk Reg.)

9. Senior Midshipman Vladimir A. Kozadiorov - technician & turbine operator (Lipetsk Reg.)

VIII compartment

1. Captain-Lieutenant Sergey V. Sadilenko - engineer (first) of remote control party, navigator's department (Ukraine)

2. Senior Midshipman Viktor V. Kuznetsov - turbine operator mate (Kursk Reg.)

3. Chief ship's Petty Officer /under contract/ Robert A. Gessler - turbine compartment commander (Bashkortostan Rep.)

4. Senior Midshipman Andrey M. Borisov - technician of equipment party of main propulsion division (Ryazan Rep.)

5. Seaman Roman V. Martynov - turbine operator (Komi Rep.)

6. Seaman Viktor Yu. Sidiuhin - turbine operator (Komi Rep.)

7. Seaman Yuriy A. Borisov - turbine operator (Komi Rep.)

IX compartment

1. Senior Lieutenant Aleksandr V. Brazhkin - engineer (second) of remote control party (Crimea Rep.)

2. Midshipman Vasiliy E. Ivanov - head of electricians' team (Mari El Rep.)

3. Midshipman Mikhail A. Bochkov - technician of bilge party of damage-control division (Crimea Rep.).